Jewelry Talks

Jewelry Talks

A Novel Thesis

RICHARD KLEIN

PANTHEON BOOKS   NEW YORK

Library of Congress Cataloging-in-Publication Data

Klein, Richard, 1941–
    Jewelry talks : a novel thesis / Richard Klein.
       p. cm.
    Includes bibliographical references.
    ISBN 0-679-44198-0
    1. Transsexuals—Fiction.   2. Jewelry—Fiction.
   3. Jewelry—History.   I. Title.
PS3561.L356 J4 2001
813'.54—dc21   00-045660

www.pantheonbooks.com

Book design by Johanna Roebas

Printed in the United States of America

First Edition
9 8 7 6 5 4 3 2 1

Contents

To Zema

I'm writing this for you, Zeem, so keep on reading. I knew you'd have to pick it up. Go ahead. Nobody's around. Just let your eyes stroll across the page. Don't you think your folks haven't known for a long time you've been checking out the videos they keep locked in the basement, or that you hide your own behind the family Bible? No one in this family would ever look there, right? Such a clever Zeem! In fact, you probably know they know, so why worry if they catch you reading this? They won't be exactly shocked—shocked! will they? Why, I even sent a piece of this to your mother's friend Shelly, who ate it up. "Shelly?" you say. "You mean p.c. Shelly?" Herself, Zeem! And you're still embarrassed? You know she's one of the strictest, most moralizing pains in the ass around. But you also grant she is one of the people least jealous of others' brilliance, and one of the wittiest. So you think you ought to be even more obtuse and disapproving than she is? C'mon, Zeem, try it on. All of it. Even the so-called theory of jewelry, the part that might require a little explanation or some interpretation. But don't worry. None of this will baffle you or corrupt your morals, as long as you don't allow it to be "explained" to you by your professors or "interpreted" by your lover.

Jewelry Talks

Jewelry Talks:
An Anti-memoir

I loathe memoirs, recollections in tranquillity by life's noble warriors, who write to flatter themselves, often subtly, all the while entangling the web of motives and embroidering deeds. But I despise autobiography. Without the excuse of celebrity, the grace of wit, or the warrant of fancy, the "auto" of autobiography rushes to write the most insidious, invidious lies, about itself and others, under the gratifying delusion, sanctimoniously sustained, that what it invents is perforce, of course, the truth. It ain't. Autobiographers notoriously are unconscious hypocrites, concealing even from themselves the profit they derive from their lies. What they write is the purest fiction—shameless self-promotion, self-righteous mystification arrayed in gaudy guises, masquerading as avowal. It is detestable. Nevertheless, I don't see how I can avoid implicating myself, my personal life or my life history, in this brief treatise on jewelry.

I abhor having to do it. I'm uninterested in memory per se, having spent my life trying principally to forget. What's past is attachment, the hook of sentimentality, the snare of nostalgia, the knot of reunion—the oppression and boredom of being tied to something that doesn't change. Sentimental memory is a form of religion, which is the overestimation of the dead. I am interested only in what's happening next.

We are forever being exhorted to live in the present, in the now. But, for me, what's next is now, already part of the present, already what the present is becoming, anticipating, generating from forces currently at work. What's next is not yet here but as good as having happened, practically past and done, yet instantly liable to change. What's next can even seem boring, if we know it already. In the rag business, next year's fashion is old before it happens, before it even hits the street. Next may not seem new, yet the next step could be the last, might be the abyss. One step ahead is darkness. But that's where I feel most free, at the icy edge of expectation, anxious with anticipation, where energy is high and risks can be taken, because the next time, the next turn, can turn everything around. That's why the prospect of writing memoirs, besides being loathsome in itself, induces in me especially deep fatigue and dank disgust.

Antithetical, antipathetic, antagonistic to remembered life, these memoirs are a sacrifice, an act of self-denial out of love for you, Zeem. I would tell you they were a gift if saying that didn't sound as if I expected you to be grateful. That would make this another hustle, no gift at all, not even a bargain. Let's just say it's part of what's left of me for you, a baroque accessory appended to my jewelry—what's left of it—which you will now inherit.

I've been blessed with the chance to live a life of utter futility, a purely aesthetic one devoted for the last forty years almost entirely to my jewelry—to what I've been given and have given myself. I have nothing much left to leave except a few pieces set with large gems by famous jewelers, and these memoirs of a life consumed by adornment—by putting it on and taking it off, all the while transfixed by the

Pelican pendant

strange light that jewelry casts on those who wear it. I've hung on to a few good things: the pavé diamond ring, the diamond-and-ruby chain bracelet, some ropes of large oriental pearls, a lot of little diamonds, and, of course, my Austro-Hungarian, ruby pelican brooch. It's worth a fortune. It will now be yours, my love, a pure gift, with no strings attached. Call it pelican charity. Early Christians took the pelican to be an emblem of Christ's love: striking its breast with its own hard beak, the bird, it was imagined, feeds its young on ruby blood from wounds it inflicts upon itself—giving up the pure gift of its own life in favor of its children. When you read this, I dead [*sic*], i.e., disinclined to be.

But my jewelry does come attached to one small impure hope, that you'll be intrigued and curious enough to read this anti-memoir, this novel thesis on jewelry—that you might try wearing it for a while and see if it changes your mood, and maybe your mind. Like all jewelry, this accessory to my legacy is intended to be attached and destined to be handed down, is designed to be given and wishes to be received. Pick it up and try it on, my love, for size, as they say, or just for the hell of it, to see if it stirs any new ambitions in your adorable sweet chest.

You may be too young to want jewelry, or even to know that someday you will. Until lately you preferred to be a little terror—wild and defiant, fresh and cynical, just the kind of kid I love. Sometimes you even dressed like a boy and called yourself Zack—among friends. But it seems you're finally growing up and out of all that—not all of it, Thank God! I love your tomboyishness, the youthful masculinity no male can ever fully experience or convincingly display. It's the very charm I admire most in women whose relation to jewelry I most admire: Mademoiselle Chanel, the Duchess of Windsor, Elizabeth Taylor (who fights like a man), Katharine Hepburn. But maybe you're not yet ready to take jewelry seriously, so I'll try to be gay to get your attention and keep you interested to the end. I think it's time you started thinking about this inheritance, which finally matters more than you imagine.

You may be disappointed, Zeem, if you expect a minute account of my inner life. I've lived so long in the presence of mirrored reflections that I hardly remember what I've felt in the past and barely know now. All that matters here is what I've learned, not what I've lost or experienced. I'll spare you the drear recital of my wretched psychology, the tedious spectacle, beloved by artists, of emotions undergone. I turn to the past only in order to instruct, perhaps to guide your future in jewelry. This memoir is anti, because it's meant to be more about you than about me, a thing into which I aspire to vanish, so that you might find instruction. If I had to find a model, I would take the lone memoir I can stand to read—the one Louis XIV wrote for his son, the Grand Dauphin of France. In a slim volume, the king recounts the principal, significant occasions of his reign for the sole and singular purpose of giving his heir the inestimable benefit of his incomparable perspective. Louis neither wanted nor required any other readers. He took up pen reluctantly: a king owes no explanations. But he recognized that he had a special paternal obligation to instruct his son, on whose good education depended the future glory of his kingdom and the happiness of his people. Louis explains to the Dauphin why only a king who has already occupied the acme of power—the throne of an absolute monarch—can possess the wealth of knowledge a new king needs in order to know how to reign. Unless you've been there yourself, actually been King—above all, King of France!—says Louis, you can't even imagine the things you will be privileged to see or the secrets you will deign to hear. Besides, he writes to his son, I am the only one in the whole kingdom, over which you will rule, whom you can perfectly trust not to flatter you. Everyone else is trying to win your favor by telling you things they think you

Louis XIV and his heirs

would like to believe about yourself. Kings, like beautiful women, Zeem, are perpetually surrounded by flatterers. Louis minces no words with his son. His memoirs are tough love. And so are mine, because they are meant exclusively for you, Zeem, my princely princess.

We've never met, but your mother tells me everything about you. I know more about you than you want to know I know, and that's a lot—things you can't recall, or won't, because they happened before you can remember anything at all. But it's not entirely for personal reasons I'm writing this; I feel no moral obligation to tell you about myself, or why we've never met, in return for knowing everything about you. I feel only an intellectual duty. If I write things you'd rather not hear, or confess to lurid perversions, it won't be for interested or sentimental reasons (though God knows I love you dearly, Zeem) but for reasons that I swear are strictly theoretical. In principle, I can hardly avoid it. I need to set down some sordid details in order to make clear why I'm writing this at all and how it affects what I'm trying to teach you. If I actually tried to recount the "truth" I'd only be making up a story, and there's a lot I wouldn't even dare to tell. Still, I always start from unvarnished anecdotes, but so narrowly selected for their illustrative charm and closely edited for their exemplifying power that they will seem to you like fiction—a novel about what my jewelry would say if it were able to talk, which it can. And since it will seem like a novel, you might as well treat it as one, and assume that what I'm saying about myself is the purest fiction. It isn't.

The way I understand jewelry, particularly women's jewelry, has got to be colored—I mean is bound to be gendered—by the peculiar fact that I, an anatomical man, have spent much of the last forty years of my life trying to live (let me get this right) as a TG-Bi-CD-TV (a TransGendered-Bisexual-fully-Cross-Dressed-TransVestite-woman). I am more than just a simple cross-dresser, since I'd love to be a woman all the time, and I don't like the term transvestite, which has come to imply a pathological condition, a full-blown fetishism, as if putting on women's clothes were all I needed to be sexually sated and emotionally fulfilled. In fact, these days, I mostly wear a sort of army jacket and slim slacks, cool sneakers or sandals in summer. My femininity is more than clothes-deep: I never look and feel more like a butch woman than when I'm dressed like a macho man. What's more, I don't happen to consider myself part of the homosexual drag community, because I am not exclusively or even exactly interested in men. I am certainly not one of those RFs (Radical Fairies), bearish men with beards, who wear dresses in public. But neither do I belong to the hetero-sexual transvestite or cross-dressing community: men, many with wives and children, pillars of the community, who regularly put on the dress or underdress of women. They have no same-sex practices, only exclusively heterosexual ones. I swing both ways. But I am not androgynous, and since I was born anatomically normal, I am not an IS, an InterSexual, like a congenital hermaphrodite. For a time I started taking hormones, like a pre-op(erative), transsexual TS, on the way, I thought, to becoming a surgically altered MtF (Male-to-[constructed] Female)—or rather, what I profoundly wanted and secretly hoped to become: a beautiful woman.

(Excuse me, Zeem, I've abused these abbreviations; they're actually used all the time in the transgender community—a kind of shorthand that quickly becomes hilarious at best, stigmatizing at worst, lumping together, under a single blunt sign, everyone who appears to share some sexual practice, genetic endowment, or anatomical configuration. In fact, as you'll learn, no two libidos are identical. So don't worry, Zeem; just ignore the abbreviations—unless they make you laugh.)

But I never went under the knife. For reasons I will postpone giving here, I have excluded the preop option. To cut them off would lend them an importance and centrality that seem irrelevant to the sensuous feelings I have when I'm feeling most like a woman, feelings that spread across my body, that have little— but not nothing—to do with my genitals. I've never thought of wanting to be a she-male, like those transgendered women in TG magazines with big silicone boobs and large cocks, sporting stiletto spikes and black latex. Although I admire them, they are a male's idea of women and, for political as well as sexual reasons, I would like to be a lesbian. Obviously (as they say when nothing is clear), I have to be included within the vast nation of trannies who have never fully settled on a single sex but spend their lives perpetually in transition from one to the other. In my case, it was practically foreordained in the very name my mother gave me.

I'm a big believer in the motivation of the name—in the way people's lives are shaped by what their names denote or connote, represent or imply. Carl Jung says, in a footnote, that people named Grosse (in German) are likely to be megalomaniacs, while people called Klein have inferiority complexes.[1] But it's usually more delicate than that. Sometimes motives are attached to the way a name sounds, or how it looks when it's written. My name covers the whole alphabet, from AB to YZ. Funny that that should also go for my sex, for my gender, not to mention my gender preferences or sexual repertoire.

---

1. Carl Jung, *On Synchronicity*. Princeton, NJ: Princeton University Press, 1973, p. 11.

The Maharajah of Patiala

My mother was a French actress of Neapolitan extraction, one of the last of the demimonde, the high-class courtesans of exceptional beauty who had no shame about calling themselves actresses or making a lush living off the generosity of rich and famous men, grateful for their little complaisances and intricate savoir-faire. My father might have been any one of her lovers at the time—a Venetian count, a Russian boyar, an Oriental prince. I rather incline to the latter, to judge from the olive cast of my skin and the unquenchable thirst I've always had for the shimmering waters at the heart of precious stones. Like an Indian maharajah, I have dreamt from an early age of being drenched from head to toe in innumerable gems sewn on silvery vestments, with the largest jewel of all, a mountain of light—an enormous diamond crystal—perched on my immaculate turban, spiked with a snowy egret plume.

I was born in Cannes in 1928, having been conceived one drunken night in Monte Carlo, when, flush with champagne and her winnings at roulette, my mother, Zizi Zinzo, flung caution aside and failed to take the usual precautions.

I was raised by a succession of nannies and never went to school until my mother married your grandfather and moved to Arkansas, metamorphosing, like the great comic actress she was, into an authentic southern belle with a drawling French accent. Needless to say, she had no need to be encumbered by a peculiar child like me. On arriving in the South, I was promptly shipped with baggage north to boarding school. Shortly after that, Zizi became pregnant by your repulsive grandfather. Their only child, my half sister—whom I saw briefly at vacations—is your own dear mother, Zanzibar. Zizi took her name not from the island in the Indian Ocean, but from a famous refrain in an avant-garde play in Paris; its obsessive, dactyl rhythm became a national obsession for a while in France: Zan-zi-bar! Zan-zi-bar! People shouted it in theaters and restaurants. (Mother shortened the name to Zanz when rumors ran that the father was the playwright Apollinaire, a famous letch, as Zizi well knew.) Besides, like her favorite eighteenth-century French writers, she thought that names spelled with *Z*s were exotic and incantatory.

Even though we hardly ever lived under the same roof, and despite the thunder of family anathema, I've stayed close to your mother, thanks largely to an unspoken affinity resulting from our having inherited a piece of the same miraculous woman, your grandmother, who died before she had a chance to know you.

Since Zanz and I are bound in our love of Zizi, we have a lot invested in you, Zeem, her latest descendant, the first and sure to be the last of your generation. I can't help feeling that, without ever having seen me, you are more my child than your father's, the lout. What are fathers anyway in the life of most little girls? Obtrusive uncles, noisy or sullen, who stay for dinner, whom you often wouldn't mind seeing less of. If you want, Zeem, you can think of me as your rich fairy uncle, fatherly in his munificence but tactfully avuncular in his gossamer reticence to intrude upon your adolescent life.

Zizi lived with your grandfather, her rich, boorish, boring, razorback boar of a husband, among the pine forests, not far from the diamond mines he owned in Murfreesboro, Arkansas, in the southwest part of the state that produces more diamonds (first found there in 1906 in four volcanic pipes) than any other in the Union. Briefly he even owned the great Star of Arkansas (47 carats). (There's probably already a Clinton diamond—a sexy oxymoron: hard and slick.) In the twenties, your grandpa bought the mines from John Huddleston with the extravagant idea that he could make them worth mining commercially. But the supply of diamonds shortly seemed to dwindle and things got very bad for him, until a miraculous fire burned all the new buildings and expensive equipment he wasn't much using anyway. Soon afterward he sold the mine to another romantic and retired with my mother to Shreveport with money from the insurance.

After the old man dumped them, the mines changed hands several times. The last owners opened one up to the public, and for a small fee you can still poke around for diamonds in the busted pipe of an exhausted mine they call the Crater of Diamonds—as if a crystal meteor had fallen on Arkansas, as if diamonds came not from far below but from far above, falling to earth like fragments of stars. Every now and then, I've heard, a tourist finds a few carats of exceptional quality, faintly yellowish or brown like those for which the mines are famous.

Already aware of my proclivities, and not wanting to distract her new husband's attention from herself, my mother sent me at ten to Baltimore, where her idol, Wallis Simpson, grew up—to a boarding school for unwanted rich boys requiring discipline. I was bullied by everyone, and sodomized by a science teacher, until I precociously escaped to Harvard, barely seventeen.

Puberty had been a horror in the boarding school dorms. The worst shame came with the discovery that sex was the answer for most of the questions I had been asking myself about adult behavior. I was mortified when suddenly it all became clear. How could I not have known *that*? So *that's* what they were doing so long in there! I was supposed to be a "smart" kid who thought he knew everything, until I started to get hair under my arms. Then it seemed I knew nothing and could do nothing right. If that weren't enough, I also suffered the revelations of my peculiar sexual preferences. My attention was constantly being snared by erotic hooks and caught in carnal chains whose flashy glamour and fiery allure I could resist for a while but not for long. Trans-sex kept turning up everywhere and returning in spades.

My childhood in Europe had been spent in delicious indolence at resorts and spas around the continent, from Antibes to Ouistreham, from Biarritz to Baden-Baden, adrift in the pampered luxury afforded by my mother, who lived very well off the proceeds of her beauty. My education was desultory and eccentric, applied by a succession of live-in hairdressers, fey tutors who embodied Mother's Rousseauistic notion that, like Emile, I should be taught not by Men but by Nature. Except that she meant Nature embellished and ornamented, supernaturally transformed by cosmetic arts, by what is decorative and adorns the cosmos created for beautiful women.

Like the philosopher Hegel, she thought that art only imitates nature badly. There are those, for example, who can imitate the pleasant trilling of a nightingale, but whenever we discover that it is only a human imitating a bird, the trilling sounds "insipid," Hegel says. Yet birdsong pleases us naturally, because we hear an animal, "in its natural unconsciousness," emitting sounds that resemble the expression of human feelings. What pleases us here is the imitation of the human by nature, says Hegel.[2] In this case, the dumb bird is more human than the human whistler, who can only do a bad imitation of a good imitation of the expression of human feelings. Only art, not nature, is beautiful, my mother thought.

She taught me to admire the beauty of an Alpine landscape for the way it precisely resembles a beautiful painting of a landscape, like the one depicted in her crystal brooch. My mother, as you'll see, had late Victorian jewelry with a few excellent pieces of Art Deco, particularly the Lalique diamond-and-emerald brooch of a Medusa head, sprouting snakes sprinkled with green scales. Her greatest treasure, which will now be yours, is a reverse intaglio (etched in) crystal, minutely sculpted and colorfully enameled by Emile Pradier in Belgium in 1864. On the back of three rounded crystal cabochons he has carved and painted scenes of an Alpine lake, each scene hollowed out of the rock to a different depth, so that when they are superimposed to form a sphere, worn as a brooch, they allow the mountain landscape to appear with startling effects of perspective. In a tiny valley, within the painted crystal mountain, is a fragment of lake, blue like the sky, in which microscopic shadows of clouds appear—as if there were a hole in the valley between the peaks through which the

---

2. G. W. F. Hegel, *Introduction à l'aesthétique*. Translated by S. Jankélévitch. Paris: Flammarion, 1979, p. 37.

sky can be seen. As if the sky were up and down, above and below, within what it surrounds and contains; like a cascading abyss or a soaring span, infinity is reflected within the smallest imaginable compass of her intaglio. The face of God-the-master-jeweler smiles from that crystal.

From an early age, I learned to love the perfumed enveloping air of a woman's boudoir, heady with the fog of hair spray and cologne, downy with puffy clouds of cotton balls and powder puffs, flounced with chiffon and goose feathers. My mother used to bathe me in milk; later she accustomed me to the enduring comfort of freshly ironed linen sheets sprinkled with water imbued with violets, to coconut oil and peppermint balms and bubbly baths fragrant with the essence of old roses poured from tall black bottles, and, above all, habituated me to the paramount pleasure—to the consoling, electric glow of precious stones, deeply colored and set in gleaming metals that were diligently cleaned and lovingly polished. I grew up in a world of women, a woman's world ("mundus muliebris," said Baudelaire wickedly, in the best Church Latin), in which all surrounding things were superficial, flimsy, soft, and pink or white. Only the ubiquitous mirrors were impenetrable, and yet infinitely penetrated by reflections, letting eyes be everywhere at once. The jewelry, however, was cold and dark, whatever dripped from the blood-red lacquered Chinese box of drawers lined with Persian silk that sat on the Louis XV dressing table marquetted in teak and ivory. She kept the best jewelry in there. She would languish in her green satin peignoir before the mirrors trying on rings and piling on bangles, draping herself with pearls and rare jade necklaces.

Fei Tsui jade is intrinsically valuable. It's the only really valuable kind. All known deposits were exhausted hundreds of years ago. Other jades are valued to some extent for the material but chiefly for the workmanship they display. Zizi had a necklace of sixty beads each about 6 carats, intricately carved, worth eighty or ninety thousand dollars. I broke the necklace over my lover Amad's head and several jade beads bounced out the French windows, through the cast-iron railing, and smashed onto the pavement below—maybe striking a lucky tourist. That's the way jewelry can vanish. It's so easily lost, stolen, or broken.

My mother loved her earrings, and when she turned her head and brushed back her thick red hair, she saw herself reflected in a hundred profiles, smiling at herself dazzled, bedecked with some ravishing pendulous pearl at her ear or some glittering golden chandelier from Spain. She also had a choker, an inch and a half wide, that was confected of diamonds and tiny seed pearls, a smaller version of the one Queen Alexandra made fashionable when she became queen of Edwardian England at the turn of the century. The ravishing, high-necked, gorgeously chested Alexandra, daughter of King Christian IX of Denmark, had, it's true, a little scar she wanted to hide, but that doesn't entirely account for the erotic value of chokers. The choker is a slave collar, and wearing it intimates the sort of sexual submission of which most men and many women dream. A choke collar, or a choker that looks tattooed, seems to say you're ready to be someone's sex slave—if the right master comes along. With spikes around, it tells the world you're a nasty dog that no one but your master can pet.

A choker may just be the most powerful way of marking the articulation between head and shoulders. A creature without a neck has nothing with which to differentiate itself into (what we call) head and body; it's the Hideous—like a slug that's all body, or a spider that's all head. A long-necked woman is very beautiful when the connection and separation between head and shoul-

Alexandra, Princess of Wales

ders are sculpted, harmonious. A choker draws attention to the intimate space of the neck, invites the eye to that delicate region of the body where the slightest peck can inflame. Anklets are for whores and odalisques. But that's another story.

You'll have my mother's choker, Zeem; it's the one I was wearing when Amad, my own Oriental prince, took me to Amsterdam; we stayed in a hotel room with a balcony that overlooked the Amstel River, where we made love one hot August night cooled by breezes coming off the water while lights from small boats cast flittering shadows on the walls, causing my diamonds to glint like phosphorescence in a Caribbean sea lit by the moon. I mounted him and rode him hard like Bellerophon racing to an orgasmic finish in a shower of meteorites and falling stars.

So you can call me Abby, my dear. Or you can think of me as Auntie Tranny, even Uncle Lou, if you prefer. That, after all, is how I think of myself in these pages—a cross (what else?) between Auntie Mame and Louis the Sun King. (Mame has some of Louis's serene confidence in his own taste. Unconsciously she seems to imitate the way he entered a room—hand on hip, she angling a long cigarette holder [he hated smokers].)

As I sit here writing this for you, it's September and there's a shiver in the air on the porch in Mougins, with a wet breeze coming up from the bay of Cannes. To the east is Monte Carlo, where Diana and Dodi bought the ring at Repossi's and where, I think, I was conceived long ago, one rite of spring. To the west, beyond there at La Cröe, lived the Windsors, in the great house with the white cupola porch on a hill overlooking the sea, where they used to sit like ancient Greek sailors, like sentinels gazing out along these shores, luxuriously at rest in wicker chaise longues covered with thick navy blue cushions piped in white while servants discreetly poured bubbles into tall thin glasses that gleamed like rubies in the oblique rays of the setting sun. Why can't I stop thinking about them? Because the greatest jewelry is royal and he was the King of England; Wallis was his tranny wife, whose jewelry I know like my own.

Noting coincidences has become an obsession. The Windsors were married in 1937, the same year my mother married your grandpapa, a scion of old money who, like the Duke, loved to dress up and, like him, had a taste for women, food, and above all gambling—after which, says Kant, the first two taste better. Gambling for money, the philosopher adds, is the best, the most exciting distraction there is and the surest relief after long bouts of reflection.[3] Like the best novel or tragic drama, gambling induces a state of constant alternation between fear and hope— the condition, he thinks, of all true pleasure.

So my mother met your grandfather in Belgium, in the spa city of Spa, where he had come for the baths and the casino, in order to lose weight and money. He could do neither until he found Zizi flirting at the roulette tables. He moved her and me to America, where she lived happily but briefly. She died at thirty-eight, leaving me an orphan bastard, personally abject but amply provided for with jewels she had stashed in vaults around the continent. Some of what she left to me I've left to you to leave.

I can't possibly pretend that the fact of my transgendering is irrelevant to my jewelry, particularly these days, when adornment is so strongly marked as feminine. There was a time when jewelry was differently distributed—in the sixteenth century, say, when women wore jeweled headbands over hair that covered their ears and men wore earrings. Later, under the ancien régime, men and women of a certain class vied with one another in their taste for jewelry. Take Liselotte, the stupendously fat Princess Palatine, who died impacted from overeating German sausage that was being sent to her regularly at Versailles by her aunt Sophie, the Grand Elector of Hanover. Liselotte detested the overrefined tastes of the court of Louis XIV, where she lived unhappily as the wife of Monsieur, the notoriously gay brother of the king. She fancied herself a great horsewoman; there are awesome portraits of her fat squeezed into impeccable riding britches, brandishing a cruel little

---

3. Emmanuel Kant, *Anthropology from a Pragmatic Point of View.* Book II: "The Feeling of Pleasure & Displeasure." Translated by Victor Lyle Dowdell. Carbondale: Southern Illinois University Press, 1996, p. 94.

whip. In fat, she wore the pants in the family—and that's often true in bi-homes: as the husband becomes femm-ier, the wife becomes more and more butch.

Besides sausage and horses, she also liked her husband's diamonds, and you could safely say she was truly in love with the king's jewels. In 1697, she wrote a letter to her aunt Sophie describing the marriage of the Dauphin, depicting the clothes at length and enumerating the jewels worn for the occasion by the noblest ladies and men at court. She herself, she notes, was wrapped in gold chenille, and wore a vast parure, a necklace-earring-bracelet set of stupendous pearls, which were then very rare, combined with huge diamonds, and a diamond stomacher that spanned the mountain of her belly and whose cost could have fed Paris for a month. Her husband, Monsieur, wore a simple gold-embroidered black velvet suit that set off richly his biggest diamonds, like constellations against a moonless sky. He had giant stones that he had paid to have diversely set on grand occasions—several of them more than 45 carats, the size of yellow plums, flawlessly colored and brilliantly cut (including for a while the giant Sancy). They were some of the first really large, well-cut diamonds brought to Europe in the seventeenth century from the Indian mines of Kollur in Golconda by the jeweler-adventurer Jean-Baptiste Tavernier. In her letter, the fat princess whines that her husband gives her no gems to wear but gaily keeps them for himself—only occasionally lending some to his *mignons,* the "young boys" he occupies his time with "day and night," she writes. Louis, the king, was of course aware of Monsieur's propensity, and while he disapproved of his brother's sexual tastes, he encouraged him in his vices—boys and diamonds—in order to keep him out of politics.

I seem to wander, Zeem. Believe me, dear, there's strategy in all this. I'm trying to impress on you how obsessively gems and

Louis XIV

jewelry have for centuries driven the dreams of the wealthy and excited the ambitions of the great, both men and women. There is a lust for jewelry that seizes hold and transforms lives. Most women have it after fifty, when jewelry becomes a supplement—not only an ornament but the sign on their bodies of the beauty they think they've lost. Where does the lust come from, and where does it lead? The mystery that draws us so powerfully perhaps resides in the power of light, reflected by metal and refracted by stone, to heal the soul through the eye, lifting spirits and brightening days. The eye springs to the light in the stone, to the brilliance of its inner fire, even as it's being soothed by the limpid luster of its watery gleam.

In texts that speak of the mystical influence and moral virtues of precious stones, alchemical wisdom before the eighteenth century associated certain gems with specific powers to heal (like emeralds) or harm (opals). Misfortune strangely surrounds the history of certain diamonds, like the Koh-i-Noor, which brings disaster to its male owners. Or like the Hope diamond, a piece of the Sancy, whose owners all suffered calamity, and which the United States of America had the folly to accept in 1958 when it was offered by Harry Winston to the Smithsonian Institute, where it resides today (causing unknown, untold trouble to the city of Washington [which hardly needs any more] and, for all we know, to the country at large). Yet those myths and fables surrounding gems and precious metals may be nothing

The Hope Diamond

more than the overheated phantasms of greedy minds deranged by the seemingly boundless wealth and almost magic power attached to these rare and precious things.

There is something miraculous about gold and diamond mines, whether it's the stock you buy in them or the places themselves; they harbor the alchemical dream of turning shit into gold. Hunks of grimy dirt are converted into gleaming flaxen nuggets or glittering crystal jewels worth fortunes. Every piece of precious metal, every gem or stone you wear, bears the trace of its extraction from the earth and its miraculous transumption into an abstract token of wealth or a refined and costly object of adornment. The rarity of precious stones and metals inflates their value, but so does the intensive labor required to mine and transform them. Their exorbitant cost reflects their incredible promotion out of mud into the universe of value and ornamental beauty, where they become wondrously luminous things that stir the blood of men and women indiscriminately.

Everything begins with diamonds. Chanel loved them for

their value and their brilliance. She spoke to an interviewer about her taste for everything that shines brilliantly—*de ce qui brille*. Of all gems, diamonds, by virtue of their great density, produce the most light; they also represent the highest value by weight in the smallest volume. They are therefore the stones that best embody a certain idea of what is most authentically beautiful and intrinsically valuable. Zsa Zsa Gabor sleeps wearing her diamond earrings, as if they would prompt her dreams. A pouch of diamonds is what rich refugees take when they leave the house for the last time. Diamonds will buy you lunch in any diner in the world. And because we so closely identify ourselves with our jewelry, Simmel calls them the last refuge of the self.

There is an innocence about the stone, the pure hard diamond. It is without the least plasticity or intention. It is only what is in itself, without deviation or deviance, without feint. Diamonds for the Greeks are "a-damantine," indomitable, invincible, unyielding, from the Greek for un-tamed. For Homer it meant the hardest thing there was, which before Greeks knew about diamonds may have been corundum (the second-hardest mineral)—of which sapphires are a crystal. Diamonds' impenetrability, their indurate density, which is ten times that of the next hardest thing, made them the weapon of an Achaean's dreams: pure crystal hardness that would break the sword of any enemy. A hoplite with a diamond sword would be indomitable, if only he ever had enough stone and knew how to fashion it.

It's not easy to work diamonds. No one who writes on them can avoid saying that only a diamond can cut a diamond. It is insecable, unable to be divided, an atom in nature, the incompressible goal of all stone, and yet merely carbon, like the softest, sloughing piece of coal, like a pencil smear of graphite.

The mystical qualities of diamonds have been observed since antiquity, when they were thought to be bits of stars fallen to earth or dew condensed at some rare conjunction of the planets at dawn. In the oldest texts, written in Sanskrit 400 B.C., diamonds are called *vajra,* the thunderbolt, the weapon of Indra. The god is usually represented as having four arms bearing three swords and two flat diamond lightning bolts, while at the level of his crotch a spiraling diamond sword juts up, elegantly twisted like a glass screw, gleaming with the delicious hardness of whatever is sharp and cruel and makes a point. Hundreds of years before the Greeks, the Indians were writing meticulous hymns to the beauty of the stone. Diamonds, in the ancient Vedic texts, were described as being "hexagonal, square or round, of a flashing color, having a suitable form, clear, smooth, heavy, lustrous, with luster inside and imparting luster."[4] That, my dear, is probably the only thing you ever have to know about diamonds: lustrous with luster inside and imparting luster.

In the Vedic hymn, the priest calls out to the diamonds: "I am a Gravastut, a Vedic priest who sings the praise of stones that speak. I invite you to speak, so that I might sing the words I need to say to make the sacrifice. I bring to the gods the gift I receive from their words, the gift I get when jewels speak, which gives immortality to the gods. Giving the gift I've received, I sacrifice it to the gods for the sake of their immortality."[5] The stones themselves are ornamented by the gold juice of the holy plant they crush beneath their crystalline sides. The beauty of diamonds causes what they adorn to be worshipped for its beauty, and only the holiest things are adored.

Diamonds have their own inner fire and they illuminate the

---

4. George E. Harlow, "Following the History of Diamonds." In *The Nature of Diamonds,* edited by George E. Harlow. Cambridge: Cambridge University Press, 1998, p. 117.
5. Ibid.

stones they surround. I'm sitting here fingering my Indian neck-lace, modestly modeled on the one Cartier fashioned for Daisy Fellowes, lavish heiress to the Singer sewing machine fortune, which in turn was modeled after one that Cartier had made the year before for the Maharaja of Patna. Dorothy Fellowes bought her "collier hindou" from Cartier in 1930, and wore it once in Venice in 1951 at a grand masked ball given in the newly restored Pallazo Labia by the Mexican millionaire Carlos de Beistegui. The necklace features thirteen faceted sapphires that hang along the bottom edge—six on each side and the thirteenth, bigger than the rest, the size of a robin's egg, suspended in the middle. It's a "Hindu" necklace that would frighten any Hindu, taught to believe that the number thirteen and, particularly, sapphires bring inexorable misfortune. I've memorized the description in the Cartier catalogue because I thought it was one of the most beau-tiful poems of jewelry I knew, full of the loveliest imagery taken from nature. Cartier's description of Daisy Fellowes's famous Indian necklace begins:

> A heavy collar with an inner row of alternate emerald and sapphire diamond-studded beads, to which is attached a narrow band of pavé-set dia-monds with an upstanding "ruff" of melon-cut emerald buds in diamond calyces, the emeralds with collet-set diamonds at the tips. From the diamond band hangs a fringe of articulated dia-mond-set stems with carved sapphire and ruby leaves and diamond-studded ruby, sapphire, and emerald beads, ending in thirteen elliptical faceted sapphires.[6]

---

6. Judy Rudoe, *Cartier 1900–1939*. New York: Harry N. Abrams, 1997, p. 184.

Tutti-frutti is the color of this mythical India, discovered in the twenties, when people in New York first started wearing jewelry of mixed colors. And I love the idea of pavé diamonds, cut flat and rectangular, making a sidewalk of diamonds, materializing the dream of walking across the sky on a crystal rainbow paved with planes of the purest light. Often many small diamonds surround large central stones, encircling or framing them, surrounding them with light, with diamonds so perfectly fitted together they seem to carpet the space around them—like the ring Diana and Dodi picked out at Repossi's in Monaco, from the collection "Just say Yes!" Hang on. I'm getting there, Zeem.

Even though we once wore jewelry equally, in the form of rings, necklaces, pendants, brooches, and buttons, today it's mostly—but, believe me, by no means exclusively—women who succumb to its allure. I know a CEO who never walks into a boardroom without 20 carats of loose emeralds in his pocket; he says they give him courage, and above all calm. Of course, it's been true since the end of the eighteenth century, since the moment of the so-called Great Renunciation, that men have forsworn diamonds on their person and dressed mainly in black, leaving finery to ladies except for uniforms of "fancy dress." Only when men are making war can they dress like ladies, wearing rings in their ears, or strutting on display in tightly fitted clothes that flatter their ass, chests decorated with braids and medals—a soldier's jewelry. I've sent you pictures, Zeem, of young Edward VIII, called David in the family, and his younger brother, the future George VI, dressed like women in bra and skirt aboard the destroyer taking them around the world in 1927, when they were sent by their father, King George V, quite against their will, on an educational progress through the British Empire. It's one of those equator-crossing rituals, a British navy occasion for gender-crossing:

David, later the Duke of Windsor and husband of Wallis Simpson, can be seen to be wearing a grass skirt, a scarf bra, and beautifully fashioned earrings meticulously crafted from bamboo. The young prince, with his small, delicately muscled, ravishingly bronzed body, smiles, intoxicated by his transvestism and shipboard male bonding, as well as by the striking effect achieved by his looping girandoles. The Duke of Windsor, you may know, had better taste in clothes than the Duchess, who was dressed by Givenchy, Balenciaga, Chanel, and notably Mme. Grès—she of the long, emaciated, neoclassical line. David taught Wallis everything she knew about jewelry; he loved to buy it for her, especially earrings. He particularly loved to see her wear a large leafy pair he had given her made of chalcedony—a (relatively) cheap blue quartz with the vitreous luster of the most transparent things—veined with brilliant diamonds and stemmed in small sapphires. They were probably made for her by Madame Belperron, perhaps the most revolutionary jeweler in the thirties, who had a shop on the rue Châteaudun, where Wallis, with her advanced taste (like that for diamonds and sapphires enhancing humble quartz), was known to shop.

Since the seventeenth century men have had few options where earrings are concerned, whereas women can put any damn thing in their ears. Jewelry is mostly for them. Lately, jewelry for men may be making a comeback. Cartier makes a chunky version of its Tank ring—a simple rectangle of onyx mounted on a massive piece of gray gold. No news: Bogart wore an onyx ring. But Yves Saint Laurent is selling swell-looking slave collars for guys—half-enameled, half-silver chain chokers worn tight around the neck—while minimal silver bracelets, cold and cool, are turning up around butch male wrists, not just limp ones, at the Dépôt in Paris.

I tried asking jewelers about jewelry, Zeem. They're often Jews. It's no accident. In the Middle Ages, gold and jewelry were the only forms of property Jews, like women, could own. The whole history of anti-Semitism is marked by the association, and the history of jewelers reflects it as well. With a lot of people I have to pronounce the word very carefully: "joo-ill-ry." My title sounds to them like *Jewry Talks,* but that's another story. Still, jewelers are all the same: they only want to talk about price, about the relation of price to value as it forms itself in the minds of their customers. One guy last week on Forty-seventh Street told me that if you want to get engaged to a nice girl on Long Island, you've got to give her at least a 2-carat ring or forget it. That's on the South Shore of Long Island. On the North Shore, he said, it better be closer to 3. In ancient times people sometimes wore money on their arms, i.e., currency bracelets whose weight in gold was carefully calculated to represent a precisely agreed upon quantity of the metal, so the bracelet could serve in the marketplace as a general token of exchange. But even when you wear jewelry like currency, like gold pieces or thick gold chains, it's always more than mere cash—and less. Try pawning some sometime.

You can't learn everything about jewelry by talking to jewelers, Zeem, but you can learn a lot. They can't tell you what jewelry means, only what it's worth. And that's important. But they can't tell me, for example, what jewelry does for a woman and why she puts it on, or the secrets it conceals and conveys. Who knows that and how do you find it out? You might read jewelry books and interview jewelers forever and never learn. Yet, in this sexed and gendered world, a woman is still defined by the jewelry she wears. Or doesn't. My thesis here is this: Je suis mon bijou; I am my jewelry.

Let me be clear right away about one thing, Zeem. We're not talking Madeleine Albright here. She allows her jewelry to talk too loud, speak too clearly: an earring quickly becomes a political icon in her ear; a brooch is a picture of what it means in a diplomatic context. She goes to Jerusalem to make peace and she sports a diamond dove; she meets Colonel Qaddafi and she wears an enameled snake, etc. That is not at all what I mean by the meaning of jewelry.

One

Giving It:
Simmel and Chanel

In a distant land, Rebecca received the servant of Isaac, and he came bearing jewelry. He sat down by the well and she offered him water and offered to bring water to his camels—the servants of his servants whom she generously serves. He knew by that sign that she was the bride chosen for his master Isaac, to whom the Lord had led him. Such a woman gives without being asked, gives more than is necessary in order to have given generously—of water, the most precious thing of all in the desert to a thirsty man. And in return for her giving, he gives her jewelry. As far as I can tell, that's the earliest moment in the Bible in which jewelry makes an appearance. "And it came to pass, as the camels had done drinking, that the man took a gold earring of half a shekel weight, and two bracelets for her hands of ten shekel weight of gold."[1] That's a lot of shekels to lay on her. The jewelers in the Bible immediately translate the worth of the ornaments into gold, into money. Of course the earring and bracelets are more than that; their great value is symbolic of the high holy destiny that has fallen upon Rebecca. She will be the mother of a race. Out of her spontaneous generosity she gives a gift that prompts a gift of jewelry and with it a promise that gives her the power to be the progenitor of "hundreds of millions," as the King James says—to give life to a nation. The jewelry she receives is the visible sign of the whole chain of giving in this complex economic exchange between man and woman and God. Rebecca accepts the gifts of jewelry and agrees to leave her land and family and go off with the servant of Isaac, across the desert to Hebron.

There may be an intention to give, but there is no gift without someone or something to receive it. (I wonder: Can you ever give a gift to some THING? Maybe not. People give their dogs Christmas presents, but that's because they treat them like humans.) If the beneficiary of a gift doesn't accept it, can it be said that a gift has been given? Knowing how and when to receive is a greater kingly art than giving, says Louis to his son. Rebecca is a hero and a founder of nations not only because she gave water to camels, but because she also knew when to accept and how to wear the great earring in her ear (one earring is enough—if it's a good one), and because she agreed to surround her arms with the precious gold of Isaac. She becomes a kind of slave to him, part of his baggage, but in becoming his wife, the Bible implies, she gains an almost infinite power of life. Not to mention a lot of shekels to keep. And, leaving town, with Isaac's

---

1. Genesis 24:22.

servant, she starts on her about-to-be-married life, weighed down with his money, already riding hard on his ass.

I start my understanding from the premise postulated a century ago by Georg Simmel, a philosopher and sociologist, that jewelry is the first form of property possessed by women. Simmel thinks that what men first possessed was not women, as Marx thinks, but weapons. For him, all sexual difference follows from that original division of property. A man in possession of jewelry is not at all the same thing as a woman owning it, since in a way it defines her as a woman—she is it. But never having been a woman (until recently, perhaps), I have therefore never really had any. How can a man—whose happiness depends on it—learn to wear his jewelry?

Men first use weapons to impose their will by force on others, above all on women; women use their first form of property, ornamental jewelry, to seduce, to charm, and to please others with their beauty, chiefly men but also other women. Ordinarily, you don't wear jewelry just for yourself, since most of the time you can't see it or don't notice you have it on. A woman's property is therefore a form of generosity she bestows on those who observe her wearing it, a gift she gives to the admirers of the beauty her jewelry enhances. Illuminated by gems and precious metals, her beauty is magnified and so is her power over others, who are reduced to awed subservience before the immensely generous spectacle of her bejeweled loveliness. In this age of late vulgarity, people cynically think that it is the cost of jewelry that impresses others with its power, but traditionally the cost of the jewel was determined by the value of its beauty. The beauty of jewelry is thus a gift that the wearer gives to those around her. Her jewelry is a form of altruism, says Simmel: Wearing it, she gives more than she gets.

At the same time, and conversely, Simmel doesn't fail to notice all the benefits in power and wealth that redound to the woman for the generosity her jewelry bestows. It singles her out, makes her "outstanding," he says—not by any manifestation of political power or strength but by virtue of the pleasure it arouses in others. What gives her power over others, over men, is her gift of beauty, inspiring appreciation and gratitude in those she delights with the glittering figure she cuts, beautifully adorned. She gets (a lot) more than she gives.

For Simmel, jewelry represents a rare point of intersection within society between two opposite human tendencies, altruism and selfishness, each in this case mutually dependent on the other. Beautiful jewelry is the image (and sound) of radiating brilliance with which the wearer dazzles the spectator; it is also—like the counterpart of men's property—a weapon that women wield by emitting a vibrant, almost palpable aura that causes the will of those who encounter it to submit to its devastating radiation. What man wouldn't give everything he could to a beautiful woman undressed, dressed only in large aqueous emeralds at her wrist, at her ears, and dangling in large drops from her breast? But why does a woman wear emeralds? To make her lovers drown?

O Esmeralda! I remember that café, l'Esmeralda, at the tip of the Ile de la Cité. Its name, you know, comes from the character in Hugo's novel, the goat girl saved by the hunchback of the cathedral on to which the café half faced. I would sit for hours in the evening and look across the water, watching barges motoring by, imagining what life was like on the river. I dreamed of living on a snug *péniche,* as it drifted past innumerable fields and crumbling city walls, never quite knowing where I was but never far from some place downstream—idly looking out for dangers or spying on lovers under bridges. From time to time my reverie was blinded by spotlights on the passing tourist boats, which would turn the dusk into noon. I drowned my sorrow for you in the green water of the Seine, Zeem. I obsessed for hours about that sonofabitch of a father of yours, who has kept me from you to the end. There's no way he can keep me from leaving you my jewelry or you from reading this once it comes into your hands. I have no wish for revenge anymore. I understand your dad was just a vessel, the enemy God put me in this world to make, the embodiment of the whole twisted system of moralizing violence and unthinking prejudice summed up by the word "straight." Like a thyrsus, he and I are locked in the embrace of the twisted and the rigidly straight.

With jewelry in mind, I spent the war pleasantly at Harvard reading widely. All my futility was supposed to culminate eventually in a senior honors thesis entitled "*Les bijoux indiscrets:* Jewelry in 18th Century French Literature." Harry Mordant, my advisor, took me aside to warn me about choosing a topic, since I was probably bound to repeat it—endlessly write about the same thing under different guises for the rest of my life. A thesis, he explained, is a kind of toy you give yourself to play with. Without realizing, you implicitly trace in its margins, beneath its topics and arguments, the shape of your own desires—sketching tracks that lead deep into the tunnel of your most secret dreads, darkest wishes, and direst imagining. An academic thesis is like a waking dream—often a nightmare. He further informed me, with a smirk, that he was telling me this knowing that if I knew it in advance, I may never actually finish. And he was right. In order to finish you need to forget what you've been told as well as that you've been told to forget your inner self and stay focused on the external topic, the ostensible thesis, not on the subject but the object of research and study. Only then, by forgetting yourself, do you allow yourself unconsciously to engrave between the lines an autobiographical allegory of your aspirations and urges. It's only after the thesis has been written, after some years have passed, that you can reread it and discover how pertinently it depicts your inner life—how well it serves as a metaphor for everything you've become and will have desired to repeat. Harry had it right on all counts. I never finished my thesis, but I've done nothing else my whole life except rewrite it.

In fact it was only many years later, after Amad had died, that I finally reread what I had written at Harvard. That's when I took the conscious decision to spend the rest of my life finishing it. What you have in your hands, Zeem, are fragments of that senior thesis intertwined with subsequent reflections and the outlines of a life devoted entirely to jewelry. It's the only thing I've ever written and I will go on writing it till the end. It's become my knitting, or embroidery, a tissue tied with innumerable knots, intricately ornamented with little roses intensely curled and intermittently lit by unexpected glints of occasional gems. My life's work, all that's left to show for it, I leave to you, Zeem, assuming that you know by now how to read it—how to draw inspiration, perhaps some courage from it. In the end, you are my first and last reader, the only one about whose judgment I give the least damn. Excuse me then if I haven't perfectly succeeded in eliminating from these pages the burden of my old thesis style, with its expository mumbling and numbing drone. Despite all my efforts to enliven and adorn it with the fruit of my fantastic reading and the highlights of my erotic career, this memoir remains pedantic, i.e., teachy and prolix, like an old academic lecture, tiresome and diffuse.

Originally, the senior thesis had three chapters, each devoted to one of the philosophers whose theory of jewelry I revered: Kant, Hegel, and Georg Simmel, the great turn-of-the-century sociologist and philosopher of money. More recently, turning fifty, I added the chapter on Luce Irigaray, the French feminist thinker on sex, who also has a philosophy of jewelry. Early on, and with growing conviction, I realized that each philosopher proposes an idea of jewelry I associate with particular women whose taste in jewelry I most admire: If Emmanuel Kant were a beautiful woman he could have been Wallis Simpson; Georg Simmel often sounds just like Mademoiselle Chanel; Elizabeth Taylor is Friedrich Hegel in the flesh (so to speak); Katharine Hepburn's cockiness might have inspired Luce Irigaray.

The title of my thesis not very slyly alluded to Diderot's great pornographic novel of 1748, *Les bijoux indiscrets*. In the novel, the *bijoux* in question are not real jewels, literal jewelry; they are something closer to what we call "family jewels." In the novel, they generally refer not to those of a man, as they came to do in English, but to that of woman. A woman's *bijou*—her jewel or jewelry—is her sex. A woman naked is already adorned.

At Harvard in those days, in order to discourage fantasies, they kept Diderot's book in the *enfer* of Widener Library, where you had to be given special permission to read. You were permitted to approach its crumbling but still sulfurous pages, in the edition of 1781, only in designated places beneath mirrors in full view of the librarian, and only while wearing white cotton gloves, like condoms, which were helpfully provided.

The significance of jewelry may lie forever beyond the grasp, even of a man like me who has spent his whole life frequently dreaming of being a passable woman. It is not that I wished to dress as a woman in order to seek men to take me as if I were a woman. Wanting that I would have been desiring not only another man like myself but one endowed with the erotic power over men that I imagine woman have—still a male fantasy. Rather, my femininity came over me in strange ways. I remember finding myself in front of the mirror, dressing my breasts in straps, and curling my eyelashes with the neatly curved instrument I plucked from my mother's dressing table. Over time, the more I put on the accoutrements of a woman, the more I began to feel the power of that strange erotic sensation that comes from expanding erogenous zones, as different parts of me became alive to sexual feeling, as the new feminine body asserted itself out of the lineaments of the old. In the slightly dazed euphoria in which I swam before the mirror I once or twice thought I saw my hips grow larger and for an instant I felt something quicken inside my body like the first signs of incipient life.

But those feelings were rare growing up. I repressed most of them (unless they weren't fully there yet) behind a normal-seeming pubescent desire to get laid. You can imagine the panic and the pain when I started to think, with the fanaticism of youthful conviction, that what I really desperately wanted was to become a woman, definitively—to transform my gender and my self. I was living in a tiny but elegant room overlooking the roofs on the rue Jarry, in the 10th arrondissement, in the middle of Turkish fast food and African coiffeurs. I climbed the walls in moments of ecstatic arousal and terror when I realized the depth and persistence of the wish that would not go away. The desire to become a woman didn't come upon me without warning; after the fact it seemed as if it had always been there—lurking, fleeting fantasies that had been flashing across my daydreams for a while. As might be expected, the crisis came around the age of twenty-three, when most men fix or freeze their sexual orientation, assuming it had been nervously floating around till then. Emerging from adolescence, men put off putting on roles, lose lability, and decide to decide. For me it was anguishing at first, the feeling that another self, an identical female other, was trying to get out of my body, was taking hold of my body, and I found it all the more terrifying as I found it intolerably arousing. All the more exciting for being so mad! I finally sought what they call professional help only after I had shaved off my pubic hair and made myself spend hours in front of the mirror "tucking" (my penis between my legs; making camel lips of my scrotum), all the while draping Turkish towels in fetching ways around my head, like the crazy nude milliner I was. Like Chanel, I also wielded a large scissors.

Eunuchs in China, like those who served the emperor in the Forbidden City, were often castrated voluntarily, intentionally immolated to escape utter misery by finding acceptance as servants in the houses of the great and powerful. Many were criminally castrated or paternally mutilated and sold to dealers for large sums. Such adolescents were in great demand by the imperial court and the upper classes, who required thousands of, in effect, slaves. Eunuchs were considered to have been "purified" (that's the awful word used to translate the Chinese), and thus thought to pose no threat to the imperial women with whom they lived domestically, on respectful and impotent terms, and whom they jealously served. Some few of these eunuchs became immensely powerful at court and in the bureaucracy acquiring vast wealth and holdings. Yet their condition brought shame on their families, who disinherited them and banned them from family graves. I remember wondering a lot about being a eunuch, since I often felt like one.

The shrink led me past the moment of self-immolation, of suicidal despair, when I thought I would rather be dead than accept my deepest wish to become a woman. Freud, said the shrink, calls this the suicide of the perverse. There were youths, even in straitlaced Vienna, who, having been raised in the most respectable circumstances, found it unbearable when they came to realize the full extent of their perversions. One day, say at the age of thirty, the dark truth that you have been trying

Chinese eunuch

to hide from yourself is unmistakably revealed and you realize, at bottom, that the only sexual practice you thoroughly enjoy is one so perverse and degraded that you prefer death to spending a life humiliated by the need to pursue its obscenities. A man's desire to become a woman is at first a form of depression, a descent into abjection, lowering oneself into a diminished state in a world where men rule. Girls at puberty often suffer mild depression when they suddenly realize exactly where they stand and the role they are expected to play.

But there are two morals to this story. The first is that you can never be a hypocrite in your pleasures, at least not for long: the truth of whatever it is you need to enjoy is irrepressible; it will out itself despite all your ingenious refusals to acknowledge it— despite all the defenses and forms of blindness you invent, the ethical or political safeguards you erect against it. The second banality is the fact that we all have a secret garden, a fantastic place of troubling sweetness that looks unnatural and filthy to someone; to "them" it's no garden, but a dump. And if, God forbid, we were to make its most perverse and evil flowers, its unspeakable excrescence, the whole focus of our erotic life, then that might very well lead to suicidal despair.

Nevertheless, the risk we run in that garden of being dirty and ashamed is also our chance, for its weird forms and corrupt flowers lend their idiosyncratic shapes to the deepest springs of our creativity and invention, to all the most individual aspects of our lives and works. Everyone is perverse; normality is a (rare) perversion. Hence there is no perversity since no one is without it: it is universal, hence normal. The word, perhaps unavoidably, mystifies what it is supposed to elucidate and conceptually comprehend; it brings together under one deprecating heading what is not marginal at all but the universal source of all individuality, of all invention. The way you take your pleasure is absolutely particular; no one gets off exactly the same way at the same time in their lives; people bring to the table their whole experience of eating.

Despite what all the sexologists want you to think, Zeem, there is no typical sexual pleasure. Its exotic forms and specific contents are what distinguish you absolutely from everyone else—the genetic, biological, historical, accidental conjunction or coincidence that makes you this particular throw of the dice, this pattern of dots, the constellation formed by the numbers on the faces of the die you are. Being creative means following the forms of your perversity (not necessarily its contents) resolutely to their ends. It's what Nietzsche calls talent—a single commanding virtue or vice, the particular knot that only you can tie in pleasure. It's the spin only you can give to whatever you turn around.

My particular genius in this matter, if I have any, resides in the fact that having been transgendered for so long in both body and soul, my perspective is not only oblique by virtue of the place I occupy on the gender line, but also motivated by an urgent need to know how to wear jewelry and what jewelry to wear— inseparable from my desire to wear it like a woman. Writing about jewelry I have gender constantly in view—and sex in hand.

The shrink also gave me the name of a cross-dressing academy in New York called Sally's Salon for Turning Little Boys into

Little Girls. Honest to God, the actual name. They shaved me closely, twice; they waxed my legs, and dressed me—in a little black dress. That was me, they thought. First they taped my chest and gave me cleavage; they blew up Baggies and filled a satin bra with them, and with lingering gestures slowly, luxuriously attached them to my chest. They gave me excellent makeup brushes and found me a short, black wig. They gave me lectures, took me on weekend seminars, and taught me about women's pleasures—about the pleasures of being a woman.

All the assistants are themselves TVs or TSs, but the instructor, Sally, is a GG (gendered girl), a beautiful woman who dominates the others: they submit to her judgments as the ultimate source of authority and authenticity, the final arbiter of taste. She repeated this every day, the first and the last lesson of every day: In order to dress successfully as a woman, to pass as a woman, you must find a model of the woman you want to be, and become her—securely.

Perhaps model is not the word she used. It is sons who mostly aim to model themselves on their fathers—to become their junior replicas. I was told not to imitate another woman slavishly: slavishness is dismissively attributed to female impersonators and drag queens. I had to find an idea of a woman that I could put on the way I had put on my face, imagining how she inhabited her dress, struck a pose, painted her eyes, chose her jewelry. I was supposed to become a woman who would allow the woman in me to speak, and speak as the woman I wanted to be—the feminine other in me, who has another name.

The school of transformation has a theory underlying its methods. It understands femininity as masquerade. The transvestite who impersonates an exaggerated feminine woman—say Diana Ross (big hair), or Bette Midler (big tits)—is putting on her Feman-inity like the mask of a mask, like a travesty of the sort of woman who already looks like a transvestite—the word for which in French is *travesti,* abbreviated as "titi." The surprise comes when the mask starts to change you, magically begins to transform your body into a more womanly one, intensifying and complicating the way it feels to enjoy.

The ultimate goal of the school was not to achieve perfect passing, which, effectively, would be no passing at all, since no one would ever know it had occurred. To be perfect, passing had to be less than perfect. The goal was not to pass but to be passable, to allow yourself to be read by the other as a man, but nevertheless to be treated like a womanly person. In this respect, the cross-dressed TV is different from a Radical Fairy, who has no intention or wish to be perceived as a woman—who wears dresses and a beard, for example. One teacher explained that the message you were hoping to receive was this: "I know that you are really a male, but I am treating you as a woman anyway, because you carry it off so well." To be a responsible TV, one cannot imitate being a woman either too closely or too casually.

Being passable is, of course, riskier than being perfect. If you are seen to be a man trying to pass as a woman, you are much more likely to be taken as the object of somebody's sexual sickness or impotent fears, and get your ass kicked. But in the end, the advantages outweigh the risks of being double, a condition a lot like that of an actor both inside and outside a role, distinctly man and yet convincingly woman. It is more rewarding, and more politically significant, than pure passing. Besides the constant sense of danger, it gives you the satisfaction of identifying your transgendering with that of millions of others like you in TG communities around the world, and of inserting your transformation into a struggle for universal recognition of the permeability of gender identities and roles.

Suppose you were perfectly a woman. No one would for a

moment ever take you to be a man. Who, then, but yourself would know or care about the remarkable journey you had made, the mountains you had climbed, on behalf of the right to recognition of tens, maybe hundreds of millions transgendered people in the world? TGs not only demand the right to live and work as they choose, they believe that who and what they are has social consequences and political implications for the way the so-called differences between the so-called sexes are understood and judged.

Many transvestites socialize only with other TVs or TSs and never test their femininity, their feminization, under the undeceived eyes of real women. Responsible transgendering requires a discipline that permits—as one transgresses societal conventions—doing it in a way that society must respectfully accept: transgression without scandal. One works humbly at developing one's own femininity by patiently attending to the ways and wisdom of GGs.

By choosing a model woman to emulate, the transvestite in a way replaces the function normally performed by an adolescent girl's mother. A girl's mother is ordinarily the person charged with indicating to her daughter how the feminine identity of her body might be construed and constructed. It is not as if the daughter merely imitates her mother; often they have dramatically different tastes. But the mother gives the daughter notions and criteria for judging how her face and body might look in the eyes of others, particularly men, in her own eyes and in those of other women.

I've often tried to imagine what it's like to discover that you have a pubescent female ass, that the thing you've carried behind and never noticed much has suddenly become the object of the most intense admiring attention. Boys' butts never get the kind of attention that girls' butts do, especially as they begin to develop and mature. It's easy for a girl to see that she's being seen as a woman, it's hard for her to understand what exactly men are seeing, and so she needs a mother to give her some idea. The conversations mothers have with their daughters are rarely explicit, barely verbal; the communication goes on at the level of the choices the mother makes for her daughter's wardrobe, the way she tucks her dress or combs her hair, gives her food or puts her to bed.

In my case, there's no mother. Or rather, my mother is not the mother of the girl I dreamed of being. Maybe she is, but I never knew it then. Perhaps writing this memoir I'll discover that my becoming a woman is the fulfillment of my own mother's wish. But a transvestite can't wait around for the time it takes to figure that out. You need to go, girl! and don an ideal. For me, there was never any doubt about who it was I had always dreamed of becoming. Her perfumed idea, her utter perfection, was so beyond my imagining that I never for a moment thought of actually being in her image—if that meant supposing some equality with her or equivalence. But I knew, with absolute certainty, with calm, smiling confidence, which distant constellation I was ecstatically destined to pursue. I knew in my heart that I dreamed only of being . . . Mademoiselle Chanel! It is the grossest vulgarity to call her anything but what she herself always insisted on being called. Coco was a name she permitted only to her intimate friends. (Or authorized for use in the title of a Broadway musical, based on her life, by Alan Jay Lerner, with Katharine Hepburn singing! playing Coco Chanel. Hepburn, Zeem, you'll eventually see, *is* Chanel in my life, but evolved, as it were.)

Jacqueline Kennedy was dressed in Chanel as she stood, bloodstained (in the endlessly reproduced photo taken on Air Force One), next to Lyndon Johnson at his swearing in. That pink

Katharine Hepburn as Coco Chanel

suit with the black accents, like the pink pillbox worn that day, was an accident that seems retrospectively like an omen, a significant coincidence, linking the obsessive image of tragedy and power to the almost bloody pink shape of the designer who had defined the twentieth-century woman. Chanel's influence on the world is equivalent in France, in the estimation of André Malraux, only to that of Picasso's and de Gaulle's. Seeing Jacqueline in that photo we realized, perhaps for the first time, that this woman of such elegance, such informed intelligence and taste, was also a soldier in politics, wearing Chanel's uniform on this occasion in which she was compelled to be First Widow, to witness and bear witness to the legitimate transfer of power to a dubiously loyal successor . . . around whom suspicion hung. Dressed like a Chanel soldier, Jackie stood next to Johnson looking not at him but at the Bible on which his hand was placed, saluting not the man but the laws underlying those that define the office he was receiving. Her Chanel suit said that she was dressed to do her duty, committed to respecting the office and the legitimacy of the officer who was assuming it. She was all courage, dignity, and beauty. For me, Chanel was on that plane in Dallas, and that's why she has been the model of my transformation into a woman.

I suppose I should point out to you, Zeem, what the recent death of Jacqueline Kennedy also revealed to me, belatedly. My eternal assumption about the suit she was wearing on that day in Dallas was actually wrong: it was not a Chanel but a pink Schiaparelli she wore, one that Jack had particularly liked and had

Lyndon B. Johnson inaugurated as president

encouraged her to wear on the eve of their departure for Dallas. It doesn't matter much. What is important for this story is that for so long I thought it was Chanel, and that it could have been. Being a Schiaparelli means that that suit could only have been inspired by—is utterly unthinkable without—Chanel, the Italian designer's great enemy and detested rival. In Paris, Schiaparelli copied other styles, shamelessly, right and left, but particularly right from Chanel.

The myth of Chanel, the one she most cunningly cultivated, is not far from the truth—like many myths. Chanel, equal only to herself, out of her rootlessness, her radical self-invention, created the uniform of the century, the form of dress that gave women the greatest possible security in a world dominated by male power. She created what women everywhere recognize as their weapon of best defense: the offensive stance conveyed by a suit made in the distant image of those worn by men.

A man does not have to compose his wardrobe every day. Even the most tasteless man can wear the same suit and tie, day after day, and appear unexceptional. A woman, when she gets up in the morning, is expected to re-create herself, Venus-like, from scratch. Chanel had an idea of what it meant to be a woman, and what it meant was to be boyish, even mannish. Chanel made possible Katharine Hepburn's freedom from style; she made women into English (or New England) boys, and liberated them. She did that by eliminating ornament in favor of a uniform, like the one, it is said, she wore in the convent school to which she was sent, in order to distinguish her orphan status from that of paying children with families. She turned us all into orphans of the state.

What is an English boy? Why would women want to dress like one—or look like one undressed? Why not? —after having been severely corseted for decades and clothed from head to toe, except on those prominent occasions when they were encouraged to display an abundantly bejeweled chest. Maybe it's the angular thinness of English boys, their regular freckled good looks and hairlessness, their *pudeur*; English boys seem free in their clothes without being louche. Cocky but decorous, the idea of an English boy is that of one who perfectly understands his place but isn't afraid to speak up, the way a German or a French boy would be afraid. He wears uniform cotton underwear under his uniform, a ribbed sleeveless shirt which clings loosely to his still developing chest, while the straps, fitting smoothly but not too tight over the back, draw attention to the Caravaggian beauty of young and charming shoulders. The drawers are slightly baggy, which emphasize his high perfectly rounded ass. He wears no ornaments except a watch, perhaps a ring (necklaces are for Mediterranean men). It may not be entirely accidental that Chanel's first important lover was an English aristocrat, Arthur Capel, whose nickname was "Boy," who gave her the money to open a shop in Deauville where she sold beach clothes modeled on his underwear. This Boy boy is Chanel's woman, and women

Prince William stamps

in the twentieth century have become—it. Not him! Something else, a kind of he-she. She made women more butch. Being butch is not at all the same thing as being a man. Believe me, Zeem, when I tell you there are female forms of masculinity that have nothing, absolutely nothing to do with being a male. A lesbian femme, for example, who loves a stone-butch dyke probably doesn't want him to be surgically transgendered all the way; she loves his butchness, not a penis. But I won't go there, Zeem, not yet; it's bound and gagged to come up again.

Taking ornaments away from women, Chanel transgendered them. And in doing that she made herself the defining force in women's fashion in the twentieth century, liberating them from the oppression of the nineteenth century's corsets and confinements, its layers and its extravagant ornamentation, its sacrifices to an idea of hobbled femininity. Women, under the blade of Chanel's iron scissors, became, not men but something else. I've modeled my own transgendering on hers. I've been looking for a masculinity that isn't male. To find it, I figured, I first had to try to become a woman.

Becoming like Chanel means trying to understand and incorporate in myself the principles of her taste in order to inhabit that look I want to cultivate. It helps that, like her, I'm tall and slender, with no hips or ass to speak of. Mademoiselle was always her own best mannequin; her clothes never looked better on anyone else. Yet despite the superficial resemblance, it's impossible to imagine her experience of being a woman. Particularly since here I am a man, imitating a woman becoming mannish. Not for the first time, of course. Shakespeare invented roles for young actors to play, like those in *Love's Labor's Lost,* where boys play at being women dressed as men disguised as girls.

Chanel had no family; the bastard daughter of an impoverished peasant mother, raised by the nuns, she almost became one.

She is without origins, of a class so low that she, the classiest, is without class, without social identity, possessing only her own fierce sense of taste. And that taste, you must never forget, is ferocious, as hard and cruel, and unforgiving, as the diamonds she loved. Her taste is profoundly negative in its virulent, ruthless rejection of almost everything, of everything other than what pleases its tyrannical judgment. Chanel's taste says NO! to this and No! to that, screams *NON! NON! NON! NON! NON!* to everything and everyone that offends her requirements for perfection. The scenes she made every day in front of her staff are legendary. She was hideously tempered, commonly striking the white-uniformed women who worked with her on the rue Cambon; all young and mostly aristocratic, they adored her. Those who stayed must have loved her tyranny. Everything in the world hinged on the cut of the jacket or the fall of the skirt. All her biographers insist on the screaming and shouting, the venomous, accurate insults she would meticulously distribute, the scalding torrents of humiliation she would luxuriously pour on the heads of everyone around her who idolized her. At the same time she was a master diplomat, briefly a kind of spy, and for a time allied with a Nazi spy during the war. She flattered and unfailingly seduced anyone who was useful to her. She herself explicitly repeats, over and over again, that she is a woman of bad character. Her greatest love is to criticize. Nothing else matters in life. To criticize is her greatest pleasure and the source of all her revolutionary creativity. Her biographers insist as well that this autodidact did not draw and never sewed. She cut and pinned, with a legendary fury and violence. Paul Morand, one of her right-wing friends and biographers, called her the exterminating angel of fashion.

She was the cruelest cutting woman. The English aristocracy into which she dreamed of marrying, whose scions kept her,

whose taste she loved, rode horses and carried small whips. Everything about her signature suit, for example, bespeaks the influence
of English equestrians: the neatness of the trim, the androgynous,
distantly military cut, the rough but expensive cloth soberly tailored and loosely draped, the colors of tweeds and flannels, the
sharp crack of leather against flesh. It was doubtless she, accustomed since childhood to the sadism of nuns, who pitilessly laid it
on her English lords, rapturously indulging their "vice anglais," as
the French used to call being whipped.

Out of the cruelty of her individual taste this orphan led a
critical life, one devoted to saying no to almost everything. And
her rage, her vicious critical tongue and her unforgiving eye—the
tyranny of her taste was liberating. It also led straight, it seems, to
collaboration. Chanel herself was a lover of Nazis and was punished by exile. Like Cocteau and many of the most refined, there
were those in France during the war whose engagement began
with the premise that the Germans had all the luxuries—food, of
course, and art and wine, paintings, clothes, and diamonds. Chanel, who liberated women, was a fascist, a racist, an anti-Semite.
Had the Germans won the war, she would have been just fine.
Does the radical disinterestedness of great taste imply the necessity
of great cruelty that leads to fascist politics? Or is this my self-
hatred in another guise? My mother, after all, had the most perfect
taste, she was once a mistress to Cézanne.

Could I become like Chanel without at the same time
becoming an elitist bigot, full of aesthetic indifference and social
despise? Probably not. Chanel, unlike my mother, hated anything
that stained the universalizing aristocracy, the rigorous purity,
of her taste with ethnic specificity, local color, surreal forms.
She loved what was purely white, and rare, and unembellished:
plus all Aryan barbarity, like ancient Syrian bangles with great
square stones sunk in purest gold, or ivory-white enameled brace-

lets imprinted with a Crusader's Maltese cross composed of large amethysts, emeralds, and carnelians. Assuming her aesthetic perspective I can hardly blame her, even if it means hating a part of myself. I have to remember that it's also the tyranny of her taste that invented a way for women to dress more freely and securely. Her cruel taste was her politics, and it became universal. She destroyed the nineteenth-century idea of woman; she invented the woman of modernity. Pale imitators can elaborate increasingly outrageous variations on her signature look, particularly on its details: short jacket, loose skirt, low heels with dark toes, chains, pearls, camellias. But no one can do what she did: revolutionize the way women's clothes are cut, changing the look of women in the twentieth century—and with that look, their possibilities for liberation. She despised her rival male couturiers, who knew nothing of what it meant to be a women, who only dreamed of becoming one. She only loved Karl Lagerfeld, a genius in his own right and a German, who succeeded her.

I think the secret of Chanel's genius was that she was the last dandy of the nineteenth century. Like French dandies, she took her inspiration from the restraint of English aristocrats, with whom she was most passionately involved, and from a Russian duke who taught her wild excess. Dandyism in France never meant spectacular exhibitionism, showy luxury à la Beau Brummel; it meant for Baudelaire and Banville the most discreet forms of tacit elegance. The French dandy dressed soberly, only in black, as if fleeing the eyes of the world, dressed in the uniform of perpetual mourning. But to the amazement of those happy few who knew enough to notice, his coat was so remarkably cut and finely tailored that its shoulders seemed to have been molded by fingers brushing the slope of his clavicle. His linen was so pure and white and it emerged so precisely from beneath the sleeve that only another of his tribe could notice and marvel at the

enormous pain and infinitely small refinements he brought to the
question of his *linge*. Baudelaire stayed in the house for days
when he could not afford a good laundress, unwilling to be seen
in public wearing linen not immaculately white.

But the essence of Chanel's dandyism is the role she assigned
to the *emmanchure*—the sleeve hole. She spent hours every day
standing in front of living models whose armholes she worked and
reworked, with scissors and pins, until the holes allowed the maxi-
mum freedom of movement with the smoothest, most unbroken
lines. There's a perhaps apocryphal story of Chanel's having
observed in Grand Central Station the way T-shirts stayed neatly
pressed to the muscled backs of GIs, even when they lifted things
above their head. She borrowed from them the gusset—the little
triangular piece of cloth that separates the front from the back of
the shirt or jacket, along the armpit—the first thing Chanel
looked at in a woman. All a woman's chic is instantly visible there.
A beautiful woman can be free only if she can move her arms. Of
course, she has to be able to walk as well; that's why the suit
always comes with a skirt that falls from the hips in easy pleats
with the military precision of a highland kilt—a skirt for making
war in.

Where does taste come from? It comes, the French like to
think, from the liver. Americans have little understanding of the
old humoral view of psychology, which has been only imper-
fectly replaced in the popular mind by scientific and psychiatric
interpretations (or vulgar psychoanalytic theories) of self. The
humoral theory of taste proceeds from a single assumption: *Cha-
cun à son goût*. No one's taste is exactly like anyone else's. Neither
the way you taste to others nor the way the world tastes to you. If
there is some organic determination of that irreducible difference
that distinguishes one from another, then it must reside in some-

thing like the complex chemistry of the liver, which receives and transforms all the products carried to it by the blood. Each liver has its own particular way of processing those products, of breaking them down. The chemistry of your liver determines, in part, why you prefer one perfume to another and, more determinedly, the way perfume smells on you. Chanel's liver told her to love the smell of Chanel No. 5. Her cubist taste for the mechanical reproducibility of the dandy's black suit made her choose to name her perfume with a number rather than one of the pseudo-poetic romantic appellations perfumes used to bear. But her most daring innovation was to combine, practically for the first time, the natural scents of flowers and oils with those that were newly synthesized by chemists and had never before existed in nature.

It is Chanel who allowed me to understand that the value of jewelry is complexly related to its equivalence in money. Before the house of Chanel launched its high-priced jewelry boutiques, it was known for its "petits bijoux"—not paste, but jewelry fashioned from less expensive stones and metals. At her shows, she draped her models with them, economizing the expense of using really good stuff; she was, of course, a monster of parsimony, except with those she loved—starting with herself. She often had the cheap pieces made over for herself using only the best and largest stones and the most precious metals. Chanel wore this fabulously expensive jewelry with her utterly simple clothes—with her little navy wool suit, her sailor costumes, over Boy's underwear. But her aim was not to be ostentatious. Great taste like hers makes expensive jewelry look like junk, something you'd throw on with fifteen other things. The gems are so enormous and the pieces so big that you think they can't possibly be real. She once said: "I gladly cover myself with bijoux (real ones), because on me they look fake."

Coco Chanel

And she continued: "Nothing looks more like a fake bijou than a large, beautiful real one" [Rien ne ressemble à un bijou faux comme un très beau bijou]. Just as any woman today with perfect breasts is assumed to have had an implant. Take, for instance, the sapphire I saw Diana wearing on television the other night, a giant sapphire afloat in the middle of a diamond choker; the stone was so big it looked like a hunk of glass. It violates your instinctive notion that precious gems are fundamentally small. Chanel concealed the splendor of her jewels, the fabulous jewelry she was rich enough and confident enough to wear. She hid them by wearing them more boldly, less decorously than they deserved.

There's the famous picture of Mademoiselle Chanel wearing necklaces with enormous real stones gleaming with iridescence, flashing their sharp refraction in the midst of strings of strass (glass paste, named for the German jeweler Irving Strass, who invented it). She wore her real big jewelry not for everyone, but for those who knew she was faking fake with the most expensive jewels in the world—all the more remarkably real for pretending to be something else.

Chanel very early in her adult life had access to unimaginable wealth. She was the mistress of several immensely wealthy men, and at one point entirely abandoned her work, into which she had thrown herself maniacally, to live with the Duke of Westminster, whose shrewd investments of his family's money made him the richest man in England, perhaps in the world; he had fully staffed houses he couldn't remember, in exotic corners of the British Empire. Chanel, in her memoirs, sums it up in the most telling enigmatic remark: "One cannot today imagine such luxury."

Chanel had the immense chic of the dandy: the art and style for making something fabulously precious and labor-intensive look like the most unremarkable familiar piece of nothing. Nothing that was important to Chanel was immediately visible; everything was obscured behind an imperious masquerade. In that she was like Louis XIV, for whom statecraft meant keeping secrets, and like him she loved the theater. He was a ballet dancer, remember, she a designer for the theater who made chiffon togas and sexy metal breastplates for heroines in plays by Cocteau set in mythic Greece. For her all clothing was a costume, or rather a kind of decor that served above all to create an illusion of spontaneity. A woman wears a dress the way an actress walks on stage, trying to look as if this is the dress she just happens to be wearing. In fact, of course, the dress and every accessory have been calculated down to the smallest significant detail.

I remember the moment in Sally's salon, after two hours of seminar, when I finally received a wig. Sally placed it gently, reverently on my head, coiffing it and smoothing it over my ears. I looked at myself in the mirror. For the last two hours I hadn't been sure what or where I was most of the time. I had been sitting at a dressing table with an old stocking on my head. The scalp above my brow was taped to the top of my head to bring my eyebrows up and expose more of the brow bone. They applied a lipstick base to cover the pores of my beard, then foundation and powder, working it all in evenly, blending, blending, always blending with beautiful little sponges to erase the visible edges that result from layering makeup on a male face. And then they put on the wig. After a few brush strokes, Sally stepped away, and before I looked at myself in the mirror I saw her smile with love at me, and I gauged the power of my transformation by the physical blow it dealt to the two other TVs. They both unmistakably reeled for a second before approaching to look more closely.

It was only then that I focused on my image in the mirror. I felt like a twin who'd been separated at birth from her sister, with whom I had been communicating all my life telepathically. And now, suddenly, I was encountering her in the mirror after we'd both become adults. She was just like me, but someone else—someone whose whole experience as a girl growing into a woman was unknown to me—unknown because it never happened. Minerva-like, she was born fully grown from the head of her father—me. I had never seen her before. But she was who I wanted to be, more me than I was—the me as whom I was most myself. I recognized her immediately, the same critical mouth (a taut line), the large watchful eyes, the slight hunching of the shoulders, and I started to laugh insanely, uncontrollably, rolling on the floor, until Sally got hold of me and calmed me down. I think she spanked me. Or maybe that's just my wishful thought. In the most common masturbatory fantasy of TVs, they are being forced by someone cruel to wear women's clothes against their will. It's only after having been coerced into dressing like a woman that you can allow yourself to feel like you need to. As I sat there, aglow with pleasure, I could tell, even under the spell of my gender euphoria, that Sally is one of those gendered girls who likes to watch men getting dressed as women principally for the pleasure of observing their erection—inevitably flaming and hard. I'm afraid I disappointed her. As I've tried to explain, Zeem, my femininity isn't phallic, the way it is with most transvestites; it's rather more cosmic than cosmetic—assuming one can ever disentangle those terms.

I sunk into the moist luxury, the pastel perfumes, the cottony hum, of women making up together; I was one of my mother's friends at the beauty parlor, or at home with Elizabeth Arden, or Mary Kay, women gathered in the living room, brought together by some shared ideal or marketable idea of beauty. That ideal, however impalpable and mostly unexpressed, perhaps ineffable, brings women together in circles of support. But it also excites in women who are making each other up (and over) a critical faculty of judgment, a ruthless determination to exclude whatever offends or diminishes the ideal of beauty to which their circle subscribes. No critic is more cruel than a beautiful woman before her glass. She tolerates nothing that compromises the look she precisely craves. How do they know what they want, where they want it? I needed to know.

After forty, it is said, a man has the face he deserves, while a woman has the face she can afford. Women's beauty is first of all an expensive gift she gives the world, an act of creative generosity—an enormous expenditure of attention, or money, or both, to remain beautiful. A woman committed to giving pleasure with her beauty carries around with her an idea of beauty that comes to her enriched by centuries of elaboration, which she works on constantly, with a kind of devoted humility, to embody in herself.

Notions of feminine beauty may very well evolve. Brigitte Bardot very little resembles the Venus of Willendorf—apart from the beauty of her swelling breasts and the perfect smoothness of her skin. But Nefertiti more closely resembles a beautiful woman in *Vogue* than she does, say, a hippy mother or a butch dyke, or some other alternative model of more "natural" or more perverse female beauty. Ideas of the feminine may not be eternal, but they are very old and change slowly.

Sitting there in their studio, surrounded by mirrors, suddenly transformed, I thought of Chanel in front of her dressing table, the one that appears in photographs all mirrored and covered with silver boxes and silvery flasks, silver brushes and scattered jewelry—nothing that does not reflect. Just imagine the prodigies of critical judgment that went into composing year after year that orphaned peasant's face, which had conquered the world and several of its richest, most elegant men. And I thought of her in that other picture, sitting at a low Japanese table, taking gems from the baskets distributed around her and pressing them into clay, composing ideas for jewelry that her artisans then superbly executed. Baskets full of diamonds, rubies, her famous emeralds, the sapphires she particularly loved—"the cold blue water of the sapphire," she called it. Cold, blue water, like what probably ran in her veins: Chanel was a witch and a bitch. Is that her secret? I felt a growing sense of desperation trying to imagine how I could ever understand the difference between what was passably correct and what was truly beautiful in a woman.

Earlier, at Harvard in those confusing days, I often dreamed of being Prince Mangagoul, the hero of Diderot's dirty novel. You might not think that Mangagoul, the sultan of the Congo, an entirely mythical, perfectly fabulous Oriental kingdom, would have any reason to be bored. He is master of a fat and peaceful land—much resembling France in the 1740s—blessed with secure borders within which learning flourishes and commerce thrives, a land distinguished by its academies and universities and graced with a capital city, Banza, which he administers liberally and generously endows. He has the most beautiful mistress in the world, Mimoza, who like Scheherazade keeps him endlessly entertained with stories she imagines and gossip she embroiders about the people of his country and the nobles in his court, all of whose bijoux are very busy. Mimoza is not only the most beautiful woman in the Congo but also the most brilliant; the prince himself acknowledges that she is, in every way, his intellectual equal, and between them exists perfect candor and mutual sympathy.

The relation between Prince Mangagoul and his mistress, Mimoza, replicates in some ways the one between the author, Diderot, and his own brainy mistress at the time, the notoriously ugly Mme. de Puisieux. The lady was married to one of his collaborators on the *Great Encyclopedia*. Diderot was struggling, on an exiguous budget, to produce the first volume, A–AZY, of the encyclopedia whose de facto editor he had become. He had just finished writing articles on: ACIER (steel), AGRICULTURE, ANIMAL, ART, AUTORITE POLITIQUE, ARABES, and ARGENT (i.e., silver, money—of which he had all too little). Mme. de Puisieux was a serious intellectual in her own write and a writer who had published several books, including a sort of mentoring novel directed at young women that was fiercely feminist for its time and heaped derision on male pretensions to superiority. How ugly was she? She was so ugly, by her own account in the preface, that she had given up even trying anymore to be beautiful, because it was so absolutely incompatible with staying up late to study, as she had been doing for years, deep into night after night.

Maybe that's my problem. If I hadn't spent so much god-damn time in those days hanging around the Harvard library, I wouldn't be looking so tired around the eyes today, despite all the plastic surgery. But there were so many things to see in that place besides the books, and so many leather chairs to sink into under yellow vellum lamp shades, holding some tome at a plausible angle while you allowed yourself to dream of the steam rooms only a block away in the vast Harvard gym. Before entering the swimming pool, men and women had to pass naked—perhaps they still do—over a little spray rising from the floor to spritz your genitals. It must have been invented by some Yankee puritan committed to public health, with the ostensible aim of controlling the spread of venereal disease but with unintended consequences that were terrifically erotic. The shower is short, cold, and hard and it makes you jump as you go across. It was the most intense public sexual experience I had in Cambridge, sunk as I was in the private absorption of study—staying up late to read instead of getting my bijoux rung.

Mangagoul is a prince the way the people dreamed that Louis XV might have turned out to be. Diderot, at the age of thirty-four, was writing *Les bijoux* in 1747. Having recently assumed the throne, Louis XV was still being called the "Bien-Aimé," though he didn't stay well loved for long. He ended up being totally enslaved to his rapacious mistress, Mme. Du Barry, whose repertoire of sexual tricks was so diverse and original (the accumulated wisdom of her long career as a beautiful courtesan) that Louis became utterly unable to live without her. He confessed that he had come to depend entirely for sexual pleasure on the "petites complaisances" she provided him. "Complaisance" is a word, now obsolete in English, that in French refers to the naughty disposition amiably to comply with some kinky demand for pleasure. The king's biographers tend to agree that Mme. Du Barry probably massaged Louis's prostate, rimmed and fisted him. She who governs the anus of the king (and kisses his ass) rules the kingdom. Remember this. It will come up again.

Madame Du Barry

So when Louis XV succeeded to the throne, all hopes were still in him. The last enfeebled years of Louis XIV's reign had been sunk in gloom following the deaths in quick succession of the king's son and two of his grandsons. Tormented by priests, tortured by the cruelty of doctors and the ministrations of his wife, the zealously pious Mme. de Maintenon, Louis XIV is reported to have averred, laughing, "I have heard it said that dying is hard, I find it all too easy." Broke, defeated, decrepit, leeched by charlatans, and drowning in sanctity, Louis was probably ready to go.

His death was followed by the Regency, the period during which young Louis XV, the last living grandson of Louis XIV, had not yet attained his majority. Charles, the duc d'Orleans, Louis XIV's dissolute nephew and the son of fat Princess Liselotte, governed the young king as regent and presided over an explosion of dissipation and debauchery, a long intermezzo of frivolity, corruption, and financial panic. It was a gay time, full of wild speculation, light furniture, and sensual excess, after the gloom at the end of Louis XIV's reign. The single most important achieve-

The Regent Diamond

ment of the Regency was the purchase, from Sir Thomas Pitt, grandfather of the prime minister William Pitt, of what came to be called the Regent diamond, the largest in the French crown jewels, 65 carats, for the then staggering sum of 1,800,000 livres. But what a stone! What glory! It came from Indian mines belonging to the Grand Mogul, and it was smuggled into France (if one believes the story told by Saint-Simon) stuck up the ass of the worker who found it and who somehow avoided the enemas meticulously administered to employees whenever they left the mine. (Zeem, I told you this would be important.)

Saint-Simon writes: "This diamond was called the Regent. It is the size of a reine Claude plum (the yellow variety), almost perfectly round, of a thickness that corresponds to its volume, perfectly colorless, exempt from any flaw, cloud, or straw, with an admirable fire, weighing more than 500 grains."[2] The regent himself was reluctantly persuaded by his finance minister to buy the stone, despite its exorbitant cost and the plight of the treasury, out of consideration for "the honor of the crown." He had the "unique opportunity" of buying "a priceless diamond, one that would outshine all the others in Europe." It would be a "glory for his Regency," and anyway, he was told, his finances were so bad that even adding this considerable debt would hardly be noticed. The crown of France is the index of the regent's glory; it signifies

---

2. Saint-Simon, *Les Mémoires du Duc de Saint-Simon*. Translated by Lucy Norton. London: Prion Books, 1999.

and materially enhances with its brilliance the reign of whomever it caps. To add an important jewel—a jewel in the crown—is the ultimate gesture, the last word, in bespeaking noble pride and enhancing royal prestige—a beacon of kingly glory.

When at last Louis XV ascended to the throne, even a skeptical philosopher like young Diderot could still dream of a king who would rule the country with justice and science, bringing perpetual peace and displaying flawless taste. Diderot imagines just such a successful, liberal prince in the guise of Mangagoul, who is so enlightened that he orders the gates of his harem unlocked and allows his wives to go where they please. He loves their freedom and is confident that if they betray him they will at least, out of gratitude, be discreet.

Yet despite having everything a prince could desire, or because of it, he has no more desire: Mangagoul is desperately bored. No one in fact is ever so bored as a satiated prince. Not even lubricious tales spun out by the most beautiful creature in the kingdom can rouse him from the intellectual apathy and sexual torpor into which he has fallen. He is unmoved by fictions; only the blunt truth still interests and arouses him. But how can even a prince discover the truth of what a woman has been doing with her bijou?

Mangagoul calls on the power of a family genie. Cucufa, a hypochondriac and sorcerer, has been spending eternity hung upside down for his health until he's summoned by the prince, to whom he proposes a magic charm—an exceptional ring. To make the bijoux of women speak he gives Mangagoul a bijou. Whenever the prince turns the bezel (in French, the *chaton*) of the ring in the direction of a woman, her *chatte* (or pussy) begins to speak: *le chaton* (masculine) *fait parler la chatte* (feminine). Puss makes pussy speak. From between its luscious furry lips there emanates, at the bidding of the ring, uncensored accounts of its lascivious adventures. The prince's jewel, like some early crystal radio, becomes a microphone and transmitter, allowing him to overhear the unspoken conversations and adorable secrets of a woman's most private parts. At last he can hear from her own lips, as it were, what no man has ever heard: the frankly indiscreet truth of a woman's jewel.

My ambition, first in the thesis and now here, has always been the same: to be a kind of Mangagoul. He pointed jewelry at a sex and the sex spoke; I want to point sex at jewelry and make jewelry talk—whatever that means! Without a genie like his, I can only reverse the legend. He makes the figural literal—bijou is a metaphor for sex; I want sex to be a metaphor for jewelry. It means that I am looking for a magic ring, a sort of "bug," with which to spy on jewelry. My magic ring is the erotic point of view of a transgendered male—the sex I can turn on jewelry, tuning in with a clandestine receiver that picks up secrets and whispers them exclusively to me. As Mangagoul mused, I, too, have wondered: "And who knows what a bijou can have on its mind?" (Et qui sait ce qu'un bijou peut avoir dans l'âme?)[3]

The magic ring I possess is a fantastic hypothesis that goes like this: Let us suppose there is one specific kind of jewelry that acts as a major megaphone to amplify and convey with perfect clarity the murmuring voice of a woman's bijou. Not all her jewelry works that way, only this particular kind. For a long time, I focused my attention exclusively on pendants; I'm not sure why. Why pendants suspended on chains hanging from necks talk more loudly than other forms of jewelry remains a mystery. Freud, of course, identifies a man's tie with his penis since both dingle-dangle. The pendant hangs at the bottom of a wide

---

3. P. N. Furbank, *Diderot: A Critical Biography.* New York: Alfred A. Knopf, 1992, p. 41.

expanse that the chain describes, as if the throat were a kind of torso and the pendant, plumped in its hollow at its base, the focus of particular erotic attention. The throat is often the place on to which sexual feelings get displaced—like nervous coughs and loss of voice. In the end, I can't explain it; I can only attest, on the grounds of my scrupulous empirical research, that it works—like a charm!

Armed like Mangagoul, wielding this magic hypothesis, I set out and soon confirmed my hunch that you can tell everything about a woman's availability by listening to the language spoken by the pendant around her neck. My interest in jewelry isn't purely aesthetic; you might say it's political. Knowing how to listen to jewelry talk is a formidable weapon in the arsenal of seduction, indispensable for adjusting strategies and devising tactics. Let me give you some examples.

Clair was very pure and lovely and wore a tiny cross studded with tiny rubies on a gold chain around her neck. Time after time, as I approached the Castle Saint Angelo of her Holy See, my pilgrim shrank and shriveled, as if in shame or horror, at the thought of violating those sacred precincts. If you go out with a woman who is wearing a cross on a chain, you have to assume she has placed this sign on her bijou like a bar, a taboo, and that her jewel has nothing to say, hums only hymns. (The same hypothesis would doubtless apply, in varying degrees, if the lady was wearing a Star of David or, in France, a Huguenot dove of the Holy Spirit.)

But, if the cross is a very large one, that's an entirely different story. Now you are dealing either with a woman who is fiercely pious and disapproving of fornication, or the opposite, a witch (like Madonna used to be) ready for any sacrilege. A moment's conversation will tell you which.

You might pay particular attention to the material of which

the cross is made: a simple empty wooden one means, austerely, that her jewel is vacant, forsaken, and unpossessed. Intensely jeweled ones, like those Chanel designed to look like ancient Damascene crosses, come very close to being pagan, evoking whiffs of sacred prostitution—priestesses in the temples of Phoenicia.

There was Chantal from Lebanon leaning across the counter in the Cheyenne Diner and shaking the perfume from her glistening hair onto the heaping plate of fries she placed before me, while my eyes were fixed on the spiked leather cross that stretched out deliciously across the expanse of her gleaming breasts, like bacon over eggs over easy.

Sometimes women wear marks of identity around their necks, often their names. I take these to be signs, clear and unmistakable, that they have signed for their jewel; for them it is a kind of possession, a piece of property they are not about to concede except in return for another signature, etched at the bottom of a marriage contract.

Conversely, if a woman wears a heart or a flower on a chain around her neck, her jewel is ready for love. If she wears an enormously big red heart, a plump curvy one, or an exceedingly pink flower, she's letting you know rather boldly that she's incandescently hot—to trot. In the casino in Biarritz I once saw a famous international whore, linked at the time to Prince Charles. At her neck was a thick gold chain from which hung a huge mound of tiny peacock feather piled on satin pink cockleshells, sprinkled with semiprecious stones—all puffed out, fluffy and furry. It announced for all with ears to hear that hers was a bijou that was generally available but at a price only few could afford.

On the street today, Faubourg-Saint-Honoré, I saw a gorgeous long blonde boojie lady (very pearl necklace/Hermès scarf) wearing instead of pearls a large 18-karat gold heart on a chain with a ruby cross in the center (the emblem of the sacred heart of Jesus)—surely a gift. Translated into secular terms, it meant she has an apartment in the 16th arrondissement, is a practicing Catholic praying to get pregnant, with a husband who hasn't taken a mistress yet. I ran up to check for a wedding band. She had one of those double rings in gold, the kind that fold inside one another: it confirmed what the pendant told me, that she's clearly intricately married.

Butterflies are a particular problem. In Freud they mean castration. But that's not my experience exactly. The butterfly speaks of a bijou that wants to close itself, like delicate wings, around a central member, and hold it tightly in its fluttering grasp. Butterflies often resemble bows (in French a papillon is a bow tie), which women sometimes wear on chains. The bow is a knot tied snugly around whatever penetrates the glassy curves of its delicious siliceous folds. To the seducer, a butterfly or knot is not a not! The bigger the fly the better the butter.

Men sometimes wear a hound's tooth, one of those wavy pointy charms in gold or silver hung on a chain. They look so much like flaccid penises you would think a guy could wear one only naively—or ironically. But if a woman wears one, it is more interesting and more alarming: it says that this is a woman who wants to hang with men. Conversely, you ought to know, Zeem, that a woman who wears nothing more than a single perfect pearl on a chain around her neck is probably hopelessly clitoral, i.e., narcissistic and masturbatory, less interested in giving pleasure than in rolling her pearl by herself.

You don't want your jewelry to talk too loud, Zeem. You might think that wearing a little heart around your neck is being discreet and tasteful, but in fact, as I'm trying to show you, the most discreet, conventional jewelry is the most indiscreet: it speaks all too clearly, lets itself be heard by anyone who wants to listen. Conversely, the rarer and more beautiful the pendant the more obscurely it speaks of desire. The best jewelry is secretive, speaks in subtle ways, difficult to decipher, open to interpretation. It's important, Zeem, for girls to know that: others, particularly men, are reading their jewelry all the time. If you are going to wear it, at least don't be naive about it. If you don't catch the indiscretions of which your jewelry may be guilty, someone who wants to seduce you probably will. If a woman (or a man) hangs a chain around her neck from which hangs a pendant pierced with a round hole, it's a way of saying "I have one" and I'm inviting you to dream of filling it. I went out with a nymphomaniac who wore two vast concentric circles on a chain, one in gold, one in ebony, as if to say she was nothing but an abyss—all shaft awaiting to be shafted.

But suppose you don't wear any jewelry at all? That's a question I'd prefer to postpone.

Diderot was in his youth a gorgeous man and an insatiable lover. Few women could resist him, except perhaps Mme. de Puisieux, who held out for more than love. It was for her he wrote his first porn novel. Later, defending himself against charges of immorality, he blamed the book on the fact that she put him up to it. In 1761, Diderot told two young German admirers: "I wrote an odious book: *Les bijoux indiscrets.* I might be excused in part; I had a mistress. She demanded that I give her fifty golden louis, and I didn't have a sou. She threatened to leave me if I didn't give her this sum, within a fortnight. I wrote a book catering to the taste of the majority of readers [to judge by *Le sofa,* the sexy success recently dashed off by Crebillon *fils*]. I brought the manuscript to a publisher, he gave me the fifty golden louis, and I came home and threw them in her skirt."[4] Commanded by her bijou

---

4. Furbank, *Diderot,* p. 43.

he writes *Les bijoux* in exchange for money he returns to her skirts—completing the circle from from lip to lap.

Loosely translated, *Les bijoux indiscrets* is *Jewelry Talks.* But in French, "bijoux" is not exactly synonymous with jewelry, there are actually two words for that: ordinarily, one distinguishes "joaillerie," which is about mounting precious stones and pearls on precious metals, like an engagement ring or a tiara, from "bijoux," which are small, artistically crafted objects of adornment, highly worked, often high priced—Chanel's frog brooch, for example, or Cartier's onyx-and-diamond tigers.

Most bijoux don't deserve to be called joyaux: stones and settings in imperial crowns, or long pendant diamond earrings with an oval emerald drop, like those Diana wore in Australia on her first great diplomatic triumph, when she was photographed dancing awkwardly with Charles, her face red with embarrassment, grinning but barely bearing it. She was dressed in an off-the-shoulder sky-blue silk organdy dress designed by McQueen, and on her forehead was Queen Mary's cabochon emerald necklace transformed into a bejeweled bandeau. The evenly spaced square-cut emeralds basked in the glow of the large brilliant-cut diamonds that surround them and lend them light. The brilliant-cut facets in the stone are mathematically calculated to prevent the least amount of light from escaping through the bottom of the diamond, allowing all its fire to flash out the visible table at the top, illuminating and magnifying what it surrounds. Jewelry magnifies what it illuminates.

Bijou, conversely, frequently connotes something small fitting easily in the hand, but cunning, complexly contrived, densely packed with the value of precious materials and intensive labor. The word probably comes from an old Breton word, "bijou," that means ring for the finger, from the Celtic word for finger, "biz." A little person is a bijou; you call any adorable little thing "mon bijou." Being small it has something particularly affecting, something that touches you closely, intimately, like a child, because so much loveliness is encompassed within something so diminutive. A woman's bijou is the loveliest thing she wears.

As you can imagine, Mangagoul can hardly contain his excitement, and at the first opportunity he turns his ring on one of the most modest and fetching married ladies at court, a model of sobriety and marital fidelity. Imagine her surprise when, without warning but unmistakably, there issues forth from beneath her skirts a high-pitched voice, only slightly resembling her own, which proceeds to recount in vivid and wanton detail her adulterous adventures with excessively prominent members of the Brahmin clergy. At this success, Mangagoul becomes an insatiable searcher after the truth of jewels. Wherever he turns his ring, women's jewels begin to speak, enumerating their adventures, judging past performances, and lewdly confessing in appalling detail delectable secrets of lubricious acts and voluptuous indiscretions.

You could argue that Mangagoul is a rapist, taking away from a woman, through magical means, what she would never willingly divulge. This moral objection, which threatens to halt the novel, is raised by Diderot. Mangagoul insists that his interest is merely intellectual, not sexual at all, and for the sake of the truth he relentlessly perseveres. Someone, after all, has to do this work.

Hearing, observing, questioning women's bijoux, I've spent much of my live dreaming I was Mangagoul, or sometimes another fictional hero, the poet connoisseur in "Les bijoux," a poem of Baudelaire. I learned the poem by heart at Harvard for my thesis (I could hardly avoid it) and I've recited it since a million times. It never fails to turn me on. It's the sexiest poem in the first edition of *Les fleurs du mal,* one of those banned by the censorious courts of the Second Empire, which deemed them an affront to public morality and an incitement to vice. The poem is a dirty postcard sent by Baudelaire to the reader depicting his Creole mistress, Jeanne Duval, disposed in the most erotic pose, undressed to kill, wearing only her gems. She was a famous "actress" in the Paris theater, of very bad character, whom he kept at great expense of money and calm. She was, however, his muse. She knew what he liked like nobody's business, exactly the way Baudelaire knew what would turn his readers on: "O memorizers of poems, overexcited graduate students sitting in plush libraries, creaming over crumbling tomes, this is for you." She is the poet's pornographer; he's ours.

In the poem she excites him not with any tricks, but simply by her attitude—the way she looks at him and the pose she strikes. His excitement is almost purely voyeuristic. Almost, I say, because it's also discreetly aural and olfactory—synesthetic: he loves the way she smellsoundslooks.

> *La très-chère etait nue, et connaissant mon coeur,*
> *Elle n'avait gardé que ses bijoux sonores,*
> *Dont le riche attirail lui donnait l'air vainqueur*
> *Qu'ont dans leurs jours heureux les esclaves des*
>   *Mores.*

> *(Knowing my heart, my dearest one was naked,*
> *Her jangly jewelry all she wore,*
> *Whose rich array gave her the conquering air*
> *Of Moorish slaves on their happy days.)*

Here's the question, Zeem: If you are wearing only jewelry, are you dressed or undressed? She's naked, but not unclothed. The jewels dress her nakedness but don't cover it; in fact, they make it more visible, more visibly enticing to this spectator whose taste she knows so well. Like a flimsy veil, her jewelry hides what it allows to be seen: now you see it, now you don't—intermittently, maddening, enticing. The jewels could be said to frame her nakedness, but not in the usual sense of surrounding around out-side. The jewelry infiltrates her form and makes it more intricate and complex. It lends the hard exteriority of gems and precious metals to the forgiving softness of her skin.

La très-chère . . . est très chère, ma chère. Baudelaire means us to hear in those words all the bitterly sarcastic cynicism he feels toward that woman, who is costing him a fortune and for whom nothing is ever enough. Women are expensive. She is very . . . very dear. But, she also happens to be sublime, because *très-chère* could also mean she's priceless, beyond all measure, equal in value to nothing except herself. She is a finite thing that gives him intimations of infinity—the infinitely self-reflexive brilliance of whatever, beyond all price, is sublime.

When I started living in Paris I began to understand what it meant to be desperately in love with a bad woman, who knew your deepest secret sexual desires. The rage and impotence, the totally humiliating self-abnegation and fury at the foot of this nasty woman, who plays with your desire like a cat with a string. You can imagine how Baudelaire must have spit out those first words of the poem: "La très-chère . . ." Reports of his lectures and readings confirm, as one might guess, that he spoke rapidly, mechanically, in bursts of acid irony. You can imagine him slyly grinning, grimacing as he drags out the two grave accents in "très-chère," opening the vowel, as if the tongue didn't want to emit the words until it had finished rolling them around in the mouth—la trèèès chèèère, dripping sarcasm. With a drawl and a wink, he became before the eyes of his Belgian audience the incarnation of a Parisian dandy just stepped out of some fashion-able salon in the Faubourg-Saint-Germain.

She wears only her jewels because she knows "my heart," the poet says. Even by this time in the nineteenth century, "mon coeur" was an expression that had become virtually useless in poetry, the pale ruin of an exhausted Petrarchan repertory of love poetry. It could only be used ironically as a euphemism for another organ of affection she knows how to touch. The editor of the late-nineteenth-century volume I was reading had illustrated the sulfurous volume with what he meant to be pornographic engravings. By contemporary standards they were pretty inno-cent, of course, but something about their muted boldness—the depth of shadows and flare of firelight roiling her body glistening with oil and jewels—excited my pedantic heart with their in-comparable chiaroscuro. Like ladies on a dirty Victorian post-card, this one is no lady, a kind of prostitute, who sells her love for money. (*Porno* in Greek means whore, as you probably know, Zeem.)

Most of all, he loves her *bijoux sonores*—"jangly jewelry" is how I translate it: bangles jangle. In French, *sonore* means noisy as well as, more neutrally, resonant. The noise her jewelry makes is all the more exciting for being aggressive, a little jarring—music that surrounds her with the rattle of castanets, irritating and arousing with its volume as well as its rhythms. The noise her jewelry makes, he says, is "vif et moqueur," lively and mocking, not just noise but something like laughter—tinkling mocking. Note that it's not she who says anything, smiling superbly, it's her jewelry that talks or, more exactly, laughs at him, runs a kind of glittering ironic commentary on this scene of conquest the Moorish slave beholds "on one of her happy days." A Moorish slave doesn't have a lot of happy days, days when she feels like the conqueror instead of the conquered. At those moments, ephemeral, illusory, she becomes the master of her master's bed, an imperious mistress with the power to provoke storms of desire and to twist his will around hers.

It's in this relation of dominated and domineering, as Simmel saw, after Baudelaire, that the meaning of jewelry resides. It is probably literally true, certainly worth speculating, that all jewelry is some form of slave bracelet, a chain or link that binds you to someone else or to yourself as someone else—your lord, i.e., someone better, more perfect, freer and more beautiful than yourself. The aim is always to enchain the other, make him (or her) submit to the beauty ornamental jewelry enhances. When it works, a creature well adorned, no matter how abject or constrained, triumphs. Baudelaire knew about the look of Moorish

"Mort de Sardanapale" by Eugène Delacroix

slaves from Delacroix, who loved to paint them in Oriental harems, like the famous one slumped at the foot of a massive bed on which her turbaned master lies serenely looking down. Her voluminous black curls and voluptuous curves lie adrift in wispy veils spread out against the snow white and gleaming gold of despotic sheets. Submission seems to make her more beautiful. Wearing nothing but jewelry, this Moorish slave, lying there on the sofa "trying poses," mocks the mute astonishment of the poet-sultan watching her—helpless in the presence of her sexual power. With only jewelry as her weapon, she ravishes the prince into ecstasy with the ornamented, ornamental spectacle of her nakedness.

> *Quand il jette en dansant son bruit vif et moqueur,*
> *Ce monde rayonnant de métal et de pierre*
> *Me ravit en extase, et j'aime à la fureur*
> *Les choses où le son se mêle avec la lumière.*

> *(When [her jewelry] dancing casts its lively mocking*
>   *noise,*
> *I'm ravished into ecstasy by this shining world of metal*
>   *and stone,*
> *And fall furiously in love with*
> *Things in which sound and light intermingle.)*

The ravisher is ravished by the jewelry he gave her. It takes him away, ecstatically, to a gleaming world of iron beds, crystal walls, and oiled satin bodies. What turns him on, he says, is her jewelry; those things she wears he loves furiously, madly—like that necklace slung over her ripe brown breast, hung with Anrézach beads. It has a pendant, a small, green silk purse in the center of which is set a faceted piece of green glass imitating an emerald. Just like Esmeralda's! Green is the color of Islam, also of witches and hope, says Victor Hugo. Esmeralda, in his novel of Notre Dame, is a Spanish Gypsy untouched by Christian reticence. The purse is an amulet. No one else may touch it; if they touch it they die.

I remember watching the evening fade and lights go on across the river in the high apartments that face the Seine. I was dressed in nothing but my black satin bikini brief that made my perfect ass the gleaming focus of the room, when she came up behind me and put his hands around my neck. (Sorry, Zeem. This gets confusing. From now on I'll mostly call her him, since that's how she thought about herself.) Before I knew what was happening he choked me back hard with a chiffon scarf he had hidden in his fist. I couldn't breathe. I saw lights, then black, I gasped, desperate, my ears ringing. She . . . he let up and let down the scarf slowly; I sank into his arms where soon he began furiously kissing me all over. Then he took out of his other fist and attached to my neck a thin platinum chain which fit very tight on my neck, like a choker, on which were strung twelve small intricately carved Burmese rubies, like wild strawberries that were good enough to eat.

He no sooner put it on me, then his whole behavior changed. Now he wanted to be *my* slave, abjectly humiliating himself at my feet, not only willing to do my will but eager to tell me how grateful he was. I told him to start by sucking my toes. I felt triumphantly beautiful, a harem queen for a day.

In the poem, her jewelry speaks as well as shines. Jewelry has always been designed to give off both sound and light (and sometimes perfume—like Etruscan earrings that had secret pockets to hold tiny sponges soaked in aphrodisiac). Today we hardly think twice about it. Baudelaire would have loved movies and video; he adored the opera, where sound and light spectacularly intermingle. "J'aime à la fureur," he says. Sounds that flash, mocking laughter, the clash of bright metal and reflecting stone, these are things that get him off on waves of fevered passion, make him mad with lust and love when jewelry laughs or music gleams.

At the end of the poem, Baudelaire's mistress has become a wild beast about to take the poet, her prey:

> —*Et la lampe s'étant résignée à mourir,*
> *Comme le foyer seul illuminait la chambre,*
> *Chaque fois qu'il poussait un flamboyant soupir,*
> *Il inondait de sang cette peau couleur d'ambre!*

> (—*And since the lamp resigned itself to die,*
> *The hearth alone lit up the room;*
> *Each time it uttered forth a blazing sigh*
> *It washed with tones of blood her amber skin.*)

His mistress knows cute tricks, some of which she's doing there, right in front of us in front of him, lying by a dying fire, with only her jewelry—"like a tamed tiger, with a vague and dreamy air," he says. Trying poses, she stretches and twists and shows herself to him from every angle. He knows what he likes. Baudelaire has left us letters with long paragraphs describing in the most haunting, lurid detail the exquisite shades of black and purple and pink that mottle the fleshy forms of his mistress's cunt.

She is all summed up in the last word of the poem as "ambre," a thing in which light and sound intermingle. The rarest amber is a shapeless, translucent, fossilized natural resin, the petrified sap of an extinct pine tree (*Pinus succinifera*) that was submerged beneath the sea sixty million years ago. The word "ambre" is very close in French to the sound of "ombre," which means shadow or darkness. The grave vowel lends to the name of the thing in the poem intimations of mortality and dark sex.

Photograph of amber

Ambre! Metrically, the sound is a single, drawn-out syllable, partly vowel back in the throat, partly consonant cluster rumbling frontally down at the teeth. "Ambre" is the last word of the poem, casually appended, as if by an afterthought, the way jewelry adorns his mistress. She is amber in all its mystery: red gold and honey, pale yellow to reddish brown, the tawny yellow of lions or blood on a tiger's mouth. Since earliest antiquity, amber has been beloved for its strange density, neither impenetrable as stone (amber is easy to carve) nor plastic as wax (it is often faceted like emeralds); brittle but soft to the touch, electrified when rubbed—like a cat. The best kind is succinite or sea amber, washed up on Baltic coasts, on the eastern coast of England, or in the Netherlands from beds of ancient tertiary seas that lie petrified and fossilized beneath the North Sea. Some of it finds its way to the surface (the destiny of sap is to rise), then, rarely, washes up on occasional shores, having been polished on the way by innumerable accidents and countless encounters with sand.

I say polish, as if I knew what it meant, as if polishing stones were not itself a mystery that has always beckoned humans. To feel its power you need only watch one of those stone-polishing machines, widely available, full of whirling steel balls, in which an ordinary gray stone picked up from the bed of a stream is transformed after a while into a gleaming translucent crystal.

Boiled in oil, amber turns from being opaque to crystal clear. It's then that you can see most clearly the insects and seeds occasionally trapped inside—victims to the catastrophe, poor saps!, that befell the primordial tree. For most of human history, amber was the most electric thing you could own; rub it with a cloth, and hair flies. Put it next to the skin on your arm and you can feel the way this stone touches you back when you wear it, communicating its energy in subtle charges. Amber's static electricity has always been seen to be the token of its spiritual power. As an amulet, it counters the insidious rays that come from the evil eye of those who mean to do us harm. Amber protects from sorcerers and witches.

Finally, the word "ambre" in French has another meaning hidden behind the first. Like an Etruscan earring, the word has a secret pocket that contains perfume. "Ambre" also means "ambergris," the miraculous waxy substance spit up by whales and found floating by sailors in tropical waters. Until recently, it was the principal fixative used in perfume to keep the delicate notes of flowers from fading away in the bottle. It has barely any odor itself, except a mildly pleasant animal scent. Ambergris has been intricately carved like wax and used as jewelry, like the pendant depicting Charity with three children in the Walters Art Gallery in Baltimore. Hard and waxy, ambergris is slippery, as if polished with oil, like the tawny resplendence of the damp and wanton amber body of Baudelaire's triumphal mistress.

In trying to become a woman, I stumbled more than once over the bitter necessity of having to choose my jewelry, not for a moment knowing what I wanted or even what I ought to want. But now, confronting that decision, I consult my own (internalized) compendium of Chanel's taste in jewelry to guide me. I've tried to allow Chanel to tell me how I should be a woman faced with the question of her jewelry.

I have conscientiously tried to read meticulously everything written about her. Some of the biographies I've practically memorized. I've tried to allow Chanel to speak through me, to inhabit me. I am a monkey of Chanel. But Chanel herself, particularly in her old age, is often seen as being simian. So I am repeating a repetition she herself insists on. She constantly maintains that she is not an artist, that her work is not an art but a craft because it deals only in models and copies. Making those, she is more like someone aping—miming the same gesture, the same look, almost mechanically—than someone inventing, creating. Her work of repetition is all about the slightest adjustments to the same suit for generations. I'm aping her aping, repeating—monkey see—monkey do—her taste, her choices, her models. Mainly, I'm trying to put into words and put into order her philosophy of jewelry—as it once may have existed, as it is still visible, readable, today in photographs and documents, as it is briefly recorded in remarks she is said to have made.

I've turned over in my mind a million times something she said to an interviewer in 1932, on the occasion of her fabulous show in Paris consisting exclusively of diamond jewelry. She is reported to have said: "Before me, a piece of jewelry was first a design. My jewelry represents *first of all* an idea."[5]

Her originality consists in bringing ideas to jewelry, and starting with them. This intellectual origin of Chanel's jewelry is the central mystery from which I begin. What ideas? What philosophy of jewelry is implicit in her style, drives the concept that creates the piece of jewelry, determines its shape and substance, its qualities and form? You see how this question, posed abstractly like that, led me in turn to Georg Simmel, an almost contempo-

---

5. Patrick Mauriès, *Les bijoux de Chanel.* London: Thames and Hudson, Ltd., 1993, p. 25.

rary of Chanel, a philosopher of money and theorist of society, who wrote a famous, wonderful chapter on ornamentation, or jewelry—the best thing I could find. It is entitled, in German, "Das Schmuck."

(Listen, Zeem, you may like me be surprised to know that the word "schmuck" is German for "jewelry," but it also means more generally "ornament" or "adornment." I never knew that growing up. I never realized that the Yiddish—and now the American English—use of the word goes back to the German word for jewelry. If I had, I would have understood that the word in German gets troped into Yiddish to mean something like family jewels, from whence "schmuck," the word for penis, or prick, which is attributed by extension to a jerk. You schmuck! The most beautiful adornment becomes the worst insult in Yiddish. Maybe it's the culture obsessed with circumcision. The foreskin is the schmuck of the schmuck, the jewel on the penis which adorns the glorious male—a dispensable little addition which must be detached in order for the penis to be found to be Jewish. When a man gives a woman jewelry, particularly when it's a ring, he can't help identifying it with his family jewels. A woman who wears "his" ring wears the "schmuck." In the case of a woman wearing a vulgar diamond solitaire, she might as well be wearing a check around her finger, says Chanel, made out for the amount it costs. In such cases, the man gives a diamond ornament (schmuck), which is a kind of penis (schmuck), equivalent in his mind to a certain sum of money with which he identifies himself, and that makes him a schmuck, if you see what I mean.)

To Simmel, jewelry, or ornament, is not an object of purely frivolous interest—mere adornment, superfluous and inessential in itself. Or rather (and this, he says, is the strangest sociological fact), precisely because jewelry is all these things—because it is in no way necessary—it serves to enhance the dignity, the visibility, the "emphasis" with which an individual imposes her personality on others. Because what is superfluous has no limits, no measure or definition, it exceeds the realm of necessity, it opens up another realm beyond it, around its narrow confines—a vaster region than necessity, which has no limit—embodied, and illustrated, in the limitless expenditure of superfluous ornamentation. When you put on jewelry, writes Simmel, it lends you the "free and princely" character that belongs to whatever is generous beyond all measure, like poets at Versailles, who poured out their gracious flatteries in floods of gratitude for the beneficence bestowed on them by a seemingly infinite source of wealth and liberality, an overflowing Sun King who gives light and life, fortune and power to poets, out of the abundance of his surplus, the pure excess of limitless resources. The more you appear covered with what is superfluous the closer you are to being that sun, that king—the ruler of the world.

The court at Versailles raised to the highest point the understanding of the power of jewelry to single out and distinguish. Louis XIV took seriously the radiant power of glory, and took his jewels to be instruments of his political power. The fierceness of the beams that shone from his diamonds, the largest in the world, flashing under the blazing chandeliers of the Hall of Mirrors at Versailles, blinded his court and its foreign ambassadors with the visual equivalent of his illustrious majesty. The world attributes the radiance of Louis's jewelry to himself; the fact of wearing large diamonds in vast parures designates those at court whose blood has been touched with light by proximity to the royal sun. In that respect, great jewelry has always verged on being a medal or badge, a sign of your belonging, an emblem of distinction and exalted rank.

A medal or badge can be made of noble matter, like the diamonds in the Order of the Garter, or of the humblest stuff, no more than the thread in a buttonhole of the Legion d'Honneur. A medal doesn't depend for its value on the stuff out of which it is made; it takes its worth from the values that it signifies, apart from itself. And yet every medal, however modest, is ornamental; it attaches onto clothes something additional and decorative: that's why medals are also called "decorations." All medals are a form of ornamental jewelry; and all jewelry is a kind of medal or badge. In fact, it is probably impossible to decide where one stops being purely the one and starts becoming the other. You might say that all jewelry exists on a continuum that goes from the merely decorative to the wholly honorific. At the court of Louis XIV, where all that matters is glory, whatever it is that raises you above others and makes you more worthy of their attention is worth the hugest sums.

No one alive today understands as well as Elizabeth Taylor the glory of gems, the power they embody, and the distinction they bestow. From an early age, and she was a phenomenally precocious star, she wanted only the biggest and the most prestigious stones, only the greatest jewelry: the Cartier diamond, the Peregrina pearl, the Schlumberger Iguana brooch, the diamond plumes of the Prince of Wales. You'll hear more about her, Zeem, because she shares with Louis XIV a royal lust for jewelry.

But the "subtlest fascination" Simmel finds in jewelry is the fact that these hard, cold substances, metal and crystal, are nevertheless bent by the person who wears them to serve their particular aims and individual interest. Jewelry never fits the curves and crevices of an individual body; it remains stiffly, coldly above the singularity and destiny of its wearer. Style, for Simmel, always has something universal, impersonal, about it. It's what makes stiff and starchy new clothes more stylish than those that have been worn a lot. Jewelry is elegant precisely, says Simmel, because it is not "specifically individual."[6] "What is really elegant," he writes, "avoids pointing to the specifically individual; it always lays a more general, stylized, almost abstract sphere around the personality." Jewelry is a form of ornamentation that says more about a person's style—the abstract, general idea of her self—than, say, a tattoo, which so closely adheres to the flesh that its significance is always intimately personal—rather than coolly elegant. These days, of course (I don't have to tell *you*), it's cool to have a Chinese character tattooed on your ass—one, for example, that means "bun."

Style is whatever in an individual decision of taste is repeatable, whatever can be copied, modeled, ordered from some top down, patronized, as the French say. There is no style if it can't be copied, parodied, or pastiched. A great work of art may be in a certain style, but what makes it a masterpiece is something irreplaceably, irreducibly individual, unrepeatable, impossible to be copied. The style of Chanel's jewelry starts with a theory, a vision of an idea or ideal of jewelry, that can be, that has been, endlessly knocked off.

In the heart of the Depression, Chanel did a show in Paris of jewelry that featured only diamonds, yards and yards of broad chains of them on necklaces and tiaras and bracelets. The diamonds were set in the most ingenious invisible platinum settings that made them appear to exist side by side independent of one another, floating like independent stars in the blinding constellation they formed. The cost of the show was so enormous, the

---

6. Georg Simmel, *The Sociology of Georg Simmel*. Translated, edited, and with an introduction by Kurt H. Wolff. Glencoe, Ill., Free Press, 1950.

wealth it represented in one place so immense, that it could not even be transported to England to be shown because of the cost of insuring the jewels. In the midst of such general suffering everywhere in the world, it took an act of the most vicious cynicism or the most expansive generosity to conceive a spectacle of such limitless luxury and unthinkable expenditure.

Think of her life at that moment. She was soon to be living with the Duke of Westminster, the richest man in the world. She was probably at that moment the richest woman, certainly the one earning the most money, largely from the fabulous income generated by her perfume, No. 5, then the most popular scent. She had limitless resources of money when most of the world had none. Pouring all that money into diamonds, Chanel was transforming it into light, making a sacrifice to light, to the prodigious luminosity of the purest crystal, to a little god of light—an intensely burning spirit wrapped in the hardest crystal, whose uncanny power to inspire reverence and nearly sexual love makes you think of animism, the worship of gods in things. I heard a Swiss jeweler tell how he loves his amethysts and likes to watch them glow at different hours of the day; he even takes them up into the mountains in order to be able to wake up in the morning with them and observe their blooming cerulescence in the palest light of an Alpine dawn.

One of Simmel's greatest insights concerns what he called, before nuclear radiation was understood, the "radioactivity" of jewelry. He understands its power to enhance the wearer by virtue of the gleaming light it radiates, the brilliance of the rays it projects. He writes that "adornment intensifies or enlarges the impression of the personality by operating as a sort of radiation emanating from it. For this reason, its materials have always been shining metals and precious stones. . . ." Simmel calls it "human radioactivity in the sense that every individual is surrounded by a larger or smaller sphere of significance radiating from him; and everybody else, who deals with him, is immersed in this sphere."[7]

We are each of us little astral suns, shining with significance. The luminescence of our personality is a function of both our anatomical, cosmetic beauty and the social distinctions we acquire and display for others. When you walk into a room, Zeem, be aware that you are wearing an aura—not some mystical emanation but a brightness you have in your power to control by what you do and what you wear, and by becoming who you are. The shiny brightness of precious jewels and metal is the outer circle of the sphere of significance surrounding human personality, radiating its energy and impressing it on others, like the aura or aureole of the sun. Wearing great jewelry, a vast diamond necklace, expands the sphere of our significance, both figuratively and literally, with the brilliance of the light it refracts. That's why stars in Hollywood borrow their jewels from Harry Winston to wear on Oscar night.

You can hardly exaggerate the magnitude and power of the light that comes from gems, a quantity of light inescapably linked to the idea of royal power. The ancient Koh-i-Noor, the oldest and most famous big diamond among the British crown jewels, dates back in Indian legend five thousand years; in 1550 it was owned by the Mogul Sultan Babur, a descendant of Tamerlane, and now is set in the coronation crown of Elizabeth the Queen Mother; its name in Persian means "Mountain of Light."

In 1730 North-West India, ruled by the Moguls, was conquered by the Persian Nadir Shah. When he examined the rich treasury he had captured, he discovered that the famous Koh-i-Noor diamond had unaccountably disappeared. He was disap-

---

7. Ibid., p. 343.

pointed; it was said that whoever owned the stone ruled the world. A concubine in the harem of the deposed Mohammed Shah, the last Mogul emperor, revealed to her new master that the emperor kept it wrapped in his turban. Nadir Shah thereupon gave a sumptuous banquet during which he magnanimously restored Mohammed Shah to his throne. Under the guise of making a conciliating gesture, he made him an offer he couldn't refuse. The Shah proposed to exchange his richly jeweled turban for the simple linen one the emperor wore. Having just received a throne, he could hardly deny him his hat. The Shah, ears ringing with acclaim for his apparent generosity, rushed to his tent, unwrapped the turban, and uncovered the hugely gleaming stone. "Koh-i-Noor," he exclaimed. "Mountain of Light."

Queen Victoria's collet necklace was made of twenty-eight round diamonds, most of them weighing between 8 and 17 carats, the size of cherries. A pendant hanging from the necklace was the huge Lahore diamond cut like a teardrop. Since Victoria, all English queens have donned it for their coronation. The enormous light streaming from the necklace is captured and reflected back in the smiles of the crowds for whom such jewelry is worn. I remember glimpsing the just-married Marina, Duchess of Kent, from my room at the Claridge, as her carriage passed through the pea-soup fog of a London day in late November on its way to Westminster Abbey. She was perched on the edge of her seat, and although much was obscured from the view of the crowd by the enveloping wet cloud, the piercing glint of her diamond tiara was visible at fifty meters, from four stories up, penetrating the adamantine gloom.

If not a mountain, a gem is often seen as a flashing eye that shoots its look into the eyes of its beholders and elicits in return their admiring gaze. That centrifugal centripetal movement, seeking in the others the reflection of one's own radiation, is the essence of vanity, says Simmel, and can be differentiated from haughty pride, which does not need adornment, which usually scorns it, and finds self-esteem in its own eyes, with no interest in the judgments of others.

Don't forget, Zeem, eyes not only see, they flash (as teeth do. A string of pearls is often seen to be a row of smiling teeth). In the language of Homer, in Ionic Greek there are two principal verbs "to see." One is "theorein," the word that gives us "theory" and is still used to mean "see" in modern Greek. The other is "drakein," from which the Greeks, and so we, derive the word "dragon," the mythical creature shooting flames at first from its eyes. The dragon eye strikes out at the eye of the beholder and fixes its fascinated gaze—the way a tube of lipstick catches the eye as it crushes into paint flowing precisely along the cruel line of the lip. Seeing theoretically is not at all the same thing as looking dragonlike—shooting a glance of fire from your eyes full of anger or love. A theory can be the most ideal speculation, the weakest way of looking at things, mere supposition or hypothesis, as when you say: "I have a theory of why John and Helen are getting a divorce." Or when I say I have a theory of jewelry.

I knew I could be a girl when I wanted a diamond. A dandy these days might covet a diamond stickpin for his tie, but most boys don't dream, as I did, of having a diamond on a chain around their neck or a tiara of starry diamonds for their hair. But I used to imagine myself wearing the tiara Chanel designed for the show in 1932, the one seen in the photograph that streaks across the lacquered black hair of the mannequin. Or the comet necklace, perhaps her most famous piece. Over one shoulder the comet's head is a platinum star filled with large brilliant diamonds, a huge one in the center and twenty-three smaller ones arrayed in descending order to compose the five points. The star on the left shoulder is trailed by a tail of six long diamond filaments that sweeps across the other shoulder and circles beautifully around it. But instead of enclosing the neck, the tail descends in a luminous display, ending in a shower of large tear-shaped diamonds, a profusion of lights!, just above the moving line of the décolletage. Chanel once told an interviewer: "I want to cover women with constellations. Stars! Des étoiles! Des étoiles! Stars of every dimension to sparkle in hair, fringes, slivers of the moon." Chanel loves what shines—*ce qui brille*—brilliantly.

What is a constellation, poetically speaking? It's the sign in the heavens of a destiny, an indication that what may seem to be only an arbitrary collection of stars obeys some obscure but fateful attraction, which corresponds in turn to the deepest impulses of individual lives. Diamonds, says the ad, are forever. Excuse me. Nothing is, least of all a material substance like diamond, subject to heat and abrasion, liable to decay away to dust in a fraction of eternity. But poetically they are forever, because their light is like that of stars—emblems of the eternity of your destiny. When you die, Sartre said, quoting a poet, eternity changes you into yourself, you become who you are—and not before: "Tel qu'en lui-même l'éternité le change." You become your destiny, seen retrospectively; and once you're dead, it's all that will be left of you. A constellation in the heavens. It will be what you are for the rest of time, for the rest of the time that you are. And who knows how long that will be?

Chanel's first idea is to make jewelry cosmic, to turn the woman into the gleaming night adorned by those matchless stellar forms scattered by chance or the hand of God across the ebony sky. Did Chanel know that the word for ornament or jewelry in Greek is "cosmos," which gives us "cosmetic," the same word for universe? What merely adorns, *cosmos,* is the most exterior, extraneous, inessential, frivolous thing, superficially decorating without essentially transforming the self. Jewelry is the most ornamental adornment precisely because it is the least part of the person who wears it; it doesn't touch, so to speak, any more than the cold hard exteriority of diamonds can touch. And yet it supplements the self, surrounds it with a cosmic aura that raises the self to infinity. Wearing diamonds, the self acquires the luster of eternity. The most frivolous is the most universal.

Ornamental jewelry, *cosmos,* the most superfluous, dispensable thing is also everything, the name of all there is, the whole mystery of woman, and hence of the universe. If a woman is the creation of her adornment, then to want to create yourself out of your cosmetics (an option not uniquely reserved to females) belongs to an idea of the feminine that wants to be universal, or, more exactly, micro-cosmic, a re-creation in miniature of what the cosmos spans. In our unconscious we may never have emerged from inside the body of the woman who gave us birth; that is why you can never kill your mother in your dreams, symbolically, the way you are always killing your father. She is forever the condition of there being any you, any universe at all, and even when we emerge from her, we live in the world as if the world were her, which it was once, literally, and is still, mythically. But what makes her a woman, our mother, is not just, not mainly, her biological function. (That, these days, can more and more perfectly be re-created by reproductive technologies.) She is a woman by virtue of how she adorns herself, and not even God can impinge on the freedom of a woman to enhance her beauty. Not even God, who knows all things, can know in advance what a woman is free to put on.

I've assumed the project of wearing jewelry like a woman because it strikes me as the highest form of prayer. It took me a long time finally to figure out that what may seem like some perversity of taste is, at bottom, the ambition to imitate God. The idea came to me from reading the *Mémoires* of the Abbé de

Choisy. As a child, heir to a noble title, he was the playmate of Monsieur (the king's brother, the gay husband of the Princess Palatine); they used to play doctor in the Luxembourg gardens dressed like little girls. Until the twentieth century, it was common for little boys in royal circles to be dressed in dresses; the Duke of Windsor wore them till he was six. But unlike many, de Choisy and his royal playmate never entirely got over it. They preferred women's clothing most of their lives. Unlike Monsieur, however, the Abbé seems to have grown up to be ferociously heterosexual, with no sexual interest in men at all; he rather used his impeccable feminine disguise to lure young girls into his confidence, in order, as if innocently, to take them to bed, where they were in for a big surprise. Destined for high places in the Church by his conniving mother, with her brilliant social relations, de Choisy was tonsured at eighteen and instantly named by the king to be the abbot of Saint-Seine near Dijon. In those more enlightened times, his ecclesiastical vocation, which he pursued faithfully throughout his life, was in no way compromised by his taste for feminine adornment or by his habit of wearing, besides his habit, dresses. The Abbé recounts in his memoirs how he particularly loved to wear jewelry, even as a young man. At twenty-two, after his mother died, he was left free of parental constraints, in possession of a great fortune, and thrilled to abandon himself at last to what he calls his "penchant" for dressing like a woman. Until then he had dressed as a male at court and in public but with effeminate affectations that seemed ridiculous to his peers. Mme. de Lafayette, a great author and one of the noblest ladies of the realm, took him aside to tell him, speaking as a good friend, that it was not at all fashionable for men to wear pendant diamond earrings or to ornament their face with tiny beauty spots, like freckles, painted on with the tip of an ermine brush. The young Abbé might be better received in society, joked Mme. de Lafayette, if he frankly dressed as a woman. Putting jokes aside, he straightaway cut his abundant hair and had it made into a fashionable wig with lots of little curls in front and a mass of big curls on the side. He donned one of his favorite dresses (he already had an important collection at home), attached the fabulous pendant diamond earrings he had inherited from his mother, hung his diamond cross on a chain around his neck, slipped into three beautiful amethyst and ruby rings, and paid a visit one Tuesday to Mme. de Lafayette's salon. When the great lady realized whom she had before her, she screamed: "Oh! What a beautiful person! You followed my advice and you've done well. If you don't believe me ask M. de la Rochefoucauld." The Duc de la Rochefoucauld was the most mordantly witty, wickedly brilliant man at court, descended from the most ancient noble family, surrounded by sycophants, but not given to flatter others, not the king or even himself. (I remember the moment years ago, when, with a diamond ring, I scratched one of his maxims on the edge of my mirror, so I would be reminded every day that "Self-love is the greatest of all flatterers." L'amour-propre est le plus grand de tous les flatteurs.[8]) But on that day, what he saw before him was a perfectly beautiful young woman, slender and supple, poetically dressed, with the most eloquent feminine grace. La Rochefoucauld assured de Choisy that he entirely approved his transformation, and like Mme. de Lafayette encouraged hir (we will never know how ironically) to continue to go out into the world dressed as the beautiful aristocratic creature s/he was. Obliged to take another name, she told her servants to call her Madame de Sancy, after the brilliant stone.

---

8. Duc François de la Rochefoucauld, *Oeuvres complètes.* Paris: Editions Gallimard, 1964.

The Sancy diamond was the biggest Indian diamond in Europe until the arrival of the Regent in 1722. Pear-shaped and rose-cut (with a five-sided table), weighing 55.23 carats, the Sancy is first attested at the end of the sixteenth century at a moment when it was also faceted and owned by Nicolas Halay de Sancy (1546–1627), a great collector and diplomat who bought it in Constantinople; he was often obliged to put it in hock to rescue the finances of his masters, the French kings Henry III and IV. In 1604 the King of England, James I, bought the diamond from Sancy and had it mounted in a pin that he wore on his hat. Later, it passed to France and around 1654 was bought by Cardinal Mazarin, the French prime minister, and it ranked number one in the group of eighteen enormous diamonds, the largest ever seen, that Mazarin collected, then left as a legacy to the Crown of France. The Sancy was stolen during the French Revolution and turned up in Spain, where it was acquired by the prime minister of Charles IV. In 1828, it was sold to the Russian prince Nicolas Demidoff, who eventually put it on the market in Paris, where it was purchased by an Indian prince or a Bombay merchant, depending on the story, who later returned it for sale in Europe, where it was bought by Lord William Waldorf Astor as a wedding gift for his daughter-in-law, later Lady Astor. In 1976 the Sancy was sold by the third vicomte Astor to the Louvre Museum, where it resides next to the Regent in immense splendor in the Galérie d'Apollon.

At one point in his *Mémoires,* the Abbé de Choisy reflects on the sources of the pleasure and satisfaction he takes in being Mme. de Sancy and in dressing like a woman. He explains it in theological terms, as if his desire arose from his religious calling. The wish to adorn himself as a woman derives, he argues, from the very nature of God. God, who has everything, wants only one thing—to be adored. We are godlike when we seek the same.

Since great beauty, like that of beautiful women, inspires the most fervent love and worshipful attention, beautiful women are the nearest thing on earth to being sacred. Any man who possesses such beauty (as Moi does in abundance) incurs a positively holy obligation to do all he can to enhance it, just as a woman would, with jewelry, cosmetics, coiffeur, and couture. As women imitate God by seeking to be worshipped, the Abbé imitates them, putting on ribbons and painting on beauty marks, the better to attract the eye to places blessed with loveliness. Self-adornment is no longer a form of empty vanity but a way of making fully present the aspect of the divine, a sort of *imitatio Christi*—in the mirror of her dressing table. Putting on drag was a quasi-religious act for the Abbé, just as it is for those gays in San Francisco who dress in the robes of holy sisters and are much less blasphemous than you think. The greatest drag queens convey the feeling that they are performing a sacred task, obeying some high calling that compels their beauty to be judged by the most absolute feminine ideals.

Remember, Zeem, you've got essentially only one alternative in life—loneliness and/or claustrophobia. Living alone, you have a shot at conquering loneliness; being married, on the other hand, is often, simultaneously, the most claustrophobic and the most lonely you'll ever be. Furthermore, claustrophobia leads fatally to murder—at least, to dreaming about it. That's why homicide, Zeem, is the only logical outcome of most domestic arguments. You get to the point where there is just no satisfactory alternative to killing the other person except perhaps divorce, which may be too expensive.

Naturally, there are sacrifices made in being alone. Overcoming loneliness means learning to love the solitude that being an orphan brings like a curse, and renouncing at some point forever the consolations of producing children, little versions of oneself. Anyway, children are only truly interesting when they become aware of vice, and at that moment they cease to be children. Instead of children, I've had my jewelry. And I have you, Zeem, my sister's child, for whom these words of caution and advice are most of what I'll leave you after the doctors consume my wealth.

I will remove my rings, too many rings, unscrew my earrings, set down my heavy pearls, and begin to write, tonight. It has been a good, a wonderful night, and despite the clear vision we now have of the end, tonight we drank champagne and laughed, and the laughter rose like bubbles in the glass, lit by the glittering light from the diamonds—the constellations of diamonds—that swept across the still ravishing necks assembled around my flower-strewn bed. I can look through the window of the little stone porch and admire how the roses, immense garden roses growing up the delicate spiral columns that support the roof, frame the landscape of fiery cedars, high, dark hedges, and red-tiled roofs leading down from Mougins to the distant swath of incomparable blue, the bay at its feet. Here I will die, but not before I've set down this lesson, the only one I think I know how to teach, on the secret language of jewelry. I have been thinking about this my whole life, surely from the moment I arrived back in Paris, an adorable little thing, all pink and sunny, with an ass that took me to the Alcazar, and a smile that made me the queen of a certain caste—the rich men with gray eyes who came night after night and stood at the bar—who required great beauty, and also something more. But I will leave that for later. For now, here's a kiss. Sweet dreams, Zeem. When you wake, don't forget to check under your pillow.

Two

Choosing It:
Kant and the Duchess of Windsor

They loved my ass at the Alcazar. I left Harvard in disgust at the Philistinism it fosters and with contempt for the vanities it inflates. Nothing interesting, I decided, can happen in a place where people only excel at doing what is most conventional. I told my mother I was going back to Paris, so she put me in touch with one of her ex-colleagues who put me in touch with the Romanian ballerina who ran the boys at the Alcazar. I went to her place not far from the whores of Saint-Denis to be viewed and interviewed. She opened the door abruptly and stood there checking me out, aglow in red-hot satin pants, with a platinum crew cut and, squeezed into a sequined top, a chest that took me aback. But I looked again and noticed she was wearing on a silver chain around her neck a small jet-black hammer and sickle, adrift in the sea of her cleavage; appearing and disappearing, it seemed to wink at me. I figured there was less here than meets the eye.

Jet, by the way, is a kind of coal formed by pressure, heat, and chemical action on ancient driftwood. Since antiquity it has been mined out of Liassic shales on the Yorkshire coast near Whitby, England. Fragile and hard to carve, its shiny blackness made it fashionable in the nineteenth century in the form of mourning jewelry—the grave ornaments you wore at times when adornment seemed vain and offensive. She made me undress down to my BVDs and, looking hard, she seemed to like what she saw. With all that swimming in the Harvard pool I had an excellent body, long and thin and lightly muscled. But it was my ass that drew her admiring attention. Genes plus the flutter kick had given it a pert little bubble roundness that used to keep its shape even sitting down, which drives the French crazy. Americans love breasts, because it's the culture of Mom, as Philip Wylie long ago pointed out. Whatever is immaculately white and pure and odorless like mother's milk appeals to Americans; the French, conversely, want it dark and smelling strong: they love organ meat, truffles, and asses. American above, French below, oral versus anal, sucking versus pinching! What else do you do with an ass if you don't pinch it and slap it and treat it a little rough. Loving asses always has a sadistic component, while breasts inspire more sweetness and generous affection. She told me I didn't have to do much dancing, mostly just a lot of parading around in black leather straps. Then she laid down the rules, like the commissar she once was: there was to be no booze, drugs, or hanky-panky among the employees, and a strict dress code at work—when you weren't undressed.

The Alcazar was my dream scene with its red plush and

gold-papered walls shimmering through the blue haze of innumerable cigarettes, the air damp with perfume and alcohol, a climate of permanent arousal. They even had my initials on the matchboxes, AZ. We were all boys technically speaking, even the gorgeous girls who were my partners. I got to see close up summits of the art of being a transvestite. These boys danced, night after night, mostly naked before the eyes of tourists whom they completely fooled and the uncompromising eyes of the crowd of discriminating men who came to the Alcazar with their special tastes. These unaltered anatomical guys were covered only with a few feathers, and yet they appeared to customers, overfed and slightly sloshed, to be the most beautiful women in the world—there at a distance across the footlights, under lighting carefully composed, under wigs, makeup, and body paint applied by costumiers who knew a million cunning ways to hide a blemish or mask an imperfection. This was Paris in the fifties, before it was easy to get your Adam's apple shaved or silicone added to your hips to soften the angles of sharp male bones. In this world, a woman's beauty was the purest theatrical illusion.

They made me up to look like one of the "girls" who was trying to look like a sexy guy. But that was fine with me, because it was sort of how I felt myself to be. I had the same foundation and lipstick they did and, like them, enormous false eyelashes; I wore sequins in my hair and on my face. I was mostly otherwise naked but for my butt which was naughtily draped—sometimes undressed or wrapped in gold braid to match my golden strap. Although I loved being loved by the "girls" in the show, I was never attracted to any of my colleagues—afraid, perhaps, that my slightest inclination would be noted and swiftly punished by Mme. Ceausescou. In any case, feeling most like a woman, I only fantasized about sex with other women.

I used to get to the Alcazar early, a few hours before the nine o'clock show. I loved to sit smoking before the mirrors in the dressing room framed in lights, basking in the infinite reflections that came progressively alive with glittering sparks from sequins and eyes and jewelry—enormous costume jewelry. *Tape-à-l'oeil,* as the French say—jewelry that hits you in the eye and knocks you out. A woman (or a boy) wearing a giant parure becomes magnified by its pure panache, like a lofty white feather, upright on a soldier's helmet, or eminent in a debutante's tiara. Big fake jewelry when it's great makes you huge, a kind of goddess. The boys dancing on the stage, bedecked in their jewels and paillettes, were transfigured; and the sodden public, weary Japanese executives and fat midwestern matrons, sitting at tables in the dark, often silently wept at the awesome mystery of their haloed apparition.

I loved my life at the Alcazar, going to bed after dawn every morning and sleeping until very late in the afternoon. I need a lot of sleep, like Katharine Hepburn. I mostly went home alone, happy to sit up late with my books and typewriter, drinking champagne until early in the morning when the sky over Paris suddenly brightens into day and I could walk to the tabac on the corner to buy a slim cigar and the *Herald Tribune* (*le Hérald,* in French), which, taken to bed, instantly put me to sleep. I felt no need to have relationships—too strange even to think I could.

I remember one night I had hung around late in the dressing room, and when I stepped out of the stage door, at four in the morning, it was dark and cold on the rue Mazarine. An icy little wind, fresh off the river, swirled around and spiked my senses like the sharp taste of cocaine. Suddenly, I caught a scent of cologne and felt something warm against my face; it was the breath of a man whispering something I didn't hear. "What!" I said. "A drink?" he repeated. I didn't even look or turn around but brushed by him. This wasn't the first time I'd been stalked by men after the show. I started walking quickly down the empty street toward the boulevard Saint-Germain when all of a sudden I heard a skipping, ringing sound of something metal hitting pavement and, as I looked up, a little flash went by and landed at my feet. I reached for the gleaming thing and picked up what turned out to be a heavy gold and pavé-diamond ring. It had a thick metal shank and, on top, a bezel carpeted with a curved plane of brilliant diamonds set so seamlessly close to one another that each prong must have touched three stones. Woven into the sparkling surface of diamonds was gold filigree that looked like some Greek or Arab script. Under the yellow light of the street-lamp, I struggled to make out what it said; and as I did, I caught a glimpse of him slouching there in the gloom, outlined by the shape of an Italian suit and a flaring Borsalino. It seemed to me his smile was wicked, gleaming in the darkness. I turned the ring and peered at the filigree, right side up. In wavy, cryptic arabesques it spelled out OUI.

You can imagine my shock—forty years later—when I first saw Princess Diana's ring. Mine looked uncannily like that. Diana saw hers displayed for the first time in the window of Repossi's— the exclusive jeweler on the Place Beaumarchais, just down the street from the Palace in Monte Carlo. She was in the midst of a yachting holiday and shopping spree that only a princess whose doting Dodi's father, Mohamed al Fayed, owned Harrods and the Ritz could afford. They needed only a few minutes in the shop to buy the ring, because they had already seen and admired it in a very high fashion magazine, *L'Officiel de la Couture et de la Mode de Paris,* which they had brought aboard the *Jonikal* (Mohamed's yacht: 200 feet, an Italian crew of sixteen, £15 million) off the coast of Majorca. Their itinerary replicated the magic one traced by Wallis Simpson aboard the royal yacht in 1936 in the company of the Prince of Wales (soon to be briefly King Edward VIII, then to abdicate and become the Duke of Windsor): Majorca, Palma, Formentor, Cannes, Monte Carlo, Calvi.

The ring had been designed by Mr. Repossi himself and made by hand in his Turin workshop. It was too large for Diana's slender fingers, so it had to be sized and sent to arrive at the Paris shop by August 30, Dodi's birthday.

Rings are oddly the only kind of jewelry that are made to fit. Because they surround the fingers of the hand, clothing them, clasping them close, they have always been the least frivolous, the most significant form of jewelry, the one which is given and received with the greatest gravity—the token of a bargain, a contract, a marriage. The hand is that part of you that regularly engages with others; it represents you, more than, say, a foot or an ear. Clasping hands is the oldest way of confirming a deal; moreover, hand and hand may be the first form of "attachment." But not the only one. I know a couple who gave each other tongue studs in marriage, and on their wedding night they clicked like crazy till dawn. A ring has to fit like a hand in yours or like a finger enclosing your ring finger—the one supposedly closest to your heart—where trust and faith in others is said to reside.

The next night my mysterious admirer was waiting at the door, as I knew he would be, and he took me unprotesting to his place on the quai. Amad was the only child of rich, fat *harkis,* Arabs who fought with the French in Algeria, a few of whom owned oil wells before they fled. He was the boyfriend from Hell—rich, ugly, and female. A stone butch, but not a lesbian, she liked boys. I tell you she was a man, with a swaggering, cigar-smoking, belching, farting confidence that fooled most people, although she didn't care whether or not she passed—at least not in Paris where no one cares. He was living on the Ile Saint-Louis facing the western tip of the Ile de la Cité and Notre Dame. It's the house right on the corner, *troisième étage,* with a view up and down the Seine from Bercy to the Louvre—better than the view from La Tour d'Argent.

Out his window Paris was born right over there in the third century B.C., when a Gallic tribe of fishermen and river traders, the Parisi, settled on the big island in the middle of the Seine. The Gauls were overrun by Caesar's centurions and the island became a fortified palatial encampment called Lutetia. The emblem of Paris is a sailing ship, perhaps because the boat-shaped island on which the city was founded, stuck in the middle of the river, lends itself to the utopian idea of a ship that would stay forever afloat. "Fluctuat sed non mergitur," is the city's motto, "I vacillate but do not sink." In the flat on the Ile de la Cité, I felt like that—nervous, always restless, threatened by the feeling I was slipping from side to side—from one side of myself to the other. But I remain afloat. Unsure of my desires, I couldn't tell from day to day which self would take possession of me, which sex would captivate me, or which orifice I preferred.

I remember watching a flight of swans below the window, arrayed in formation around the western tip of the Ile Saint-Louis. Advancing toward the east, like an armada, they swam past an oncoming barge, making way slowly as if afraid of nothing so much as ruffling their dignity or besmirching their navy whiteness. The whiteness of swans is ghostly, unreal, against the muddy green water of the Seine, against the tans and browns of water and stone. The birds emerged like ethereal emblems of some poetic allegory of Paris. I think of you, Swans, whenever a barge, long, deep, and empty, comes pushing into my life, at a breathless clip, with the force of the ineluctable. The swans composing arabesques against the double darkness of the vault beneath the bridge pay ironic homage to whatever is the opposite of their immaculate grace. When love barges in, there's nothing to do but be beautiful.

As the swans pass indifferently beneath the little bridge, a saltimbanque above is doing his bicycle show for a crowd that he's gratefully gathered. They make a square around him inside of which he turns in circles while sitting backwards, doing handstands on the handlebars. On this chill, very gray January day, he's dressed all in white, in shorts and skimpy T-shirt like a clown, invulnerable against the elements, the laws of gravity, and the risks of mortality. Yet on his head he wears a funny soldier's hat, a memento mori—an old khaki thing that men might be wearing this day at war. He does his little act three times an hour—most of it not performing but gathering the crowd and making it stand where he wants in a square around him. He calls to every passerby, orders them like a traffic cop to take their posts along the side, swinging his arms in order to prod them along. He knows that if people stand where he directs, thereby becoming spectators at the performance he provides, then they acquiesce in the implicit contract not only to applaud, which they do vigorously, but also to deposit a few francs in the hat he passes around. The audience, no dupe, is happy to pay for the serendipity occasioned by this little fragment of urban circus. Or rather, they pretend to be duped in return for the unexpected gift of him and the dramatic space he conjures up, on a public thoroughfare in the midst of their Sunday promenade. It's another allegory, this for the air of theatrical illusion you encounter everywhere in the streets when you first arrive in Paris. After a while, for many who live here, the magic disappears—but returns like magic every time they get away and come back. Amad's apartment, overlooking the river, came close to the center of the city's power.

Repossi's Paris shop lies just across the place Vendôme, obscurely set into the formal façade of that arrogant, imperial space, where once a mob cut down the phallic column Napoleon had erected to his glory. Only one small window, softly lit, allows the eye to penetrate behind those august walls and to imagine the splendors within. Written on a card in the corner of the window is the Repossi motto, which makes me dream: "The most secret of the great jewelers is also the most creative." I've always wondered what exactly that "also" is supposed to mean. Is it a contingent connection or a necessary one? Just a lucky accident ("By the way, besides being secretive, Repossi's happens to be the most creative") or the very reason for its genius ("Our secrecy makes us creative")? The latter would imply that Repossi thinks that all great jewelry is made to reveal that it has a secret it will not tell. And a great jeweler knows how to give shape and lend substance to the most beautiful secrets of all. (Without ever, ever disclosing its price.) A beautiful woman adorns her beauty with intimations of her deepest secrets, disguised as her jewelry.

Keep this in mind, Zeem: Whenever you wear jewelry, you are telling the world you have something to hide—a mystery whose shadows lie deep in your heart. It's a bold way of keeping a secret. Of course, if you're a Hollywood star at the Oscars wearing the Harry Winston diamond necklace he lent you for the evening, there's less mystery than if you own it and it's yours. A piece of jewelry that's a piece of property is usually more expressive than one you've borrowed and put on. Although maybe things are changing now: it's more and more the case that you are what you lease. Particularly, where jewelry is concerned: you only attach it, don't use or consume it. It may well have preceded and will almost certainly outlast you. The only way you might actually be said to possess a diamond is if you burned it up with fire blown by your last breath. Then you could honestly claim that you had never rented; it was yours exclusively to the end. Alas, you wouldn't be around to enjoy the pleasure of that thought.

Jewelry is forever attracting and attractive by virtue of the enigmas it discreetly advertises, intimating, whispering—implies. You might think that the best way to keep your secrets is to never wear any jewelry at all, but, as you'll see with Katharine Hepburn, it's not quite that simple. Women who don't wear any jewelry, and there's a class of them like her, are communicating just as loudly about what it is that adorns them.

Whether you know the secret your jewelry indicates is not as important as knowing you are being seen to wear one—on your sleeve, as it were, on your neck or arm or finger. It's almost a provocation, an invitation to the viewer to ponder and dream. After all, secrets are made to be told: keeping one means it can always be betrayed. Wearing jewelry is thus an open invitation to curious, cunning minds to penetrate the mystery of, say, this Repossi ring, ringing with implication, to extract its content, and make jewelry talk.

Mr. Repossi opened his shop for them two days early before the end of the summer vacation so that Dodi, it is said, might slip it on her finger in the Imperial Suite, the darkly glittering night they ate their last meal at the Ritz. He took it from the jeweler without paying. It was the rule: for years Dodi had been living a life beyond his means but not beyond that of his father, who always paid in the end. This time Mohamed was more reluctant than ever. What father, even the richest and most loving, would be happy to shell out a quarter of a million dollars for an engagement ring his son couldn't afford? In the end, the father said he was glad to pay; he said this was his son's dearest wish, and his last, and he would respect his son's last wish to give this ring to her who had accepted it.

The ring is supposed to have been handed to Diana's sisters at the hospital when they arrived to bring back the body. But that is disputed. It is rumored that the ring was entombed with her, the diamonds and platinum returning to the earth from which they came in a form unlike anything they were for hundreds of million years. No longer merely stones and precious metal, but a sign of royal romance, they are endowed with world historical significance, ablaze with tragic beauty. The whole history of the story of Diana and Dodi is only a vanishing instant in the geological life of the diamonds, but the ring, which marks that brilliant instant, may endure in the earth for hundreds of millions of years to come. If someday the story is lost, the same indomitable, unconquerable, impenetrable substance will persist. Nothing can penetrate it or cause it to decay. That's why Tutankhamen wore diamonds in his tomb. Beloved by pharaohs to whom they spoke of eternity, they were lavishly set into funereal jewelry designed to be worn exclusively by the corpse. The pieces were more hollow and less sturdy than those intended for the living, but the diamonds endure. Nothing lasts forever—except maybe a thought.

Diana's family insists that this was an engagement ring; her friends speak of her resistance to marriage and call it a "friendship" ring. Since Roman times there are examples of betrothal or friendship rings decorated with an engraved pair of clasped right hands—the one you always give to shake on. Jewelry collectors in the nineteenth century gave them a specific name, taken from the Italian term for them: *mane in fede* (hands in trust). The rings were widely popular in Europe from the twelfth to the eighteenth century. The motif of clasped hands was often used in wedding chains in the sixteenth century, and on wedding rings. Sometimes the hands are clasped at the bezel and are surmounted by a precious stone as if the hands were giving birth to an opal. The ring on the finger is an index of hand in hand—the way we signal peace and union, not war, say, between the sexes. In French, a wedding band is called an "alliance."

Diamond ring given to Princess Diana by Dodi al Fayed

They had known each other only a couple of months; Diana didn't like him pressuring her. But all agree she was prepared to wear it. She's supposed to have told her closest friend, Rosa Monckton, the granddaughter of Walter Monckton (the Duke of Windsor's trusted aide): "He's given me a bracelet. He's given me a watch. I know the next thing will be a ring. Rosa, that's going firmly on the fourth finger of my right hand"—as far as possible from the fourth finger of the left.[1] Notice too, Zeem, the order in which he gave her the presents: a princess might at first accept a watch, only then a bracelet, and finally a ring. A bracelet, a pure ornament with no utility, speaks more intimately—bears more weighty significance—than a useful watch, but less than does a ring.

It seems certain they were planning to live together in the former house of the Duke and Duchess of Windsor in le Bois de Boulogne (with the spiraling staircase in the trompe l'oeil entry). It's hard to believe Diana and Dodi would have chosen to live in sin in that place of all places of abomination, the spot on earth

---

1. Thomas Sancton and Scott MacLeod, *Death of a Princess: The Investigation.* New York: St. Martin's Press, 1998, p. 144.

that for decades had been the object of the royal family's obsessive distrust and loathing. In those ghostly rooms, Diana would play the Duke of Windsor, casting herself in the role of the beloved royal who gives up all rights to the throne and suffers exile for love of a pariah, the twice-divorced Wallis Simpson—an Arab businessman. The repetition is uncanny. Could it be purely accidental? Mythically, it makes the Princess of Wales into the ex-Prince of Wales. And what if Dodi, like Wallis, had been a sort of cross-dresser?

What exactly were they planning? Repossi won't tell! The jeweler, true to his motto, insists that he will never ever tell us the secret the ring congeals. He even declined to reveal the number of its carats. Of course, anyone who announces publicly that he can keep a secret has already made it obvious that he can't. To reporters Repossi's spokesman coyly avers that the ring came from a collection of engagement rings designed by Repossi himself, in a series entitled "Dis-moi, oui." This is a ring to strike a bargain; it gives incomparably much (estimates go up to $250,000) in order to elicit from her a single little word. Say Yes to Me! he says to her, as he slips it on her very slender finger. You wear my ring that speaks, that says to the world you said yes.

When they saw it in the window of Repossi's she exclaimed, "That's the one I want." What does a Princess see? And what does she want? To judge from the picture in the *Times,* it's an awfully large ring: in the center looms a 3- or 4-carat, emerald-cut, flawless white diamond solitaire surrounded by four triangular diamonds whose points make a star around the central fire; the shape is outlined in the band of platinum that runs from point to point. The star is set in a pavement of brilliant diamonds, like those that should have been sunk in the sidewalk of Grauman's Chinese Theatre in Hollywood. Diana saw herself already enshrined in the celestial vault of our myths. The ring marks her emergence as a fully independent, finally matured, universal celebrity. The star ring seems to confirm in advance that in losing her royal highness she had risen above mere royalty to become a perpetually burning candle in the night of our dreams.

Excuse me, Zeem, for having to say this: Royalty is predicated on hierarchies. Whenever royals go looking for someone to marry they measure their requirements in terms of a pyramid of dignity, rigidly in place, with kings and queens and emperors at the highest highness of the pinnacle, the pointy point that seems like the whole point of a pyramid. In the two great crises that have beset the British monarchy in this century, the central issue was the honorific HRH, the right to be addressed as Her Royal Highness. How sweet it must be, to judge by the incessant, fruitless energy the Duke of Windsor expended during most of his married life trying to acquire that title for his wife. It was only at the end, after having exhausted every possible avenue of appeal to the sympathies of his family, that the Duke allowed himself to abandon his bitter efforts. Wallis wrote him several letters encouraging him to let the matter drop, but he persisted almost to the very end in seeking royal "recognition," as she called it, of her noble position as the bride of a king.

HRH has always struck me as looking like INRI: Jesus of Nazareth Rex of the Jews (*I* being *J* in Latin). To be addressed in the third person with respect to one's highness has intimations of divine elevation. Those who bear the initials HRH participate in the mystery of royal succession—the ineffable power of continuity that resides in the body of the anointed king. The body is only a vessel through which sovereignty continues to dwell eternally: the royal stand is never at half mast over Buckingham Palace; the king is dead, long live the king, etc. They were obsessed with the royal prerogative. The Duke always dreamed of sitting again on the throne. He loved coronations, especially the robes and clothes.

A Wallis Simpson biographer insists she never planned or wanted to marry the king. Others, particularly the royals, see her from the beginning as having ruthlessly intrigued. To them she was a monster, an embodiment of the crass ambition and sexual corruption their piety proscribed and dignity abjured. Its faintest odor was contaminating, and so they would never so much as allow her in their presence, or even in the same country, if they could help it. In her dreams, Wallis probably saw herself as Queen of England. She might even have hoped, at one point, that Hitler would put her on the throne. But that came later. It's possible to believe that at the beginning she longed only to be the king's mistress, until he found someone suitable to marry; then she intended to withdraw with her memories to the security of her comfortable second marriage with Ernest Simpson.

According to her flattering biographers, Wallis resisted for a long time the idea of divorcing Simpson. He represented the stability and safety to which she aspired in her old age as strongly as she had wanted in her youth to breathe free and take risks. In letters chronicling her adventures to her aunt Bessie, she barely bothers to conceal her glee at the way she has squandered her youth. She writes as if youthful charm and beauty were a kind of capital to be spent extravagantly while you had it, in the hope of finding in time a man to take care of you when it was gone. She married a wealthy, reserved, Anglophile American named Ernest, who was serious, truthful, predictable, and had excellent clothes; he was also quietly witty and a good dancer, "obviously well-read," she writes (it's not obvious how she would know): "He impressed me as an unusually well-balanced man." That certainly implies he has money. Could she also be intimating, well-hung?

The Duke and Duchess of Windsor

The Prince arranged to meet with Wallis's husband in order to ask him to give her a divorce. Simpson, having himself taken up with another woman who would become his second wife, agreed, on the condition that the Prince settle on Wallis enough wealth to secure her future. The divorce proceedings were a night-mare because of peculiarities of British law and the rigid require-ment that she be under not the slightest cloud of adultery. For months she was unable to be in the same country with the Prince, in order to forestall any hint of impropriety. Unlike Diana, she wasn't chaste on their marriage night, however much she might have wished to be; for the wedding she wore a long straight skinny dress confected by Mme. Grès of palest blue that in the black-and-white photos of Cecil Beaton looks creamy, virginal white.

Diana, who was allowed to preserve the title of Princess of Wales, was stripped of HRH, as a condition of the divorce, by the current Windsors. Technically, from then on, protocol required that she curtsy to her own children, who, as princes of the blood, outranked her. Diana was allowed to keep all gifts of family jewelry (estimated to exceed $100 million) for herself, and she agreed not to lend or sell any jewels given to her by the royal family, including the 30-carat sapphire brooch that was the Queen Mother's wedding present. Upon Diana's death, the jew-elry passed to her son William, for the future Princess of Wales.

If Diana had died a year earlier, she would have been enti-tled to a royal funeral. Instead, she was attributed a private cere-mony, a personal burial with elements of royal pomp. There was no lying in state, but there was Westminster Abbey and a funeral for the ages. HRH may finally be about nothing so much as where your body rots. The Duke of Windsor had to plead with his niece, Queen Elizabeth, on his deathbed, gasping with emphy-sema, to permit Wallis to be buried with royal ceremony next to him in his English grave.

Add to the mix the passionate depths of resentment and loy-alty that the Fayeds felt, father and son, toward their adopted

Queen Victoria and servant

country. Who knows what it would have meant to have had Diana permanently linked to a man who could stand for all the un-English English, all the immigrants and colored who have made London vibrant and chic again. For centuries, their dark skins have been utterly absent from the caste of royals, even from among its servants, excepting Queen Victoria's highly personal collection of handsome, turbaned Sikhs. Currently, there are only a handful of colored servants in the little army that waits hand and foot on Queen Elizabeth, and most of them are in menial positions. But think what it would have meant to the Windsors if Diana had married Dodi. One of those dark strangers, a keening Muslim, emerged from the unfathomable depths of Egypt, was about to take a step that would have elevated him to the position of being stepfather to the throne, forcing the British monarchy to take within its circle a family that had exposed its xenophobic, racist nerve. Their wedding might have meant the end of the monarchy, the last whispered hurrah of the old idea of sovereignty linked to the permanence of soil and blood. For republicans, like me, who hate the monarchy and fear the tyranny of class its principles entail, the end can't come too soon. Shortly, as Stalin said, there will only be four kings left, the only ones that deserve to remain: the King of Hearts, Spades, Clubs, . . . and, of course, there will always be a Queen of Diamonds. Take Elizabeth Taylor. No. Wait.

Diana's diamond ring was supposed to be her lucky star, not the emblem of her star-crossed doom. Repossi had introduced this line of rings with the slogan: "A little yes for the most beautiful day of your life. It was worth waiting for!" "A woman has only two good days," said Palladas, the fourth-century cynic, "the day she marries and the day she dies." For Diana, with this ring, they sort of coincide. It is not the first time. In fact, it's the most poignant theme in *The Greek Anthology,* a Renaissance collection of inscriptions found on antique Greek tombs. The most touching epitaphs record the tragedy that befalls a bride who dies on her wedding day—whose marriage veil turns into a shroud. When the moment of greatest joy becomes the worst horror, life and death seem to exchange place: love kills and death smiles. Remember Medea, my dear, who soaked the marriage dress of her rival in poison that turned the young girl's flesh to fire and burned her to a lacy crisp.

Sorry, Zeem. Ignore the pathos. But look at Diana's ring again. The four points of the star, the diamond triangles surrounding the rectangular solitaire, can also be seen to be double deltas doubled: the diapered cipher of Diana and Dodi, set in a carpet of diamonds.

Sometimes I think that Edward VIII believed so strongly in the necessity of marrying Wallis Simpson because of the mystical bond their ciphers made. On their first Mediterranean cruise together he started compulsively entwining her W with his E. In their correspondence, he regularly, adorably refers to the two of them as "a girl" and "a boy," as if they were any little boy and girl in love, anywhere in the world. He wrote to her in 1935:

> A girl knows that not anybody or anything can separate WE—not even the stars—and that WE belong to each other forever. WE love [underlined twice] each other more than life so God bless WE. Your [twice underlined]
> David

Not even the stars can separate them, their love is more powerful even than fate, which governs love. In practically every letter he writes her between the time of their first Mediterranean cruise and their honeymoon, he asks God to bless WE. God blesses the king, of course, but if it were only the king using the royal "We," he would have written, God bless Us. But he is nothing without her; the king is two, first person plural, joined together like the king to the kingdom he exchanges for her. After the marriage she started using it herself to refer to them. Their initials make a funny sort of rebus: WE is both a pronoun and a picture that paints the way Wallis entwines with Edward. An E, you see, also looks like a W, turned around 90 degrees, and he liked nothing better than to pen them gracefully together, indistinguishably. He further didn't fail to notice that W stands for Windsor, the couple's civil name. They were both obsessed with the royal cipher. Every piece of linen that went on their beds (they slept apart), every piece of porcelain and napkin in their kitchen was mono-grammed with WE surmounted by a royal crown. It must have seemed—especially to Edward, who was full of mystical intima-tions (as are most who play the kingly role; otherwise they'd laugh all the time)—that the combination of their initials was a signal that this marriage was made in heaven, sanctioned by the genius of the English language.

Diana's ring, with its double deltas set in pavé diamonds, recalls to mind the Cartier brooch the Duke gave the Duchess on their twentieth anniversary, in 1957. Shaped like a heart, it's paved all over with circular diamonds into which are set the intricately intertwined monogram of their initials and the roman numerals XX, spelled out in small square-cut emeralds. The heart is surmounted by a gold and calibré-cut-ruby crown, shaped just like those on their dishes. In 1957 the pavé setting of circular dia-monds to create a uniformly brilliant surface into which other gems are set was big news: twenty years later the style seems tired, even a little vulgar. Diana never had the sort of brilliant creative taste the Duchess did, much less the Duke, whose powers of discrimination were nurtured in surroundings of royal wealth, especially gardens, and fed on the jewelry of Queen Mary, his mother, and on the memory of Queen Alexandra's, his infinitely elegant grandmother. Like Benoit, the Paris bistro where they were planning to eat the night they died, Diana's ring is no longer really fashionable.

No one may ever know for sure what transpired between them when he slipped her the velvet box from Repossi's. Given Dodi's taste, he might have presented it with trumpets on the stereo—all the more lavishly proffered because it wasn't paid for. But maybe the moment of giving the gift wasn't all that different from the casual one recounted by the Duchess of Windsor in her memoirs, when she first received a piece of jewelry from her prince: "The Prince took from his pocket a tiny velvet case and put it in my hand. It contained a little diamond and emerald charm for my bracelet."[2]

Maybe it's the velvet box that makes a woman's heart leap. The smallness of the box is an icy thrill to anyone who knows that the very best things come in small packages. It may be true that no child ever wanted a smaller Christmas present, but adults look hardest for very small gifts under the tree. Smaller is bigger. It's a principle which belongs to the logic of jewelry. Compared to other gems, diamonds have the greatest density and hence the highest value in the smallest volume. Costume jewelry needs to be big to compensate for being (relatively) cheap. The little velvet box gives you a shiver. Maybe it's the idea of stone and metal against velvet, the royal cloth, used to line the crown, worn on state occasions. Velvet has a gleam or sheen that lights the background. Set against the plush velvet of the crown, the jewels gleam with unusual splendor. Which is why all the ladies at the marriage of the Dauphin wore velvet with their giant parures.

Liselotte, the Princess Palatine, continues imperturbably her exhaustive account of the jewelry at the engagement ceremony of the Dauphin in 1699. She writes:

> My son [the future Regent, Charles d'Orleans] wore a suit embroidered with gold and different colors, and all covered with gems; my daughter wore a green velvet dress embroidered with gold, whose skirt was entirely garnished with rubies

2. Wallis Simpson, *The Heart Has Its Reasons.* New York: David McKay, 1956, p. 125.

and diamonds as well as the bodice; her coiffure consisted in several sprays of diamonds and points of rubies with a golden ribbon all garnished with diamonds. The king had a suit of gold cloth, lightly embroidered on the side with golden blond thread; Monseigeneur wore a similar suit of gold on gold. The fiancé was in a black cloak embroidered with gold, and a white blouse embroidered in gold with buttons of diamonds; the cloak was lined with pink satin embroidered in gold and silver and golden blond thread. The fiancée had a dress and a skirt underneath in silver cloth covered and bordered with rubies and diamonds. The diamonds she wore in her coiffure and everywhere were those of the Crown. The dress of Mme. de Chartres was black velvet, like the suit of M. le Duc d'Anjou, her parure was in diamonds. Madame la Duchesse had a dress in velvet the color of fire embroidered with silver and a diamond parure. Mme. La Princesse de Conti had, like my daughter, a dress and skirt of green velvet embroidered with gold, a parure of pearls, diamonds, and rubies. Mme. La Princesse had a blue velvet dress, a skirt garnished with golden ribbons, and a parure of diamonds; the dress of Mme. De Condé was in velvet color of fire, her skirt was embroidered with silver and her parure was in diamonds. Those are all the outfits I remember.[3]

3. Princess Palatine, *Une princesse allemande la cour de Louis XIV: Lettres de la Princesse Palatine.* Paris: 10/18, 1962, pp. 81–82.

All she remembers! You'd think she'd need a video camera to record all this. At least, pencil and paper. Why does she go on like that? It tells you how intensely curious and fascinated they were at court with the spectacle of royal jewelry. Its enormous social power is felt particularly at this moment in history, in the middle of the seventeenth century, when Louis the Great is at the height of his absolute power, bringing the sunshine of modern, rational methods to bear on questions of economy, power, and glory. The beginnings of science flourish at this moment, at the birth of Modernity, when simultaneously gems suddenly become available in profusion, in large sizes, shaped by technologically advanced forms of faceting. Using principles derived from the grinding of lenses, they began to calculate the nature and angle of the cuts that could be made in, say, a diamond, so that light entering its limpid crystal water would emerge as little as possible from the bottom, while intensifying the light coming out of the top and sides. The power of that reflected, refracted light to fasci-nate the eye of a princess sharpens her memory and motivates her exhaustive descriptions. It's not just the aesthetic power of light from gems that moves her, it's even more the aura of social prestige the jewelry emits.

There's no jewelry without a state of society, says Kant. Who would wear it if they lived all alone? Hermits don't. Well, maybe once some Robinson Crusoe on a desert island slung a string of cowrie shells around his neck. That may only mean he was expecting to be picked up one day by strangers and didn't want to be caught without his pearls. You don't even put jewelry on for your children, Kant thinks, or for your intimate friends; jewelry is worn only for strangers. He wouldn't necessarily disagree with Simmel, that wearing it is a way of giving pleasure to others, an act of altruism, of what he calls sociability. But barbarians wore jewelry well before they were sociable, before they had any idea of participating in the pleasures of convivial social intercourse. In its most primitive uses, jewelry was first of all a way of showing oneself off to best advantage, not for the purposes of pleasing others but in a gesture of competition. Jewelry is a sign—an honorific sign like a medal or a trophy. The jewelry I wear or that I drape on my women enhances my prestige, my aura of power and wealth and beauty: it commands respect. It means that trophy wives are the earliest form of male competition. It's why the blondes who wear the biggest rocks to the health club are the ones who work the hardest on the StairMasters.

Before humans could carve stone or shape metal, they were wearing beads and making little pendants out of shells. In a London museum (Victoria and Albert), there's a gorgeous one, circa 28,000 B.C., from an Upper Paleolithic site in Moravia. It's made of fossilized shells strung together on a string, long tubular ones alternating with cockleshells, all the same size, and in the middle a pendular spiral shell hangs down. You could say that all necklaces, ever since, have been some version of this one. Fashion in jewelry hardly ever goes out of style, and old styles endlessly return.

Not only in the history of the human species but in the life of the individual, we affirm ourselves as human in the signs we sign on our body or our surroundings. A child, says Hegel, throws stones in a pond not just to see the pretty circles, but to see that they are mine. The barbarian necklace, like the circles in the pond, exteriorizes the self and makes me visible to me. Maybe it was only by ornamenting themselves that humans first understood the difference between a thing and a sign, a first sign to myself of my being human, essentially different and hence superior to those animals I paint on the wall, whose power and cunning I fear and admire. Maybe jewelry, which seems to be such an unnecessary inessential part of culture, is the first cultural arti-fact of all. I attach an ornament, therefore I am. There is no tribe anywhere that does not decorate itself. Not to paint your face and adorn your body is to remain in the condition of nature; wearing a necklace identifies me as human—an indispensable first step on the road to Cartier.

Self-consciousness is acquired along two paths: either by internal reflection, by representing oneself to oneself, or by exter-nally transforming the world, stamping it with signs of the self, giving it one's personal cachet. But in the act of transforming the world in order to make it reflect my self, I am changed by the new conditions I've created in the world of which I am a part. The self is both author of its creations—the source reflected in its works—and authored by the external transformations it itself produces. What's the aim of this self-reflection? To recognize one-self in the forms of external things, in order to enjoy oneself as if one were an external reality. Jewelry arises out of a play impulse that is serious, says Hegel. Wearing jewelry is a serious form of playing with yourself, of taking yourself as a thing to be play-fully, beautifully adorned. For Elizabeth Taylor jewelry has every-thing to do with that primitive impulse to flash, the exuberant display of her self-conscious desire to enjoy and share with others the joy of her divine beauty. I promise. I'm getting there, Zeem.

The ugliest girl in her French school and already butch, Amad was obliged to marry a distant cousin, before coming to Paris during the Algerian war, where he quickly divorced. With his parents' money s/he bought herself an apartment, and began permanently cross-dressing. For a while he used to hang out at Chez Moune's, the Lesbian club in Montmartre, where the *patronne* greets you at the door in a tuxedo and monocle, Mar-lene Dietrich style. He felt comfortable there with other women dressed as men, but s/he was such a stone butch the lesbians were all in love with him. She got tired of trying to tell the lipstick femmes she liked it only with boys. She spent days upstairs at the Café Flore and nights in caves in Saint-Germain where thin girls in black sweaters wearing white makeup played guitars and sang about death. In the sixties "he" started coming to the Alacazar. (Sorry, again, Zeem, about the pronoun confusion; I guess it's unavoidable when someone is anatomically one sex, socially another, and psychologically somewhere in between. From here on in, Amad will be masculine, which is how he referred to himself and impressed himself on me. You'll just have to deal.)

I fell in love with him in his place on the Quai d'Orleans, a vast old apartment he had converted to an Oriental loft, with Persian carpets covering the walls and low plush couches drowned in pillows covered with metallic fabrics from the Orient, from Palmyra, Kush, and Bangalore. You would of thought it was the apartment of a gay guy with its photos and statues of mostly naked men. But he was she.

In the evening lying there in the enveloping darkness lit only by the streetlamp down below and the smoldering flame of incensed candles, it felt like a magic carpet where any dreams were possible. The magic I think has something to do with the coming together of the two islands, almost but not quite touching. Like boats in a race, the two islands lap in the middle of the Seine, so you need to cross three bridges to go from one side to the other. Below is the pedestrian bridge, called the Pont Saint-Louis for the saintly medieval king who used to wander in the cow pastures on the island behind Notre Dame reciting prayers from his breviary. A bridge has been there, more or less unsteadily, since 1634, since the first one was built by Jean-Christophe Marie, the developer of the Ile Saint-Louis, who erected luxury houses called hotels on the island, which until then was still pretty much empty fields and a few huts. The first bridge Marie built collapsed the day it opened, killing scores, and there have been twenty-two different bridges ever since. Something about that span doesn't like a bridge.

Where was I? Plush velvet is the cloth of princesses. It was an inevitable accompaniment to the new fashion at the court of Versailles when people began wearing large single gems in minimal settings and wanted, advantageously, to display their fire. That fashion was made possible by the development of trade in large diamonds with India—by the near mythic success of the adventurer and gemologist Jean-Baptiste Tavernier, who braved unimaginable perils to visit the Indian mines of Golconda and return with enormous diamonds.

Jean-Baptiste Tavernier was born in 1605, the son, not surprisingly, of a geographer. In several volumes of his voyages, he recounts the six arduous and dangerous trips he made to Turkey, Persia, and India between 1631 and 1668, carrying silk and perfume and gold to trade for stones. He justifiably boasts of his courage, claiming that he never once was prompted to turn back by natural or human threats along the way. His aim was to visit all the great diamond and gem mines in southern India, located "in a barbarous country where one could proceed only on roads that were very dangerous."[4] As he wrote in his memoirs: "I am the first person in Europe who opened the path to these mines, which are the only ones on earth where diamonds are found." Visiting the fabulous Kollur mine, he saw workers striking rocks with hammers while sharp crystals flew off, glinting and potentially dangerous. About the diamond workers he wrote: "Since their wages are so small they have no scruples about trying if

4. Jean-Baptiste Tavernier, *Six voyages en Turquie, en Perse, et aux Indes.* Rouen: J.-B. Machuel le Jeune, 1724, p. 378.

they can to hide a stone in the sand for their own profit, and being naked except for a little cloth that hides their shameful parts, they try adroitly to swallow it."

Tavernier negotiated an enormous purchase with the Grand Mogul of Persia, who had seven thrones, some covered with diamonds, others with rubies, emeralds, and pearls. But it was for the diamonds Tavernier had come. "The diamond," he says, "is the most precious of all stones and the one to whose commerce I am most attached." And what an ornament of commerce he was. From Kollur he bought his most famous diamond, the deep blue one, the Tavernier Blue, 112 carats, faceted asymmetrically in the Indian style, and sold it to Louis XIV in 1669. He sold others almost as big to Colbert, the minister of finance, and to Monsieur, the brother of the king, and still others, on his way back to India, to the Medicis in Florence.

Legend has it that a thief once stole the dark blue diamond from the eye of a statue of the Hindu goddess Sita, wife of Rama, and ever since the stone has borne a deadly curse. In 1673, Louis had it reduced by half and re-cut into a heart-shaped brilliant weighing 67 carats and officially named "The Blue Diamond of the Crown." Shortly thereafter began the sinister series of personal and political catastrophes that afflicted his reign—the death of his son and heir, of his two grandsons, and the loss of all the lands he had conquered to the east and south. "The Blue of France," as it was also called, was worn by his red-haired mistress Mme. de Montespan, who shortly fell from grace and was replaced in the favor of the king by Mme. de Maintenon, the very woman Montespan had engaged to baby-sit the king's bastard children. (Let that be a lesson, Zeem: watch out for the babysitter. To your man she looks both like a desirable child and the mother of his children.) Some claim that Mme. de Montespan wore the blue diamond to a black mass, and hence cursed the stone forever. Tavernier, after he sold the Blue to Louis, returned to India, where he was eaten by a pack of wild dogs. Louis himself had the cursed stone mounted as a pendant which he wore—like an albatross. Louis XVI and Marie-Antoinette took turns wearing it, then they were executed. During the Revolution the diamond was stolen from the Garde Meuble of the king and disappeared. One story has it being halved again in Holland by Wilhelm Fals, a diamond cutter, who died heartbroken when his son stole the diamond; the son committed suicide. It's thought it was taken, if not to Amsterdam, to England, where it was cut into two or three smaller stones, the largest of which (44½ carats, cushion shaped) reappeared on the market in 1830 and became known as the Hope diamond after Lord Henry Philip Hope—a famous sonofabitch—who bought it and was run over by a carriage. One assumes, perhaps too quickly, that this was another accident in the series of uncanny calamities that have befallen the owners. But who knows? Maybe Hope's long-suffering wife, bereft of hope, had something to do with it.

Have you heard the story, Zeem, about the big blonde at the party wearing an enormous diamond? "The good news," she told its admirers, "is that this is the Lipshitz diamond, the third most famous in the world. The first is the Hope diamond, the second is the Koh-i-Noor, and the third is the Lipshitz. The bad news is that the Lipshitz diamond comes with the Lipshitz curse."

"What's the curse?"

"Lipshitz!"

Proving again: The bigger the diamond the bigger the schmuck.

The Hope is classified as a type IIb diamond, which is semi-conductive and therefore usually phosphorescent. Its dark steely gray blue color is attributed to trace amounts of boron. After exposure to shortwave ultraviolet light, the Hope diamond phosphoresces a strong red color, lasting several seconds. Perhaps that explains why Tavernier describes its color as being a "bleu violet." The Turkish sultan bought the Hope in 1909 and a few months later was overthrown by an army mutiny. In 1913, it was purchased by Evelyn Walsh MacLean, an extravagant Washington socialite.

The setting Cartier designed for Mrs. MacLean surrounds the stone with sixteen white pear-shaped and cushion-cut diamonds and is attached to a necklace of forty-five graduated white diamonds. A bail was attached to the pendant so that she could clip on the other huge diamonds she owned—the MacLean diamond and the monstrous, pear-shaped Star of the East—all together weighing well over 150 carats. Mrs. MacLean's son was killed in an automobile accident, her husband died in a mental hospital, and her daughter succumbed to an overdose of sleeping pills. A decade or so after the untimely death of Mrs. MacLean, Harry Winston bought the Hope and promptly donated it to the Smithsonian. Why would anyone buy the damned diamond? you ask. It merely proves that Hope springs eternal.

After the queen's death, Louis secretly married his mistress, Mme. de Maintenon, as everyone suspected he would. Her dress the Princess Palatine doesn't record and won't remember, because she loathes her with the enthusiasm of passionate envy, her bitterest enemy, a petty noblewoman, a baby-sitter, who had captured *her* king's affection and gained his trust at her expense. Anyway, the king's wife had by that time become so pious that her dress and parure were probably not even worth mentioning.

Queen Victoria is at the origin of the present British collection of royal jewels. It was she, and more particularly her husband, Prince Albert, who despite their disinclination to self-display were passionate admirers of great jewelry. Albert himself designed some of the most important pieces that the queen bequeathed to her descendants. The nineteenth century was a time when great wealth began to pour into the heart of the British Empire, notably from their colonial holdings in India, where maharajahs had fabulous wealth in gems and gold, and from South Africa, where the Kimberly mine, the greatest hole in the world, was dug to exploit the treasure of the blue kimberlite soil—mafic, igneous crystallized rock, once molten, thrown up from plutonic depths, carrying with it crystals of carbon in gem-rich pipes of hardened lava.

Her daughter-in-law, Princess Alexandra of Denmark, was the wife of the rakish Prince of Wales. Alexandra was a gorgeous woman, a wife befitting the king of the Edwardians. She was tall and stately, with an hourglass figure, that was stringently corseted. She had what her contemporaries considered to be the perfect chest and throat for wearing jewels. And she covered herself, sometimes to an alarming degree, with the greatest jewels in the royal collection. She had the head of a Gibson girl, with thick black curls that she wore up, showing her extraordinary little ears. Nietzsche thought that small ears were beautiful and large ears grotesque, for moral reasons. Big ears are promiscuous and hear everything; small ears are delicately attuned to catch only the range and frequency of what they want to hear. Alexandra's daughter-in-law, Queen Mary (the current queen's grandmother), began by imitating her, eventually simplifying and refining the royal taste in jewelry.

Take a look at this coronation picture of Queen Alexandra. She was mostly deaf and blithely blind to her husband's faithful infidelities. She was, it seems, a sweetheart, who loved her children and grandchildren. There's a note she wrote to David, her grandson, the Prince of Wales, the only one I've read with the

Queen Alexandra

ring of real warmth, so rare in the usual formality with which royals commonly address their descendants. It begins, "To David from his loving Mummy."

Wallis Simpson means more to me than her jewelry, which I love. Her quasi-royal collection was sold in Geneva in 1993 for $55 million—the best pieces were given to her by David when he was king and later Duke of Windsor. After a while, Wallis started choosing her own jewelry in collaboration with the Duke, whose highly evolved taste and imaginative daring can be judged by the revolutionary influence he had on clothing. A Windsor knot or a Windsor coat are tributes to the transformations he achieved in men's wear—mostly in the direction of more relaxed, sporty, "American" style within the rigid conventions of English royal life.

There was something more about Wallis Simpson than her jewelry which got my attention. It hit me like a smart crack against the side of the head when I read the blurb on the back of her authorized biography by Michael Bloch. The blurb was taken from James Pope-Hennessy, the biographer of Queen Mary, the Duke of Windsor's mother; he is quoted as having said, "I should classify [Wallis Simpson] as an American woman par excellence, were it not for the suspicion that she is not a woman at all."

An enigma tears open a tear in the fabric of reality. The love story of the century is suddenly a mystery crying for a detective, someone to reweave the threads of an explanation across the rent, to restore an unbroken web of cause and effects where the scandal has erupted. Like the cadaver in a detective novel, the mystery of her sex won't die until it is put to rest. Not a woman at all? If not, then what? Can this superb woman, whose name topped the list of best-dressed women in the world for decades, have been an American man? Can it be she was he? Bloch is coy about saying so, but his innuendo insinuates it everywhere.

Not entirely a woman, perhaps, but certainly not a man! By compensation for her mannishness she was the most girlish girl, the most feminine woman. You only need to take a look at the picture on the cover of Bloch's biography. It's one of her most fetching. She is twenty-one, and perfect, the new wife of her first husband, Major Winfield Spencer, commander of a naval air training station in Coronado, California. In 1917, he was considered too much of a drunk to go overseas and fight. He was brutal and beat her; she shortly left him. Maybe he was driven to drink by what he discovered on his wedding night beneath her skirts. But in the photo, leaning against marble stairs, framed by mimosa, she looks adorably girlish in a long blue wool skirt buttoned up the front and a high-necked long-sleeved sweater scalloped at the neck and sleeves with cotton doilies. Around her waist is wrapped a pleated cummerbund of black crepe; on her head sits a large black straw hat with a high crown banded around by the same dark pleated material. It looks like she's wearing a delicious chocolate cake. Half leaning against the stone, she is posed. Her arms are arranged to make a kind of frame around herself, which is framed in turn by the marble pillars behind her head. She is a picture, picture perfect, naive and cunningly contrived, like the best fashion photos. The pose requires that her left forearm cross in front of her body in order to grasp the middle and index fingers of her right hand whose elbow makes a right angle against the marble banister. She is framed by fronds of delicate leaves hanging from the planted urns on either side. She seems to be playing with the tip of one plant, whose branch has occasionally slipped over her right shoulder and splays its self against her dress like a large leafy brooch. It is as if the very plants want to embrace her, to swirl their leaves in arabesques around the elegant clarity of her narrow, slender form. The pose serves to hide her wedding ring but it hitches up the sleeve in a way to display to the camera the bracelet she was wearing. Wallis Simpson never looked more beautiful.

In the slightly blurry print, it's hard to make out many details, but the bracelet does appears to be double. It looks like a

Mrs. Wallis Spencer

single band of gold around the wrist intertwined with a string of beads; the gold band was probably bought for her by her drunken lout of a husband. He and she, the frequently abused wife, got to live a chic officer's life in California during the war—about as far as any soldier could get from the trenches of Verdun. It was probably she who had the idea to buy some glass beads and to twist them seductively around the conventional solid gold bracelet he had given her, probably with his army company insignia inscribed.

The crystal beads twist loosely around the gold band complicating its simple brightness with the sinuous weave of their darkly glittering opacity. The bracelet is a thyrsus, the wand of Bacchus, a hop-pole encircled by convoluting grape vines, an emblem of divine intoxication, or the caduceus of Mercury, who wields a central, straight unbroken rod intertwined with double serpents. There's a prose poem of Baudelaire written in honor of the thyrsus—an immaculate symbol of poetry itself: around the firm rod of the poet's creative will spirals intricate arabesques of poetic ornament. The male principle is mute without the female genius of adornment to unfold and express it in circling rounds of verse; conversely, poetry without the straight hard aim of poetic intention is limp and aimless. I know it's perverse but I can't help reading that bracelet in the photo as an androgynous emblem of her trans-sex—a whirling reeling wheeling gyre.

Later, after the war, Major Simpson and Wallis, posted to China, served their country leisurely. Wild rumors have her accompanying him to his favorite Peking bordellos. If the even wilder rumors were true, she was able to observe there, and learned to practice, the most obscure and refined arts of sexual pleasure. David's father, King George VI, is supposed to have received a secret report from Scotland Yard on her whoring in Peking, a complete and intricately detailed account of her lascivious education. Those Chinese techniques of pleasure, invented and refined over thousands of years, have been meticulously recorded and ritually taught by masters or madams for centuries. Of all the secrets in that incredible arcana, the rarest may be the ars erotica involving sexual encounters with hermaphrodites and the secrets of vaginismus. In some women the clamping of the vagina is uncontrolled and potentially deadly; in some, however, the skill can be acquired.

I can't stop thinking about Wallis Simpson, Duchess of Windsor, in the brothels of Peking, learning exotic secrets of the intersexed. What forms of pleasure did she provide, so excellent and rare that a prince might renounce a kingdom? Imagine the sensibility of the woman, with her edge of cruelty.

I like to think I can see inside the sadness in David's eyes, which was remarked in him even as a young man: it's the sadness of the perverse, the pain of someone having to deal with his own transsexual impulses. It lets me understand what led him to her, a kind of she-man, who wanted only to be the perfect woman in the eyes of him who, in her eyes, was the perfect man—since kings are always supposed to be men. There's no knowing what turned Edward on, but he says over and over he can't live without her. We know, if you believe Kitty Kelley, that David, like his brother Albert, was disastrously small in the penis. If you put that fact together with her talent for vaginismus, you can imagine her clamping down on the king and pulling that little thing into her vise (or vice), in order not to devour but to massage it, procuring for him the most intense pleasure he had ever been able to know, while she hums the solemn cadences of "God Save the King." Don't forget, Zeem, that Elvis had a micropenis. It may even be the ironic condition for being the king. He who, metaphorically, wields the biggest scepter in the kingdom must have a trivial little literal rod himself. David needed a woman like Wallis to give him what some think he never had before she came along, the feeling of being (with) a man, like her, whose enormous clitoris is indistinguishable from a small penis like his.

According to one of the cruelest biographies, the Duke, who slept with a Teddy bear his whole life, never made love in his own bed. Well into his sixties, he would sneak into his wife's bedroom at night, being sure always to return to his own room before dawn. He's obsessed both with the guilt and pleasure she manages to supply. Besides, she's so cruel.

Wallis was bossy and cheeky, from the beginning. All the biographers speak of her imperious, maniacal domesticity. Before she was even divorced, she was writing David firm little notes instructing him to tell the butler to find dinner chairs without arms and to remind the prime minister to consult the Cabinet about the Prince's plans for a summer cruise. He admired her boldness and he liked to be ordered around. He complains all the time about how she treats him, and yet he loves it more than his kingdom. The king, who rules, needs to be ruled over by someone immeasurably beneath him (a twice-divorced American commoner)—in the eyes of his family, beyond the palest pale.

Eventually, Wallis had enough of bordellos. She left her first husband, but stayed in China for a year playing around the diplomatic set in Peking. There's a picture of her at the races with her young boyfriend, an Italian diplomat, who is as elegant as she is. He's slim, limp-wristed, sports a pale, floppy Borsalino hat and a gray herringbone suit, double-breasted with large loopy lapels, and a flowing white hanky that drips over his heart. His shoes are very long and pointed. Chinese jockeys are riding by, with their little whips.

She held the tightest rein over every moment of their life and they had the best servants in the world. Their butler was the model Wodehouse used for Jeeves. She didn't scream like Chanel, but she was hard and cutting. They shared the compulsive desire to attend to every detail. Couturiers, by definition, are obsessed with finish, with every last button, every hair in (or cunningly out of) place: the mannequin is an icon, frozen in her perfection. Wallis had no sports. Movement didn't interest her, only staying and decorating. Her monument is the house in the Bois de Boulogne, which remained untouched for ten years after her death, every dish and towel in its place, until it was all shipped out and meticulously catalogued by Sotheby's to be sold lock, stock, and barrel, and all at once disappear. Sotheby's re-created the rooms of the house in its showroom, using painted backdrops but the real furniture—many of the familiar pieces one has seen in all the biographies. The auction, to be held in October, was postponed until February. Dodi Fayed's father, remember, owned the house in the Bois de Boulogne; he had preserved it as the reliquary it was, until the moment his son and presumptive daughter-in-law decided it was there they would re-enact the Windsors in exile.

In 1956, Wallis wrote about her sadness at having finished the decoration of their country retreat, the Moulin de la Tuilerie, where Edward loved to come to garden and do a little embroidery. She writes in her memoirs:

> There can be little more that I can reasonably do to it. . . . No longer can I justify to myself the endless afternoons given to combing the antique shops and the art galleries of the Left Bank, picking up here a piece of Sevres or Meissen for a table or a vitrine, there a still life—what the French call "la nature morte"—to hang in the dining room.[5]

While he delighted in growing things, she appreciated nature when it was dead. She paid lavish attention to her cut flowers, whose ghostly beauty touched by imminent death seems to defy it—posthumously alive, not quite dead. She loved white chrysanthemums, Chinese flowers of mourning, and she was fanatical about her arrangements. Servants had to fill the flower vases twice a day so that their water would be always crystal clear. She was a creature of vitrines, of shop windows. She loved everything frozen in ice, under glass. Her taste in paintings ran to still lifes of shocking mediocrity, fruits and vegetables frozen in a pitiless

---

5. Simpson, *The Heart Has Its Reasons,* p. 13.

glaze of photographic realism. They loved snapshots. The king himself was a compulsive photographer. Every room of their house had multiple portraits of her. Their lives were those of the first modern royals, who spent their time in front of cameras and fleeing from them.

They were probably fierce anti-Semites. Her racial bigotry goes back to Baltimore where she was taught disdain for Jews and for what she casually called "niggers." She and he were notoriously patronizing to the people in the Bahamas where he served as governor during the war. The Windsors were sent there ignominiously by Winston Churchill to prevent them from falling, more or less willingly, into the hands of the Germans, who entertained ideas about making him a quisling king after the German invasion of Britain—in the place of his patriotic brother, George VI. On at least one occasion, hearing of that possibility, Wallis was seen to smile broadly. Her biographer quotes her at the beginning of his book: "I have always had the courage for the new things that life sometimes offers."[6]

Emerald Cunard, the famous hostess, who was smitten with Joachim von Ribbentrop, the new German ambassador, was a frequent guest at the Fort with David and Wallis. Gossip circulated about the king's "Nazi leanings" as early as June 1935; he was less fearful of the threat of Germany than he was of the spread of Communism. In 1939, Wallis and Edward accepted an invitation from the führer to visit Germany; her smile is never more radiant than in the famous picture of her shaking hands with Hitler. The Duke and Duchess traveled in a circle which included many sympathizers with Nazi Germany and much admiration for the disciplined way Hitler raised his people out of

---

6. Michael Bloch, *The Duchess of Windsor.* New York: St. Martin's Press, 1996, p. 11.

The Duke and Duchess of Windsor with Hitler

defeat. The best man at their wedding, "Fruity" Metcalfe, had Nazi connections. They were close to the Mosleys and to those who were close to him. Mosley, a lord who renounced his title when it suited him, was the leader of the pro-Nazi party in England, the Black Shirts, for whom black was beautiful, but who bashed blacks and Jews in the streets after rowdy party rallies. The Windsors' love of uniforms and the snap of leather, the sharpness of their taste, resemble Chanel's; with her they share an infallible nose for smelling out a Jew. They were not murderers, but their taste was killing. They were scions of the higher anti-Semitism, which is distinguished from the vulgar Nazi variety by the refinement of distaste and cool indifference with which it regards any Jewish production.

I'm sure Wallis was furiously but discreetly political. Hitler is reported to have said to his entourage that the Duchess "would have made a good Queen." A compliment like that from Hitler is no compliment. In *A King's Story,* Edward writes: "Wallis had an intuitive understanding of the forces and ideas working in society. She was extraordinarily well-informed about politics and current affairs."[7] Royals, after all, can hardly avoid being diplomats, and in Bermuda she was indefatigably active as the governor general's wife. They were restless schemers and relentless dreamers after political power and influence.

Deprived of normal human contacts, they lived in a world of generalized suspicion. As do many royals, they considered only dogs and horses to be perfectly loyal—especially dogs. Royals look to animals for the trust which they rarely find, or place, in those around them, even in those closest to them. Humans, unlike dogs and horses, are all too ready to flatter and conspire for advantage—especially the members of a royal family. The Churchillian pug dogs the Windsors loved to death were the dearest things in their lives. They decorated virtually every room with their ugly faces—in paintings and photographs on the walls, on couch pillows in her bedroom, and on every surface there proliferated little pug figurines made of the finest porcelain.

---

7. Duke of Windsor, *A King's Story: The Memoirs of the Duke of Windsor.* New York: Putnam, 1951, p. 21.

The Duchess of Windsor

They preferred dogs to humans, like many English animal lovers. It's not surprising that, like many of them, they were also crypto-fascists.

Cecil Beaton, who had an eye, found her "brawny and raw-boned in her sapphire blue velvet." The pictures he took of her in 1938, in an effort to speed her public rehabilitation, are almost cruel for the way they display her brawny shoulders in a sleeveless gown and the raw-boned thickness of the hands she hated and always tried to hide. She often looks like she's wearing drag! In this photograph her hands are featured in the foreground, crossed on her lap, but they appear almost slender under the weight of three enormous stones—the two giant, 18-carat cushion-cut

Miss Wallis Warfield

rubies, surrounded by diamonds, set in the Cartier bangle bracelet the Duke had just given her on her anniversary, and the enormous rock of her emerald engagement ring.

As a young girl she liked to dress up in men's clothes, and according to her biographer, she understood how attractive that was to a lot of men. "In an effort to attract boys, she tended to play up this masculinity: she often dressed mannishly, parted her hair, and wore a monocle. She developed a somewhat bossy personality."[8]

Who knows such things? Did you know that by playing up your tomboyishness, Zeem, you make yourself more attractive to boys? But how high up do you play your masculinity when, like Wallis, you're also trying to play your masculinity down? That's the question. It's a question and a problem for bull dykes who are feminists but whose girlfriends are often precisely attracted to their macho swagger. How far can you switch without switching?

Sometimes switching sex improves the people we love. When I lived in Cambridge I knew Elizabeth, an early MtF (Male-to-[constructed] Female), who used to tell me stories about her

---

8. Bloch, *The Duchess of Windsor,* p. 16.

mother while she was fitting my skirts in a boutique where I could safely buy. Before Elizabeth had her sex change, the mother had been a major pain in the ass—rigid, moralizing, humorless, incessantly nagging and criticizing her son, hating his effeminacy. But the instant Irving transsexed to Elizabeth, her mother underwent a moral transformation. She began smoking cigarettes, going to bars all the time, saying fuck this and fuck that. Her aggressions vanished, and she became generous, tolerant, uproarious. It was as if the ambiguity of her son's transition had introduced into her overrationalized, hyper-controlling self a little grain of madness that loosened the constraints she had been imposing on her own desires and her son's.

I remember the time in the toilet of Wiggles, a bar off Harvard Square, when she let me see her g-string, which was famous in Eliott House. Elizabeth had been to design school in Philadelphia and knew how to cut and sew. I was in a dress but she was squeezed into jeans and a cunning torn cotton blouse. Sweaty from dancing on the bar, she pulled me into the ladies' room and with strength surprising for a girl forced me to my knees, while she slipped her jeans down over her incredibly slender waist. At her crotch I was blinded: on blue-velvet plush strewn with semiprecious stones were traced the letters "EI," i.e., Elizabeth, the First (also Iorio). Kneeling at her feet, a little stoned and stunned, I began to lose myself in meticulously observing the way the moonstones, aquamarines, and opals were cut—some faceted, some en cabochon—in every imaginable shape. There were baguettes, and lozenges, cushion-shaped, and brilliant-cut stones: topaz, tourmaline, beryl, and garnets. They seemed in that dim light like dozens of colored fireflies flashing against the dark blue shadows of a lawn. I knew she was already close to having the second surgery. She had spent the required year taking hor-

King Edward VIII

mones, getting implants, living as a woman, but not yet castrated. On the floor of a bar in Boston, kneeling reverently before the jewel between her legs, I never even thought to wonder whether there was something or nothing behind the veil.

Switching sex is like turning your profile. Traditionally, the official portrait made of the king's profile on British stamps shows him facing opposite the direction of his predecessor. Edward VIII broke with this convention: he thought his left profile was his best side and insisted that he should be depicted facing the same way as his father, George V. Hugh Cecil was commissioned to take the photographic portrait to be used for the new issue. Edward obviously liked the open-necked informality of the picture, since he inscribed two prints for Wallis Simpson and had them set in a double-fronted gold Cartier frame.

The new stamps looked very modern, compared to those of his father's reign. Edward's brother, George VI, quickly reverted to the older style when he succeeded to the throne, following the new king's abdication. Dumb brother Georgie, the father of Elizabeth II, may have been stuttering and stodgy, but he knew what he hated—namely, his brother and his ilk, with their chic cult of breezy insouciance and open-shirted intimations of Hitler youth. Like many English aristocrats, David and Wallis were drawn to the modernity of Hitler's taste, which, like Chanel's, was liberating in relation to the opulent, ornate pomposity of Edwardian taste that preceded it. Hitler proposed a less-adorned, more dynamic aesthetic ideology based on the beauty of cruelty and hate.

Of course, not all Nazis, like Hitler, once were serious paint-
ers in Vienna or imagined themselves to be architects. But he was
not alone in his artistic temperament. We would love to know
more about the large brooch that Goering wore attached to his
green velvet smoking gown, when he descended the staircase of
his country house to greet Speer, who was there on business.
Speer tells us, in his memoirs, that later, while they talked, Goering toyed on a table with handfuls of loose cut gems.

Modernism is the aesthetic of industrial capitalism. It takes
mechanical machines as its ideal of beauty. It desentimentalizes
the picturesque piety of fin de siècle Romanesque and straightens
up the arabesques, the smarmy swirling lines of Art Nouveau.
Its purity purges the heart-felt profundities of late Romanticism
and restores the superficial values of anarchic spontaneity and
senseless repetitions. Modernism grants freedom and promotes
autonomy by encouraging anonymity and anomie. Paranoid,
tormented by its obsessive thoughts, modernism lives off suspicion, feeds on narcissism, violently fractures relations among
people along lines of hierarchy and identity. It believes only in
numbers and worships money; it promotes the ideology of pluto-
crats: only the rich are free. Modernism is the aesthetic of bad
mechanical machines, whereas postmodernism, if it exists, has
the beauty of good electronics. It may only be dawning, this new
age, and we may never live to see it in full flower. What's left of
modernism may kill us all yet.

If you look closely at the picture on the stamp of Edward in
profile, he appears to be wearing a single, slim gold chain slung
adorably across that fully exposed, elegantly muscled neck, infor-
mally undraped. How modern is that? It looks queer. The neck of
a queen, not a king. Turned to the left (a *Linker,* as Germans say),
David leans the other way. He was, of course, German through
and through like the rest of the royals. Even today, whenever

paparazzi in London spy a royal, they warn each other by yelling, "*Achtung!*" No protocol hinders English royalty from marrying French, Spanish, Italians, or Russians of equal dignity. But because the Church demands that they marry Protestants, they've generally found their spouses beyond the Rhine. As Prince of Wales, Edward often visited Germania, particularly Austria for skiing. He loved the German language and as he grew older sought more and more frequent occasions to speak it.

He is turned to the left, in the same direction his father turned. He never escaped being in the shadow of his severe, overbearing father. In his first address to the nation, after having become king, he insists that he is the same man as before, before and after his father's death, unchanged by having become what he no longer is—still facing in the same direction.

> I am better known to you as the Prince of Wales. . . . And though I now speak to you as King, I am still that same man who has had that experience and whose constant effort it will be to continue to promote the well-being of his fellow men . . .

"I am still that same man who has had . . ." In his clipped voice the single-syllable words, enunciated slowly, have a martial cadence, as if to emphasize his undeviating uniformity with himself. The motto of the Prince of Wales is *Ich dien*—in German, I serve. I submit myself to the obligations of my royal blood, remain obedient to my destiny. Except that he took it to be his highest duty, not a derogation, to serve love before serving his kingdom. Once he gave his promise, to her and to himself, no power in heaven or on earth could sway him.

His father loathed his taste. He once called him sissy-boy to his face. At the funeral of the miserable sonofabitch, David appears unaccountably stressed. People always thought of him as eternally boyish, full of fun and energy, always laughing, noblesse oblige; the new king was wan and troubled from the outset of his reign. It's no wonder: he was faced by the dilemma he had contrived for himself, deciding whether to marry Wallis before or after his coronation. There never was any question of giving her up, or conversely, as his mother proposed, of keeping her for a mistress. He intended to marry her at all cost. The question was whether to avow, before the coronation, that he fully intended to make her his queen, or be crowned and keep secret his secret intention.

Harding, one of the courtiers, thought that "his mind was at least temporarily unbalanced." Queen Mary went further, describing him as "absolutely unhinged." They kept on coming to him and reminding him of his duty, of his motto, of the dignity and historical importance of the role he was about to assume compared to the trivial question of his domestic happiness. Nothing prevailed over his mad insistence that he couldn't live, as he said, "Without the help and support of the woman I love." Unless she weren't a woman at all.

In many ways the Duke of Windsor reminds me of Georgio Armani. They are both small men, with vivid smiles, sleek and elegant. When they walk into a room, it freezes conversation, heads bow and eyes avert their gaze in the presence of so much commanding style. No other designer makes such a towering impression, not since Givenchy who in the fifties, at the height of his success, was charismatically handsome, but looming six feet six inches tall. Power often goes to tall men—de Gaulle, Chirac, Kohl, Clinton. But Armani is regal and slight, like Edward, or, another Italian, Napoleon. If you look at the Armani face, you notice first the perfect nose that tilts up as if it were bobbed. It isn't, as one can tell from a youthful picture of him on the beach with his mother, his elegant and influential mother, at the family compound on the island of Pantelleria off the coast of Sicily. Like Edward, Armani was destined to be beautiful and to love the beauty of powerful women. And so, I imagine, was I.

Three

Wearing It:
Hegel and Elizabeth Taylor

No one's lust for jewelry in this century has been more notorious, ambitious, knowing, some would say vulgar, than Elizabeth Taylor's. How vulgar? There's a story about the time Princess Margaret asked to try on the Krupp diamond, the 33.19 flawless emerald-cut carats, which had belonged to the widow of the German steel and crematorium magnate. Elizabeth VIII wears it as a ring that stretches from knuckle to joint. (I always call her that to distinguish her from Elizabeth's I and II, but also because of her Henryesque tastes in power, love, food, and marriages, eight of them.) Burton had "won" the gem in a bidding war with Harry Winston at the Parke-Bernet Galleries in New York in 1968 for the then bargain price of $305,000. Princess Margaret

Elizabeth Taylor wearing the Taylor-Burton diamond

looked at the ring on her own hand and said in a joshing tone, "How incredibly vulgar!" And Elizabeth replied, "Yeah, ain't it great?" The Princess probably didn't realize she was looking right into the depths of what is probably the clearest, whitest, large diamond in the world. Elizabeth Taylor, on the other hand, knows exactly what she's looking at in her vast collection of diamonds and other great gems and pearls, including, besides the Krupp, the 69.42-carat pear-shaped Taylor-Burton diamond (now sold but once suspended from a diamond necklace after Liz had decided it was a little too large for a ring) and La Peregrina, the most famous black pearl in the world.

There was the time in Geneva, near the end of the marriage, when Eddie Fisher, wishing to surprise and mollify her, purchased a diamond necklace chez Vacheron Constantin. She received it, examined it, and asked how much he paid. "Fifty thousand," he was pleased to say. She looked again, turned to him, and said, "Eddie, there's not a decent stone here. You've been taken."[1]

The point of the story seems to be that she just was being a bitch, since Vacheron Constantin is a great jeweler. But it also tells you that she can look at a necklace of diamonds and distinguish the good stones with an appraiser's eye. It also suggests why money is always spoken of in the same breath as her jewelry. Those violet eyes know what things are worth, and she defies all taboos about keeping it a secret. Eddie Fisher complained that she needed to be given diamonds before breakfast in order to have a good day. But she never gave love for diamonds. Elizabeth Taylor is not a whore.

When she was seventeen, and was already a great star, a luminary at MGM, Howard Hughes, who was forty-four, decided to marry her. He had already had affairs with the hottest women in Hollywood: Lana Turner, Ava Gardner, Ginger Rogers, Yvonne de Carlo. He promised her a million-dollar dowry and discussed buying her her own film studio, if she and her parents agreed. She loathed him. One day, to prove the sincerity of his intentions, he filled an attaché case with loose large gems and carried it to the pool where she was sunbathing, clad in a bikini. He came up behind her, opened the case, and poured out onto her brown little

1 C. David Heymann, *Liz: An Intimate Biography of Elizabeth Taylor.* New York: Birch Lane Press, 1995, p. 242.

belly a fortune in emeralds, rubies, sapphires, and diamonds. "Get dressed," he said, "we're getting married."

Elizabeth Taylor stood up, eyes flashing, and, brushing a ruby from her navel, told him, "I am not for sale!"

No one knows for sure when her passion for jewelry began, but it is often dated from the public occasion in 1949, at the age of seventeen, when she was crowned princess of the Diamond Jubilee at a celebration of the Jewelry Industry Council. Her crown was a diamond tiara worth $22,000 in 1940s money. She instantly asked: "Can I keep it?"[2] They let her wear it around for the day but it wasn't long before she had one of her own.

In an interview, she recounts an even earlier memory, when she is not being given but gives jewelry. "I remember the first piece of jewelry I ever bought," she says. "It was a costume piece I got for my mother for Mother's Day when I first became successful in films. I saved up money and bought her a very pretty bow with flowers of simulated sapphires."

The bow is an old motif in jewelry that became popular in the seventeenth century. Ribbons back then were worn as ornaments, on men's clothes as well as women's, while ornaments, like jewelry, were attached to the clothes (sometimes the ears) with bows. Eventually the bows themselves became jewelry. When you wear a bejeweled bow you attach an attachment. In giving her mother a bow, she displays, touchingly, the force of her wish to remain lovingly attached to this overbearing woman. Elizabeth's first gift of jewelry to her mother is also a prototype of all the gifts of jewelry she will receive from men in order to keep her bound.

Sara Taylor had a brief career on the stage in New York and London where her greatest moment came playing a crippled girl

2. Ibid., p. 76.

who throws away her crutches in the third act. God knows Elizabeth herself has risen from crutches plenty of times. The mother
gave up her career when she married but burned with ambition
for the daughter that was born, a Pisces, on February 27, 1932.
Like most Pisces, the last and oldest sign in the calendar, she was
a precocious child, already an adult practically at birth. Elizabeth
was named for both her grandmothers and was given a middle
name of Rosemond, her father's mother's maiden name. All the
women on both sides of the family lend their names to this
mound of roses or rose mouth—this miracle of beauty she has
been since birth.

Elizabeth once said that she did not choose to have a career:
it was forced on her by a mother who wore the pants in the family. The father was off tending his important art gallery and pur-
suing his boyfriends on the side. Her long-standing personal and
political sympathy for gay men is often attributed to that. But
you bet I'll get there.

Her mother pushed her ferociously to grow up and be a star.
Faced with that kind of pressure, a child can either passively
resist, openly revolt, or, alternatively, completely identify with her
mother. In the earliest movies, *Lassie* and *National Velvet,* you already see her preternatural confidence in her beauty and seductive charm; she knows how attractive she is because her mother
hasn't stopped telling her. You can see she sees the effect her presence has on those around her. Her mother, like JonBenet's, must
have been teaching her to be a beautiful woman from the time
she was born. Like her, Elizabeth was a gifted pupil and learned
early to confirm her mother's impossibly strict notions of how to
look and act grown-up—or else! Elizabeth also learned from her
mother that great actresses deserve the solace of great jewelry.

Little Mary Pickford, who in films played unadorned innocence, in life loved very large rubies and star sapphires. She

Elizabeth Taylor with her mother and brother

owned both the 60-carat Star of Bombay and the 200-carat Star of India; she wore both all the time.

Theda Bara said she hated diamonds. Instead, she wore an engraved emerald ring and a turquoise ring she called her talisman, which she never took off.

Gloria Swanson's taste in jewelry was so lavish she had to rent it. One year, she spent half a million dollars leasing her jewelry. In 1920, in *Affairs of Anatol*, Gloria Swanson wore an important emerald, amethyst, and gold necklace by the great designer Iribe, starting a fashion for colored jewelry.

Joan Crawford was so tediously known for wearing sapphires that the press called them "Joan Blue," as in the sentence, "She's wearing the whole schmear of 'Joan Blue' tonight." One of her favorite pieces was a bracelet set with three star sapphires of

73.15 carats, 63.61 carats, and 57.65 carats. From her second husband, she received a 70-carat star sapphire engagement ring; next to which, on the same finger, she often wore a huge, cerulean emerald-cut stone, blue like the sky bumping up against the sea. In the forties, Crawford added to her collection a 75-carat amethyst ring and a huge 100-carat citrine ring, both emerald-cut with a simple setting.

Jean Harlow also loved sapphires; her engagement ring from William Powell was a 150-carat cabochon sapphire she wore in her last movie, *Saratoga,* in 1937, before her tragic death at age twenty-six.[3]

Marilyn Monroe sang "Diamonds Are a Girl's Best Friend" in *Gentlemen Prefer Blondes,* and became eternally their icon. It was she, glittering in sequined white, suspended overhead, who sang that song on video over and over again at the great exhibition of diamonds in New York at the American Museum of Natural History.

Diamonds, taken in themselves, are not friendly to girls. They weigh them down, and their sharp points frequently prick the skin. They are hard and unyielding, not at all fuzzy and warm the way you might imagine a girl's best friend to be. But diamonds are friendly precisely because they are cold and hard, indomitable and rare—can be counted on to keep their shape and value even when the girl loses hers. They are practically liquid cash; at least that's the idea. The reality, of course, is quite different.

Buying diamonds is one thing, trying to sell them is another. Still, it's what you take when you flee for your life. Holocaust narratives always note the role of jewelry as the possession of last

---

3. Internet address: http://www.gemstone.org/famous.html/. International Colored Gemstone Association: Gem-o-rama.

resort. When even currency may not be convertible, gold and diamonds preserve their value in easily portable volumes that can be secreted away and universally accepted in exchange. When the Bolsheviks led the tsar and his family downstairs to a large room with few chairs, in the house in Siberia where they were being held prisoner, it was ostensibly to take their photograph. The only shots taken were fired out of the barrels of pistols, unloaded indiscriminately on the adults and the children, three young girls and a small boy, killing them all, it's said. But several of the assassins were themselves wounded, because bullets bounced off the bodies of the royal family, as if they actually possessed the magical properties mystical Russian royalists traditionally attributed to the family of the tsar. The explanation was more prosaic: The tsar's family had large diamonds sewn into the lining of their clothes, which turned bullets away as if they were rubber and sent them flying back to strike their executioners. Like a girl's best friend.

Elizabeth Taylor doesn't just want jewelry, she wants the gift of it, i.e., with no strings attached—with only the wish for her love in return. Marc Bohan always had to give her a gift whenever she bought anything at Dior. "I love presents!" she exclaimed.[4] Like a goddess, who has everything, she above all wants to be adored. Like a tough businesswoman, who can calculate costs to the last centime, she loves to get something for nothing.

Elizabeth Taylor is the opposite of Chanel, who also wore big expensive jewels, but discreetly, as if they were junk. Elizabeth Taylor's vulgarity consists in the way she indulges her love of everything that flashes, everything that is overabundantly visible. She is always bursting at the seams, exteriorizing herself in the most extravagantly excessive ways. At puberty, already irre-

---

4. Heymann, *Liz,* p. 163.

pressible, she insisted on wearing strapless dresses and peasant blouses, heavy makeup, and lots of jewelry—big, jangly bangles, the bigger the better, and earrings the size of curtain rings. Her style is hyperbolic. She told a reporter she thought her marriage to Nicky Hilton would last because they both "adore [not just like] oversize [extra large] sweaters, hamburgers with onions [big and sloppy], and Ezio Pinza [huge voice deeply enchanting]."[5] When she gets fat, she literally bursts out of her bras; people always used to

Elizabeth Taylor, 1979

be shocked by the tightness of her sweaters and by the way her big tits always seemed to verge on escaping their décolletage. She presents herself abundantly, and that amplitude is her genius.

Her language is excessive. She's famous for the way she curses. She has the foulest mouth in Hollywood and that from an early age. She is known to have addressed an MGM executive, oximoronically, as you "Shitassedmotherfuckingfaggotcock-

---

5. Ibid., p. 112.

sucker."[6] Since her adolescence, people have noted how bizarre it is to observe such black streams of vile language issuing forth from radiant perfection. Because she does everything to excess, transgresses every taboo, she likes everything big and bad. When she decides to eat, she gains fifty pounds. At one point, she became Miss Piggy, or Miss Piggy was modeled on her, a beautiful woman who is also a pig, who, like her, eats pizza before going to bed and craves fried chicken and mashed potatoes. She became sublimely, awesomely fat when she was married to Senator Warner; she blamed all those campaign luncheons, dinners, barbecues, for having put more than 180 pounds on a five-foot two-inch frame. But she was still Elizabeth Taylor, squeezed into dresses, like Divine, or draped in caftans, the whole nine yards.

She had a wooden leg, by all accounts. She could drink Richard Burton under the table, whose drinking killed him—not her. Sipping champagne all day long and knocking down vodkas, she had long periods when she would start boozing at ten in the morning and, to observers, often seemed stupefied by the alcohol and the prescription drugs she was doing. She spent many months in rehabilitation, not to mention hospitals of all kinds. She has been near death several times, suffered a brain tumor and hip replacement and tracheotomy. Her face seems to be a document in the modern history of plastic surgery. Her health is a permanent catastrophe; she is accident prone and liable to serious disease and major dysfunction. It's a form of hysteria; everyone's noticed how frequently the illness or accidents coincide with the breakup of one of her marriages. In order each time to love as fiercely as she does, she must forget the last husband and all husbands past and promise herself, with absolute conviction, that this time is the first time—again. She is never

---

6. Ibid., p. 171.

bothered by questions about her exes, whenever she introduces a new one. She expects diamonds—uncrushed by time that crushes us all. And when she ends the marriage, it is she who pays the price, who almost dies—but whose near death is the condition of being reborn to love again, forgetting absolutely what went before and promising to love till (another) death do us part: eight marriages, if you count as two the twice she was married to Richard Burton. I learned from her that the best time to love is the next time, and all that matters is to believe in love as blindly, as purely, and excessively as she does.

She knows her taste is vulgar; and she likes it. (I mean, she did in her heyday; she does everything more "appropriately" now.) Noël Coward and Cecil Beaton, giants of refinement, despised her gross American style. But they never understood the difference between European taste and American. The Old World, cramped and refined, has a taste for small differences; in the empty vastness of America we admire large ones. Elizabeth Taylor likes big jewelry, lots of it, all the time, and big cocks the same. Her lust for one apparently corresponds to her passion for the other. Some of her biographers even tell you about the size of the cocks she married and the amount they paid for the jewelry they gave her.

She received sixty-nine graduated pearls from her first boyfriend, Glenn Davis; it may be a sign that their relation remained at the level of oral sex. In her teens, she would always tell reporters she didn't intend to give "it" away until the wedding ring was on her finger. Tit for tat. Pearls, by the way, are like living things. They are happiest in contact with flesh; they absorb its oils and share its sheen, and, like the most delicate creatures, they are poisoned (they discolor and dissolve) when sprayed with perfume.

In 1949, when she was only seventeen but already a great star, Bill Pawley, her first fiancé, gave her a 3.5-carat emerald-

Elizabeth Taylor applying makeup for a scene

cut diamond engagement ring worth $16,000. When his high society parents broke them up, she was quickly betrothed again to Nicky Hilton, the profligate, violent, heroin-addicted son of the hotel king, Conrad Hilton: "the man with a thousand bedrooms." On February 20, 1950, Nicky gave her a set of diamond-and-emerald teardrop earrings and a matching square-cut diamond ring, bought at Headley's, the jeweler in Beverly Hills. She married him three months later, and they began their nightmare honeymoon to Europe on the *Queen Mary*. On their first romantic night aboard, Nicky lost $100,000 in the ship's gambling casino and punched his new bride in the stomach. The Windsors were on ship, and Elizabeth spent her second night in their company. The Duke and Duchess consoled the young bride and established a bond that culminated many years later, at the fabulous Geneva auction of the Duchess of Windsor's jewelry, in Elizabeth's buying the Prince of Wales's diamond brooch: three white-diamond feathers set in a crown (the Welsh emblem of royalty).

In Paris, the Windsors gave a dinner-dance for Elizabeth Taylor at their salon in the house in the Bois de Boulogne (where decades later Diana and Dodi planned to live). The next night, Elsa Maxwell feted the unhappy couple, Elizabeth and Nicky, at Maxim's in the company of Orson Welles and Maurice Chevalier, the Maharajah of Kapurthala and . . . Jimmy Donahue, a dear dear friend of Wallis Simpson and her frequently noted escort in the fifties, when she was stepping out in New York and Paris, unaccompanied by the Duke. Jimmy Donahue was heir to the Woolworth fortune, obstreperous, and notoriously gay. But there was talk he and the Duchess were having an affair, because they were seen so often in such high spirits in swank nightspots around town. Her biographer speculates that he was drawn to her masculinity.[7]

Donahue was just the sort of naughty, rich gay guy who would appeal instantly to Wallis and Elizabeth, for quite different reasons, big and small. When it comes to her bed or her diamonds, Wallis Simpson preferred what is small and cunning. If the Duke of Windsor had a micropenis, Nicky Hilton's shlong was huge. One of his ex-girlfriends paints the picture of something that was thicker than a beer can and "much longer."[8] Joan Collins, another former lover, said that he was not only a "sexual athlete" but between his father, his brother Baron, and himself "the [Hilton] boys possessed a yard of cock."[9] Implying she's taken the measure of them all.

Michael Wilding, Elizabeth's next husband, on the verge of bankruptcy, couldn't afford an engagement ring, so she bought her own expensive cabochon sapphire from Cartier on Rodeo Drive, and she gave it to him to slip on her finger on February 29, 1952, a leap year. "I leapt," she told an interviewer.[10] She gives it to him to give it to her. We know nothing reliable about the

7. Michael Bloch, *The Duchess of Windsor.* New York: St. Martin's Press, 1996, p. 190.

8. Heymann, *Liz,* p. 83.

9. Ibid., p. 102.

10. Ibid., p. 111.

Wilding penis; maybe because whoever buys the ring has the penis. On the other hand, his name is Wild-ing and she named one of her cats Fang. To witches of all kinds cats are familiars—little emanations of their most wicked impulses.

In October 1956, husband number three, Mike Todd, gave her a huge 29.4-carat diamond engagement ring (worn previously by an earlier fiancée, Evelyn Keyes). The bauble, measuring an inch across, had cost, according to Todd, "in excess of $200,000," even though when he had given it to Evelyn Keyes, it was insured for only fifty grand. Billy Paley couldn't help telling Elizabeth that the ring was too big and vulgar. She let out a raucous laugh.[11]

Before leaving on their honeymoon Mike Todd also gave her a $350,000 pair of double-tier pendant ruby-and-diamond earrings and a matching bracelet and her own movie theater in downtown Chicago.

Sex with Todd was all about fighting. Eddie Fisher reported: "Elizabeth fought over anything and everything. I couldn't deal with it, so I tried to appease her, but she would become even more ferocious." She and Mike Todd were famous for slugging each other and then falling into bed. Eddie Fisher complained about her abusing him with her fists. "Elizabeth loved to fight. I'd give her my shoulder and let her punch away. Next I'd get on top of her and pin her to the ground, and she'd burst out laughing. Finally, we'd make love. But she still wanted to brawl, and unlike Mike Todd I was never much of a fighter."[12] Her greatest moments on the screen are when she's angry, slashing, murderous. She is Martha in *Who's Afraid of Virginia Woolf?* and Maggie in *Cat on a Hot Tin Roof;* she has another cat—called Mike Tyson.

---

11. Ibid., p. 111.
12. Ibid., p. 188.

Truman Capote may have understood Elizabeth Taylor better than anyone: "She will risk everything yet at the same time worries about some of the most trivial matters; she has the utmost courage, but the merest trifle can throw her for a loss."[13] The courage is extraordinary. She fights like a man. She is ferocious with reporters who intrude upon her privacy, chasing them with knives and throwing things. At the same time, she is the most vulnerable beauty in the world, prey to every infirmity and calamity.

After they were married, Eddie Fisher gave her a $270,000 diamond bracelet, a $150,000 diamond-studded evening bag, and a $500,000 emerald necklace from Bulgari, a store whose existence he had never suspected until he met Elizabeth Taylor. Richard Burton once said, "I introduced Elizabeth to beer; she introduced me to Bulgari's."[14] Some speculate that she married Fisher for his sexual prowess. Not only was he well endowed, with what one biographer calls an "impressive organ,"[15] but no sooner did he climax than he would get another erection. Some people attributed that to his addiction to amphetamines, at a time when Hollywood doctors were handing them out like candy to keep their clients happy.

In 1968, to cheer her up after the death of her father and news of the death of Nicky Hilton, Richard Burton, her fifth husband, went on a spree. He bought a diamond-and-ruby necklace for $100,000, a sapphire-and-diamond brooch ($65,000), and La Peregrina ($37,000), one of the largest and most historic pearls in existence—a pear-shaped drop weighing 203.84 grains. Burton also gave her a heart-shaped yellow diamond ($900,000)—originally a gift in 1621 from the Mogul emperor Shah Jahan to his favorite wife, Mumtaz Mahal, who inspired the Taj Mahal. The

13. Ibid., p. 224.
14. Ibid., p. 271.
15. Ibid., p. 188.

Cartier diamond, 69.42 carats, renamed the Taylor-Burton, cost the actor a cool million and a half.

Elizabeth's beauty is often seen like a gift from the gods, such perfection, everyone attests, as to take your breath away. Critics naturally insist on her stumpy body, her pudgy hands, and fat legs, but no one denies that in her youth and prime she had the most perfectly beautiful face and shoulders and chest—whatta chest! Breasts assertively pointed and boldly plump, skin as smooth as almond milk. The face is classically proportioned (before and after surgery), yet with features strongly marked. Those violet eyes, as fierce as hurricane skies, framed by the two abrupt circumflexes of her thick, dark eyebrows, are set widely apart above a delicate, slightly flaring nose beneath which gleam the fullest reddest lips, the rosy bow of her mouth, inviting kisses. There's no way language can describe it; poets have been trying forever and they only keep repeating the same formulas and clichés. She has the look of the divine; features like hers in their perfection remind me of Lakshmi, the Hindu goddess of beauty, wealth, good fortune, bounty, pleasure, affluence, and abundance.

In India, some women are worshipped because they bear the distinguishing marks of the goddess: a certain golden glow to the skin, a widow's peak, a way the nose looks at certain angles. Men on the street and in trains come up to such women and fall on their knees in adoration, persuaded they have come into the presence of an incarnation of the goddess herself—a living, breathing avatar of Lakshmi. People often speak that way of Elizabeth Taylor, as if seeing her in her splendor was like witnessing some epiphany, an appearance of Venus on Mount Vesuvius. Such beauty is independent of class or social station; the gift descends from unfathomable realms of the collective unconscious, where archetypes of beauty dwell, to impress its universally acknowledged forms on serendipitous flesh.

As an engagement present, Richard Burton gave her an emerald-and-diamond brooch, which she wears with the emerald necklace he gave her as a wedding present. He later added earrings, bracelet, and a ring, some of whose emeralds were from the Grand Duchess Vladimir of Russia, the inheritor of the tsarist jewels. Elizabeth once told Burton she would rather have emeralds than a Lear jet: "You can't wear a Lear jet," she said.[16]

Elizabeth Taylor understands that time casts a palpable glow over jewelry, lends it depth or volume that haloes it with a kind of temporal gravity. This stuff has been created in stars, lain buried under great pressure for hundreds of million years, has been stubbornly dug from the earth at great expense of lives and wealth, and worked intensively for long periods in a small space over short distances in order to be nothing but the gleam in my sweetheart's eye.

Jewelry is haloed by geological time, but also by history, if you think of famous gems and jewels, like La Peregrina—the great pearl found in oyster beds off Panama in the sixteenth century and presented to King Philip II of Spain. Pearls in those days were vastly more rare and precious than they are today (there were no cultured pearls), so in 1554 the king himself took it across the channel and gave it to Queen Mary Tudor, the homely, cranky, austerely pious queen of Catholic England, whom he married and whose bed he briefly shared. Longing for home, and despising her embrace, he left it—on the first boat back to Salamanca. Queen Mary, of course, kept the Spanish pearl. At her death, the pearl returned to Philip, however much Mary's half-sister and successor, Elizabeth I, would have loved to keep it in England. The virgin queen herself was famous for her immaculate pearls; she covered herself from head to toe with them, and

---

16. Ibid., p. 288.

rivaled the queen of France, Catherine de Medici, in the brilliance and size of her collection. The Spanish royal family passed down La Peregrina from generation to generation of queens, and to an occasional "queen," like Charles II, in the eighteenth century, who rather fancied wearing the pearl himself. In the nineteenth century, the Bonaparte brother who conquered Spain, I forget his name, took the pearl to France, where it stayed in the family until it was bought by the Marquess of Abercarn in Wales, whose husband, the Duke of Omagh, Northern Ireland, had it set in platinum and diamonds and sold it at auction, on January 23, 1969, at the Parke-Bernet Galleries in New York, to Elizabeth Taylor Burton for $37,000. Like a gypsy, the pearl has peregrinated over four and a half centuries of intricate royal history, as Elizabeth Taylor fully knows in detail, before coming to adorn

Queen Mary

this Queen of Diamonds, whose beauty makes her royal, an incarnation of those beings, reborn in every generation, who shed their blessed light on mere mortals.

In 1976, October 10, Elizabeth Taylor and Senator John Warner, currently head of the Armed Services Committee, formalized their engagement in her Vienna hotel suite with a ring that featured a red ruby, a white diamond, and a blue sapphire to symbolize their meeting in the Centennial year.[17] Who knows if Elizabeth didn't dream of being First Lady one day—ruling the country by ruling her husband, the way she probably imagined, and envied, Nancy running Ronnie? She could have been queen over our necks as well as our hearts. It's true she hated Warner's right-wing, sexist politics—particularly his opposition to abortion—and all the campaigning made her fat, but she has always understood the political power her beauty wields and never ceased to use it for her causes.

Warner's sexual prowess was widely bruited around Washington and, according to Elizabeth Taylor's hairdresser, "John Warner was big." But then so were Nicky Hilton, Eddie Fisher, and Henry Wynberg, her ex-lover and business partner in the scent business ("Diamonds"/"Elizabeth Taylor's Passion"), who is said to have had an organ of "almost equine proportions—long and thick and hard."[18] Elizabeth Taylor's most recent husband, Larry Fortensky is a big guy but "normal size," according to reports.[19] Like her great good friend Malcolm Forbes, he also drives big motorcycles. However, he never gave her big diamond earrings the way Malcom did, but neither is he gay. He used to make $40.00 an hour doing construction work, maybe more now.

Elizabeth Taylor has recently said, after divorcing Larry Fortensky, that she will never marry again, but she won't stop falling in love. How do you keep on falling? That's the question. It's something I've been trying to understand for a long time. Love, in the West, begins (we know) at first sight, with what the French

17. Ibid., p. 356.
18. Ibid., p. 321.
19. Ibid., p. 427.

call a *coup de foudre*—a thunder clap, a lightning flash! Troubadours in Provençal courts wrote the first love poems to go with songs they used to sing to the gaily bereft, war-widowed wives of lords gone off to fight Crusades. In her husband's absence, the lady of the castle was no lady; she was lord of it and all its surrounding domains, and she took her pleasures like a man. The poets called her "Domina!" Lord-esse, the vulgar Latin word that gives us Dame.

For at least eight hundred years, it's been the same story: love always comes in an instantaneous flash. You look into her eyes and suddenly your head begins to spin; you lose your head, falling head over heels in love. And it all happens in the moment when two looks collide; before a single word is ever exchanged, everything is understood. In that dizzying instant, your life has been changed forever; you may even faint. Petrarch fainted dead away by a fountain in the Vaucluse on Good Friday, when he first glimpsed Laura. When he recovered his senses, he discovered that he had been transformed—born again in a sacrilegious conversion, having become not the lover and obedient servant of Christ but of his new lord, Laura. He also acquired a new vocation; he became a poet—her troubadour, dedicated to writing poems in verse that sing her praises.

Exactly the same damn thing had happened before forty years earlier while Dante was walking downcast in Florence. As he tells it in *La Vita Nuova,* he lifted his head and his eyes met those of Beatrice. There was a flashing exchange of looks, his head began to spin, and when he came to his senses, he was converted to her love; he would follow Beatrice beyond the grave, pass through Hell and Purgatory out of obeisance and love for her, as if she were a god, were the embodiment of God. And it all starts in the moment when lightning strikes. Today we call it chemistry, Zeem. It's probably hormonal. You'll notice your hair has gotten shinier.

Love is a fair fiction, a happy illusion that enters your life through the eye, and the fiction becomes fact—becomes a precipitating agent, a proximate cause of real, physical, as well as psychic changes in your life. A fiction changes your life. While the illusion lasts, your body chemistry changes. For eighteen months hormones rage. You can't stop thinking about the other person, and thinking about her arouses you. Sometimes, maybe often, people get married in order to stop thinking about each other. But at the beginning, at the moment of the *coup de foudre,* love takes over all your thoughts and all your time—not only the present and the future but even the past. I think I read it in Benjamin Constant, a French Romantic: you know you're in love when it feels like you've known the other person your whole life, AND YOU HAVE! Even your past is changed by falling in love: you understand who it was you've been carrying around with you all those years, like a little stencil in your eye that you've cast on everyone who comes near, until the right one comes along and fits the silhouette you've always known.

For Elizabeth, each new love into which she falls erases the past and replaces it with a new one—as if everything that happened till then was insignificant, except as part of the destiny her new love comes to fulfill. That's what happened to me when I picked up the ring and put it in my pocket and continued on my way, knowing this was the beginning of a story. I never even saw the guy's eyes, only the smile. But the sparkling ring was my lightning flash. I got the message and I elected to receive it.

It took me many years to realize I couldn't understand Elizabeth Taylor's relation to jewelry without first grasping G. W. F. Hegel's philosophy of piercing. He's the nineteenth-century German idealist philosopher, with scintillating ideas about the relation between art and champagne. In Part I of his *Aesthetics,* Chapter II, under the heading "Empirical theories of art," in the course of discussing the causes of inspiration, he makes this ebullient point: "A genius can be put into the state of inspiration either through an act of will or through some exterior influence. (In this respect, one ought not fail to note the good office that may be performed by a bottle of champagne)."[20] After reading Hegel, I decided that whenever I sit down to write, I would make a habit of imitating Faulkner (excuse the flattering comparison), and, instead of sour mash bourbon whiskey, I would open a cold bottle of Veuve at my desk, letting Widow Cliquot be my muse, and drink those small bright bubbles until I could no longer see the page. That's why you may notice that from time to time the writing here gets a little fizzy.

But Hegel also thought about other things, like piercing. Here's the operative passage:

> The barbarian practices incisions on his lips, in his ears; he tattoos himself. All these aberrations, however barbaric and absurd and contrary to taste they seem, however deforming or pernicious, like the torture inflicted on the feet of Chinese women, have only one purpose: humans do not wish to remain the way nature made them.[21]

Hegel seems to be reflecting the prejudices of his age, by calling these practices barbaric, seeing in them only deviant acts that are cruel, pointless, and contrary to good taste. But in the end, he contradicts the conventional wisdom by lending these primitive acts of adornment some higher human dignity, and showing

---

20. G. W. F. Hegel, *Introduction à l'aesthétique*. Translated by S. Jankélévitch. Paris: Flammarion, 1979, p. 57.
21. Ibid., p. 27.

them more sympathy than did most people of his age, or do ours. Far from being aberrant, they represent for him the most basic way of signifying our humanity, the very first thing that distinguishes us from more or less unconscious natural beings, like animals. The ornament I incise in my lips, or insert in my nose, or attach to my neck is not just frivolous decoration; it is a mark I make upon myself that says I am different from nature, that I am a self-conscious human being—not beast. For Hegel that necklace is a sign, maybe the first sign, that I am not merely what I am, but also what I make myself (out) to be: It means I take myself, my body, as an object of contemplation and admiration.

In China, noblemen much admired the tiny, deformed feet of women mincing as they tried to walk in shoes that were very high and impossibly small: their feet had been tightly bandaged since infancy to make them cruelly fit. Man cripples woman, then worships her shrunken, twisted limb, treating it as a fetish, loving her painful infirmity and identifying with the cruelty that produced it—ornamenting her with this hideously unnatural refinement. However vile it seems, the practice is motivated by this most primitive impulse to adorn, the desire to separate the self from nature, to distinguish human beauty as independent and free of the obligation to be only what nature made it. There are many tribes that disfigure themselves with lip plugs distending the jaw, head-binding to narrow the skull, ear plugs stretching lobes, and other horrors, which, in their own eyes, make them beautiful. It's the same instinct that makes some women want to wear rigidly tight corsets and hobbling high heels.

Amad treated cynically my desire to dress as a woman and loved my boyishness. But he bought me jewels because he lived to give me things I loved. To me wearing jewelry was the externalization of everything I longed to be but wasn't yet, it was the attachment I attached to myself that made me feel most like a woman. I needed the jewelry the way Hegel says you need a tattoo or piercing, something on your body that tells you who you are—externalizes your sense of yourself. Without a bijou of my own, I wanted desperately to wear one. In my ruby necklace I felt like the most beautiful woman in the world, particularly when I wore it making love. Amad was the perfect lover, himself a beautiful woman and a cruel guy, who loved my ass for the jewel it was.

Amad kept me a virtual prisoner there. I used to sit and wait for him to come home from the club where he spent most of the afternoon playing golf, and evenings playing bridge, after having briefly passed by his office near the bourse, to clip coupons and cast an eye on the Bourse. I was in love with his dyky woman's body, and his taste. He wore no jewelry, but he was meanly pierced. He wore his body like a jewel and everything about him looked, smelled, and tasted very good. The smooth tightness of his dark-skinned body let me imagine Oriental eunuchs lying with their furtive mistresses, exercising their surprising male strength on bodies they left unpenetrated. And I wondered how a woman like that could let herself be loved by a man like me, who was trying so hard to be a woman like her. She would knee me incessantly, subtly striking me harder than I liked, on my ass or crotch. As if she couldn't find any other way to poke me, till it hurt. I learned to love it.

I don't know what possessed me the night he came home later than usual, and I was feeling even more like a sex slave. I started in telling him I had seen some gorgeous silk wallpaper on the rue du Bac, creamy white sprinkled with large, faded gold lozenges. He understood I was alluding, not too obliquely, to the paper in the hall, hung on those walls which were four meters high—paper I detested and he loved. It was Moorish, with tightly geometric figures in bordello red, black, and gold. It was probably the principal pretext for the occasional arguments that rarely disrupted the largely untroubled arrangement we shared. His eyes flashed, he let out a bark and grabbed my wrist. But I just continued, as if I didn't know what I was doing, babbling on about how I had bumped into Claude de Monrichard coming out of a shop, looking great, who smiled and showed me a gold cap on her large front tooth (she's a boy), which had been delicately incised with her heraldic crest: in the middle was a diagonal bend sinister, the bar of illegitimacy, with three pricking lance heads below, and above a tiny boar rampant sable enraged. It was the only jewelry she wore.

Amad had heard enough. He wrenched my arm hard and pulled me down on the bed, and told me had something he wanted to show me. He tore off his beige linen pants and introduced me to the newest member of our ménage.

In the world of piercing there's something they call a Prince Albert. It's when you get a thin gold ring inserted vertically at the tip of your penis, piercing the urethra in the process. When it's worn by women it's called a Queen Victoria. Genital adornment is the ultimate jewelry, a bijou in your bijou. A bit much, no doubt, gilding the lily. What could be more beautiful in itself, less in need of ornament? The beauty of genitals is diminished by whatever presumes to enhance it. No ordinary ornament, a Prince Albert hurts like hell; soaking the scar to promote healing and check infection is a long and disagreeable process, but the payoff is incalculable. The Kama Sutra says you've never really had sexual pleasure, a really ecstatic orgasm, until you have had it with a ring in your thing. By inserting cold, hard, unyielding metal under the skin of erogenous zones, like tongue and nipple, through penis or clitoris, via testicle sacs or labial lips, you aggravate their sensitivity and exasperate nerves lacerated by the violent intrusion, igniting excitement. The mind is compelled to focus more intently on the source of this painful pleasure, so intensely confined that you lose yourself, ecstatically, outside yourself with pleasure the first time you make Prince Albert work. What other jewelry can do that for you? The only trouble is: it doesn't last. That's the trouble with piercing and tattooing—after a while the pleasure you take from radically transforming your body diminishes. Like a contact lens, that makes eyes water until the cells on the retina grow accustomed to its rigidity, the penis or clitoris ring stops irritating after a while; that means the pleasure is diminished too. Any habit grows dim. The same is true of tattoos. Getting up in the morning with a masterpiece on your body must eventually begin to pall—no matter how great the art that produced it. There is bound to come a moment when you wish you could be looking at something else. Jewelry, conversely, doesn't give you the kick you get from piercing or tattooing, but jewelry doesn't grow boring in the same way. Today's another day, and the pearls you wore yesterday get put aside for the silver necklace with the gold embossed shield, and a different look.

But the principal advantage of ornamental jewelry over tattoos is that you can bestow it; you can't pass on tattoos. Now an old lady at the end of my life, I'm ready to give my jewelry away to you, Zeem. I haven't needed it for a while. Jewelry, worn conventionally, is a sign that a woman accepts to be the object of a male regard. I've become a woman who isn't bound to male ideas of what a woman is and how she should look and be. My jewelry has a whole other purpose now. I'm getting ahead of myself. Let me dwell a little longer. I've got so much—too much to say, before the end.

The very idea of piercing jewelry, the wish to be penetrated by your adornment as a way of setting or displaying it, would have seemed vulgar to Chanel. Having jewelry be part of your flesh seems like a form of the bourgeois desire to make all orna-ment more like property, more "personally" yours, like mono-graphed towels or a tattoo. At most Chanel might not have despised the fake studs and rings made by Jean-Paul Gaultier, which attach to the body with a clip. If you have to wear it, fake it.

(You know, Zeem, I'm venturing on to delicate ground here. There were things even Chanel didn't understand or didn't get, like the irritating pleasure of skin pulled back and forth against metal. Piercing jewelry gives you something like a new organ, the way Proust dreamt of an organ for kissing, one better suited than the overburdened mouth—already being used for too many things. A kissing organ might not only allow you to caress, but to penetrate the skin of the one you love. Have you ever considered that whales, with their sonar, are doubtless able to observe the organs beneath the skin of their partners—to "see" and caress (maybe tickle) the viscera of their lovers with rebounding electro-magnetic waves? Piercing with a ring means you are ornament-ing some tiny area beneath the skin that no one, not even you, can observe. But you can feel it, and so can your lover, and you can fantasize a place of hitherto unexplored intimacy—a deeper mutual penetration. But don't rush into anything, Zeem. Before you do anything drastic, consider there's more to it than that. Of course, everybody notices you can't stop talking about Myrna's nose ring, not to mention her new nose.)

It's often true that piercing is apotropaic: it serves to ward off evil spirits. That's why it's usually done at orifices, like those above the eye or in the mouth, or below. The body protects itself against the menace of the external world by externalizing itself at the places where the most feared and the most desired dangers dwell, where I need most protection from my own impulses to incorporate or expel. Piercing participates in witchcraft. Often it's seen as sacrilegious, a crime against the handiwork of the Lord. Leviticus says: "You will make no incisions on your flesh, nor will you imprint figures on you." No piercing, no tattooing. Jews who are tattooed can't be buried in Orthodox cemeteries. To pierce or prick the body intentionally is a form of rivalry with God, a self-creation that gives you a godlike sense of possessing your body—an ecstatic appropriation of yourself. For many people it's a sort of religious experience, where you take yourself for a little deity. Piercing is often a rite of passage, that takes the individual out of childhood indistinction and integrates it into the group. It puts a mark and inflicts pain as a sign that one has left one world and entered another.

Nevertheless, the current vogue of piercing would be seen by Hegel to be a regression, a nostalgic return to a primitive state of self-consciousness when the human spirit, emerging from nature, seeks to imprint itself on the world, make a mark upon the body that reflects the self to itself. Barbaric taste has become chic again—or kitsch. But the difference between putting on a great piece of jewelry and getting pierced has everything to do with the way the experience changes you. Here's an example.

In Appenzell, Switzerland, mature men pierce their right ear and wear a special earring, an *Ohreschuefe*.[22] It represents a milk ladle. There are lots of cows up there. The earring is supposed to protect against diseases of the eye, strengthen vision, and dampen irascibility. Actually, it seems to be a guy thing in this village, a macho way of being one of the boys. But maybe it works. Acupuncturists, after all, correlate the same precise point in the earlobe with vision, and there's a lot of anecdotal evidence to

22. Véronique Zbinden, *Piercing: rites ethniques, pratique moderne*. Lausanne: Editions Favre, 1997, p. 53.

suggest that getting your ears pierced improves your eyesight, at least temporarily. Could it be that people pierce their bodies dimly aware that they are healing themselves by pressuring vital points? Piercing may be good for your health. Trouble is, I know people who have had to soak their belly button for months when it became infected.

Four

Giving It Up:
Irigaray and Katharine Hepburn

At my age, I think much on suicide, particularly lately. Flesh has grown stale and I've read enough books. I've lived too long anxiously alert to what comes next to feel any inclination any longer to care. When looking into the abyss, next has little appeal. Besides, I fear we are on the verge of some great ecological catastrophe; I'd sooner not be around to see it. It's bad enough that frogs are dying everywhere; for I do love frogs—in every way: hearing and catching them, eating their little legs with garlic, admiring them splayed on a shoulder as an emerald brooch by Chanel. My fear of catastrophe may be only the consoling pessimism, the presumptuous vanity of someone who is anyway close to dying, and wishes her personal apocalypse to coincide with world historical annihilation. It's said that decrepitude has its melancholy charms, as eighteenth-century taste in ruins attests. But I'm only interested in the swerve of positive entropy, what Lucretius calls clinamen, whatever there is, in a universe of decline, that defies the odds, flouts the general tendency, springs up alive and growing. I'm too old to care for babies; chewing on memories holds no interest for me at all. At this moment, given the state of the world, and the shipwreck of old age, there's only one good reason not to commit suicide: the effect it has on children. It's a burden on them; they brood about it, and worry it might be a lesson to them. But I have no children, except maybe you, Zeem—a niece who has never known me, and will inherit all I have. In fact, it's only after I'm dead that you'll inherit this memoir and discover who I am—at least something about me. I've only told you all you need to know, and it's probably more than I imagine. Now I'm in a hurry to die, so you might enjoy what I'm past enjoying, my jewelry and this memoir, the news that someone in the world you've never known, maybe a little posthumously, has loved you very much, my sweet little pelican.

For decades, at the worst moments, only Richard Nixon's mantra sustained me. He who rose so high must know something, I thought, about being low. "Never, never, never give up," he used to say. But giving up, I've decided lately, can be a kind of victory too, particularly at my age, as my eyesight fails and my jewelry is more and more only an image of itself in my mind—still very beautiful but without the surprises that a different light, another dress, a great occasion can always produce. As I've gotten older, I don't care to please others and what little beauty is left hardly deserves to be enhanced.

Life without jewelry doesn't seem worth it, and suicide ought not to be painful: you drink a small crystal pitcher of chilled Negroni—bittersweet cups of Campari, vodka, Martini & Rossi red vermouth, and thirteen Phenobarbital. You put on Mozart's *Requiem* and offer yourself the potion, like Cleopatra tendering Antony a cup of wine into which she had dissolved her pearls. Far from doing any harm, my death will only do some good, to you, Zeem, who will inherit this rather sooner than later, will read this memoir in time, perhaps, to appreciate the options you are inheriting.

As I said, I hardly wear jewelry anymore and, to tell the truth, I've come most to admire women, like Katharine Hepburn, who don't, or almost never, put it on. It's not her style; she's not that kind of girl. In many ways she's more like a guy—not a man but some beautiful "he-woman," as she gets called in one of her movies (*Adam's Rib*)—a guy as only a smart, confident, strong, and beautiful woman as she is could be. A "he-woman" could be thought to resemble a "he-man," someone bigger and stronger than life, but it isn't used as a compliment. It's what Spencer Tracy calls her in disgust when he wants her to stop being so competitive, to be a wife, not "a competitor, a competitor."

You might think that a "he-woman" is the symmetrical obverse of a she-male: those men who have become pre-op transgendered women, hormonally and plastically enhanced. Not at all. A he-woman is not a stone butch.

In the movies Katharine Hepburn usually plays a woman who takes charge, doesn't need a man to tell her what to do, who takes initiative, rights injustices, discovers solutions that no man could find. In *Adam's Rib*, playing a lawyer, she beats Spencer Tracy at trial; in *The African Queen*, she takes on the German navy; in *Woman of the Year*, a film made in 1941, she's a celebrity journalist who practically runs American foreign policy. Thirty years later, life imitating art, *McCall's* magazine actually named her its first Woman of the Year. The award said in part: "She is a raving individual . . . Her beauty is her reality; it ages but does not grow less. She is a creature without creams or formulas, a woman un-made up."[1] An un-made man, it's said, is an impotent, castrated one; an un-madeup woman is a he-woman, in a cosmos where cosmetics and adornment have always defined womanliness.

A raving individual? What does that mean? Maybe it has something to do with her being so selfish—"a totally selfish person," she says about herself, repeatedly. She could have found a pleasing or thoughtful title for her memoirs. No problem: she settled on *Me*. What does she think the word "me" means? It doesn't necessarily mean, "I, Katharine Hepburn," as she seems to think. Any fool can write "me." Only an egomaniac thinks that the first-person object pronoun refers exclusively and solely to her. Of course she knows that "by Katharine Hepburn" is also on the cover of her book, to help the reader. But at some moment she had to think that she liked the idea of a book, her autobiography, simply, boldly, solipsistically entitled. It's a joke, of course, but the joke of someone who feels deeply that when she speaks, hers is the only voice in the universe. In fact, she writes: "Now I still think [at eighty-five] that if I don't look at something, it doesn't exist."[2] She reminds you of Oscar Wilde, who once said that "Other people are quite dreadful. The only possible society is oneself." Katharine Hepburn says, to explain a failed marriage: "My hitch was that I was in love with myself."[3] She is, she admits, "a terrible pig. My aim was ME ME ME."[4] She only has one word to say, interminably repeated. That's her problem and her chance.

She writes: "That was the spring of 1930. I seemed to be get-

1. Garson Kanin, *Tracy and Hepburn: An Intimate Memoir.* New York: Viking Press, 1970, p. 79.

2. Katharine Hepburn, *Me.* New York: Alfred A. Knopf, 1991, p. 92.

3. Ibid., p. 94.

4. Ibid., p. 154.

ting nowhere. That summer I went for two weeks to Europe."[5] Not only did her family's money secure her against the Depression, she never even noticed it. She writes a sentence like this: "It was wartime, 1942, and it was also rush hour." Getting across town to the theater is in her mind of the same order of importance as the Second World War. I can appreciate that. It used to be that the two worst catastrophes I could imagine were total nuclear war and my own death. Now, having grown so old, the one is improbable, the other, surprisingly, desirable.

Unlike Wilde, or most egomaniacs, Hepburn's style is not conspicuously ostentatious; always understated. She has the virtue of Puritan New England where she was born and where she's always lived; she's parsimonious. She gives nothing away; everything is always more than meets the eye. Her clothes are radically simple: tapered beige pants, short beige jacket, high-necked short-sleeved blouse, a scarf in her hair, white socks, moccasins or simple sandals. She wears a sort of leisure suit, vaguely military, a casual, female uniform—her defining influence on modern women's style.

She barely writes a complete sentence.

> I'm back in Fenwick. From my bed I see the sun rise. Between the inner and outer lighthouses. Across a field of marsh grass. Birds circling. A family of white egrets. Swans go honking by. Even an occasional osprey.[6]

Among all the multiple families, a lone, occasional hawk is ME herself, singular and rare, unobtrusively stalking at a great

---

5. Ibid., p. 111.
6. Ibid., p. 329.

distance. In her clothes and her language, in her acting and her life, her beauty resides in always seeming to be elsewhere, somehow withheld. She's the symmetrical opposite of Elizabeth Taylor, with all the signs changed. She can be the pure embodiment of Yankee meanness—in both senses: tight with love and money, cruel to those around her. Her mother was the head of the Connecticut Woman Suffrage Association. Her father was a crusading doctor. She grew up with philanthropic parents, but she is totally unengaged and self-absorbed. No Elizabeth Taylorish AIDS work for her.

She was raised in a large family with five siblings, but never had children of her own. The other two girls in the family were much younger, so she grew up surrounded by an older brother and two younger ones. "Being a girl was a torment," she writes. "I'd always wanted to be a boy. Jimmy was my name, if you want to know."[7] (How did she know I wanted desperately to know?) She regularly shaved her head. When you see some pictures of her, in pants suits and short hair, you can start to believe that Katharine Hepburn grew up to be Jimmy. "I love diving. Hell—I love all sports. I was skinny and very strong and utterly fearless."[8] The opposite of what girls are supposed to be. As an adolescent she was tutored at home. She decided she didn't want to be in any school. "Too many girls. Too much curiosity."[9] She wanted to play golf.

The death of her older brother isolates her even more. Her older brother Tom hanged himself in the attic, for no apparent reason; it was she who found him and cut his body down. He may have been playing a fraternity party game he'd heard about

---

7. Ibid., p. 39.

8. Ibid., p. 43.

9. Ibid., p. 43.

from his father. You put a rope around your neck, tuck your chin and stiffen the muscles, pull the rope tight, and scare the Hell out of your friends. Sometimes, the rope slips. "This incident," she writes, "seemed to sort of separate me from the world as I'd known it."[10] "Seemed to sort of" is the closest Hepburn ever gets to being analytical.

Many people think that was the defining moment in her life. It's as if, holding him in her arms, his body entered hers. She became the man Tom might have been if he were named Jimmy. And, in turn, Katharine Hepburn, having become Jimmy, taught me, who thought he always wanted to be a woman, how to become a man. At the end of my life, I think I've finally learned how to be a he-woman, a man like Katharine Hepburn, who doesn't wear jewelry.

Becoming Tom or Jimmy, Hepburn reinforced her commitment to playing deadly serious games—like acting, like all sports. She is a fanatic tennis player, playing ferociously, mostly with men, every morning of her life. Her friends say that, in her prime in the thirties and forties, she might well have been one of the best women golfers in America. She is always playing. She knows the rules of the game and applies them to herself with ruthless conviction and uncompromising determination. Even to the death. "I didn't care what it was in," she said. "Win the race."[11] *The African Queen,* the movie named after the boat on which they travel down the river, might slyly refer to Humphrey Bogart, who plays the wuss afraid for his life, rather than to her who unhesitatingly goes to war and takes command.

---

10. Ibid., p. 49.

11. Joel Ryan, *Katharine Hepburn: A Stylish Life.* New York: St. Martin's Press, 1999, p. 7

Katharine Hepburn playing golf

She went to Bryn Mawr and wasn't happy "with a lot of strange girls." She'd go to bed early and get up at four to "have solitude" [*sic*] in the john. Maybe that's what she calls masturbation, Zeem. She avoided the dining room entirely. She played the leading man in one play. Her mannishness has often been noted, particularly her voice with its bark and depth (although she can also purr adorably). Above all, the articulation, the diction is always precise. But what kind of man is one of the most stylistically influential women of the century? Her dress is a kind of transvestitism. It's often been noted that she can wear anything, from the most feminine skirts and veils to pants and sneakers and

Katharine Hepburn playing tennis

T-shirt—and always looks good. She even carries off the dopey hats she wears in forties films—bizarre creations: a tall black cone trailing veils, or a striped Santa Claus cap with pom-pom, or stocking numbers that fall limply over her shoulder. Remember in *The African Queen,* the more her layered, frilly Victorian dress becomes ragged and ruined by life on the Congo River, the better she looks.

Playing deadly serious games is what she grew up to do, in place of her brother, whose game turned deadly. She went to see a movie in which a famous actress played a sappy woman. Hepburn emerges furious: "I hate sappy women," she told a friend, "sleeping around and then whining when they get bruised—there's not a game in the world you can play without the risk of getting hurt some— That's what makes it fun—worth doing—

playing—what was the *matter* with that damn woman? Dumb. *Dumb!* What's the matter with her?"[12] Playing games at risk of being hurt, that's what makes them fun—she says, as if she had become her brother, playing with fire, with hanging, and made his death into the rule of her life as a man—no sappy woman.

Hers was the fierce originality of taste that comes from old Yankee stock having large houses on the shores of the New England coast, with enlightened parents telling you to consider yourself equal to any man, and, above all, to become who you are. She refuses to enter conventional female roles, to adopt the assumption that women should be the way men think they're supposed to be. She won't wear their jewelry, because wearing it is generally a sign you've agreed to play at being feminine. She won't play that game and is no such woman; being ME is prior to being male or female.

It was once rumored that she was a lesbian; she shared a house for a while with a friend, Laura Harding. But she has spent most of her life with men, or alone. She seems to like to spend a lot of time at home alone in bed. Just Me.

Told to buy her own costume for the first Broadway play she was in, she went to Mrs. Franklin's in Philadelphia and paid a fortune for a sweater suit—the kind of suit women wear when they mean business. When she tried out for parts in New York, all the other girls "dressed up fit to kill." She'd wear her "slouch" costume: "an old stocking cap . . . or not hat in a day of hats. And an old green tweed coat. I would pin the coat together with a safety pin. Throw a sweater over my shoulders, string my hair a bit . . . very casual for those days."[13]

---

12. Kanin, *Tracy and Hepburn,* p. 66.
13. Ibid., p. 105.

You notice that her only jewelry is a safety pin. The piece of jewelry we call a brooch was once a tool, a *fibula* the Romans called it, a garment fastener with a spring attachment—a sort of large metal safety pin that was used to hold togas in place. A straight pin is curled back several times to form a spring, while a catch plate at the other end holds the pin in place. The rich and powerful commissioned golden fibulae, which were intricately granulated and filigreed, aiming more to please the observer than merely to fasten garments. It seems clear that what we call brooches, which women pin on their dresses, are nothing but fibulae that have lost their function. At first, the safety pin was merely a tool that happened at times to be decorative. Eventually, it became purely ornamental, became jewelry, and turned into a brooch, losing all practical utility. Form took over function. Just as shirts no longer require cufflinks, some are made to allow men to display their collections.

The British royal family on state occasions wears oval brooches bearing photos of their dearly beloved on ribbons they attach to the broad ribbon they wear across their chest. I'm seeing Goering again, descending the stairs wearing an emerald brooch on his green velvet gown—in a snit at having to meet with Speer. By 1943, the second most powerful man in the Reich had sunk into total torpor, sloth, debauchery, gluttony, and drug addiction. He was embittered when Speer forced the closure of Horvuth's, Goering's favorite Berlin restaurant, as a measure of austerity. Secretly, he was probably madly in love with the artistic, handsome, ruthless minister of industry and was trying to attract his admiration. Fat Goering found himself fetching, in emeralds.

In the Renaissance, a figural brooch was a little stage or temple on which the artist placed small scenes with tiny figures perfectly rendered in enamel laid over gold and surrounded by precious gems, cunningly set. One of the great mysteries of these brooches lies in the way they always have hanging from their base, on small chains, three drops— usually pear-shaped pearls. A distant allusion to the marriage of the trinity (of cock and balls), or a purely formal device, the sketch of an inverted pyramid on whose pedestal the pendant is displayed? It's as if one cannot create such a brooch unless it

The Canning Jewel

is finished and framed at the bottom by those three hanging drops. Often the elements hung from the brooch are unequal, the

Hans Holbein brooch designed for Henry VIII and Jane Seymour

middle one longer than the two at the sides. They have a visual rhythm, a sort of lilting beat: one and two, two and three. It reminds me of the brooch that Holbein made for Henry VIII, and Jane Seymour: three bars of diamonds, like this, III. The first two bars are decorated to allow you to read the brooch as HI (Henry Iane): Three is Two. But Three is also One: After all, thinks the king, there is really only me myself, I-H enry. Like the Trinity, One in Three: Me. Me. Me.

The fibula was replaced in medieval usage by the coat hook, called in French a *fermail,* which itself became the principal medieval form of jewelry. However, once the fibula turned into a brooch, purely an object of adornment, no one, unless you were a slouch, would think of wearing a safety pin on your coat. But few slouches have the taste of Katharine Hepburn, a sort of punk ahead of her time; from her, it's only a step to wearing safety pins where they have absolutely no utilitarian function, attached to your nose, or pinned to your brow. It is difficult to know at what moment ornamental jewelry becomes a useful tool, or a tool is transformed into jewel. Virtually anything can be taken as an object of the jeweler's art. The most famously eccentric thing ever gilded appears in *Against the Grain,* Huysmans's perverse novel, whose infinitely tasteful hero finds the colors in his priceless Oriental rug seeming somehow too dark in the sumptuous room he's decorating. He decides he needs something moving on it, something brilliant and gleaming to heighten the rug's tone. We watch as a fabulous turtle, expertly gilded in thin gold plate encrusted with diamonds and rubies, staggers across the carpet under the burden of its bejeweled carapace; it is found, next morning, dead.

Watches, which are tools, are often considered to be jewelry and exquisite ones like those Cartier made are triumphs of the craft. Elizabeth Taylor gave Eddie Fisher a Cartier with the inscription: "When time began . . . ," during the time when she was still wearing Mike Todd's wedding ring on her right hand, Eddie's on the left. She also gave him a platinum Piaget watch engraved: "You ain't seen nothin' yet." Little did he know she had just met Burton. Combs, too, are jewel encrusted, like the ones that the Duchess of Windsor received from the Duke while she was waiting in England for her divorce.

Compacts for lipstick and powder may be thought of as

tools, what the Germans call *Gebrauchkunst,* use(full)-art. The one David gave Wallis in 18-karat gold, en lunette, shaped like a half-moon, fits in the hand very nicely. On one side it is pavé-set with sapphire, ruby, emerald, citrine, amethyst; on the other side is the map of Europe in yellow gold, inlaid like marquetry against a background of red gold (an alloy of one part copper to three parts 24-karat gold). The itinerary of their cruise in 1936 is traced in red enamel with brilliant little gems—diamond, ruby, emerald—set to signal the ports of call. Perfume flasks can be blown of the finest Venetian glass, then engraved with floral spray motifs. Wallis had one whose stopper is a large pale, pale blue aquamarine briolette, a long oval crystal, surrounded at its base by a band of cushion-shaped rubies and brilliant-cut diamonds.

Now that a brooch has come to seem too fussy, too intrusive on a blouse or jacket, a safety pin, pinned to a coat, can look cool and chic precisely because its utility as a fibula becomes apparent again. It undresses the brooch, eliminates its inessential ornamentation and restores it to its minimal, elegant simplicity of form and function. Safety pins, in the noses of young women, are jewelry that's lost all utilitarian function, but not yet its utilitarian appearance. Already the punk look has become high fashion and soon safety pins in the nose will get bigger and bejeweled, until they turn once more into body brooches. In fact, body jewelry is already the rage—not to mention tattoos, or chokers that resemble tattoos, or henna-painting applied to hands, feet, and breasts in the intricate Indian manner.

Dressed to slouch, Katharine Hepburn wore safety pins before they became fashionable. But even in the movies, when she's dressed in fancy dresses and feminine costumes, she hardly ever wears jewelry—only once in a while some small earrings. Sometimes she'll have a flower at her throat or a little black bow tie. In life, the single exception I found is a photo taken with

George Cukor in Wales when they were making *The Corn Is Green*. In the picture she is looking very elegant, in her sixties, sitting on a stone step in front of a brick church. Her hair is upswept and coifed, the slacks and sweater look expensive. The body language tells you she's not happy at all about whatever Cukor is telling her with barely restrained intensity. He can hardly control himself. She's turned to look away from him, her right arm crossed in front of her, knee raised, the Hepburn mouth drawn down tightly. Her left hand is up at her ear distractedly playing with what looks like a thick round gold earring. Maybe it just feels funny on her ear, since she wears earrings so rarely. But given the situation, it may be her body language saying: "I may appear to be listening to you but I'm really mainly listening to myself. Touching my earring, I'm not tuned into you but to what I'm telling myself, as I sit here half listening and seeming totally, narcissistically self-involved. Especially, with that camera pointing at me." She understands, instinctively, what earrings are for. What it means when a woman puts them on.

Wearing a ring in the ear tells the world that you like to listen to the sound of your own voice. You want to hear it first! before any other. Putting on an earring is a form of seductive narcissism. You see this all the time. Like when I'm in a bar and want to attract someone's attention. I touch my hair, adjust the dress, take a long puff on a cigarette. If none of this works, I take a compact from my purse, gaze at myself in its mirror, turn my head slightly once or twice to check the coif, briskly apply the reddest or blackest lipstick I have in my purse in a few long strokes, and then plump my gleaming lips for a last brief second before the mirror. It gets them every time—women as well as men. All those little gestures are means of attracting the other's desire by making it seem as if you only truly desire yourself. People are immediately attracted to narcissism; that's why they love little children. What we all desire is the unembarrassed self-love of the child, or any little animal, for itself. Katharine Hepburn made a career out of the seductive narcissism which consists in artfully seeming not to care how you look to other people, only how you look (or listen) to yourself.

Touching her earring, in that pose of self-absorption, she illustrates what earrings are for. They've been around for a long time, at least since people have been living in cities. In Mesopotamia, nearly five thousand years ago, in the royal graves of Ur, Sumerian women were found wearing crescent earrings, the earliest and most persistent form of decoration for the ear. A hoop or circle of metal is tapered to a fine point where it pierces the ear but made thicker at the bottom where the crescent hangs down from the hanging crescent of the lobe.

The crescent form since earliest times has been a hallowed sign in the Orient, a partial thickening of the circumference of a circle that evokes the moon—the emblem of the prophet Mahomet. According to the Koran, God made the sun and moon subservient to man; they are regular in their movements in order that man might mark time and make calendars. The waning and waxing of the lunar year prepares the return of the prophet in the holy month of Ramadan, the month of fasting and of reckoning the time when man will meet his God. The moon regulates the occurrence of those holy times and pilgrimages, when we are lifted into another time, above the clouds, to whatever lies beyond the noisy here and now of finitude, mortality, and death.

Sometimes, the bottom of the hoop, where the crescent thickens, resembles a boat. The most beautiful earring ever made is an ear boat found, not surprisingly, in Tarentum, in southern Italy, dating from the second or third century B.C. It's not surprising, because this is the region of Italy, south near the heel, settled by Greek sailors, where Pompeii and its ruins remind you how much beauty and pleasure have been lost to understanding, how far we've fallen from the pinnacles of refinement and sensual delight attained in antiquity. Those subtle, decadent Italian Greeks, at the confluence of the Mediterranean and the Adriatic, with enormous sophistication and passionate natures, knew erotic and aesthetic pleasures we can't even imagine. This is not nostalgia. To be sure, we've learned things the ancients never dreamed of; but we've lost much more—particularly in the erotic arts, which once were more closely linked to the cultivation of all kinds of knowledge, musical, biological, rhetorical, martial. You get a hint of what that means at those rare moments, for example, when reading a book is more exciting than touching the naked woman at your side. We've neglected Cupid, the god of love and luxury, at our peril.

A boat in the ear is an invitation to dream of departing. In our myths, the sailor is the man in love with the moon and the aimless crossings of the sea, with no end in sight, where one can go for days in boats without ever going anywhere or ever having been. The sailor has no home but changes place as the moon evolves its forms across the face of a month, a boat afloat above the clouds that billow and crash above the horizon below.

From the beginning the earring is a hoop, hung on the ear, or a disk covering the ear, and held in place by a plug. The earliest ear disks already display the impulse to cover it with swirling circles of filigree. The circles in the ear repeat the shape of an ear, a lovely circular ear, that is small. Small ears, remember, are lovelier than big ones, and are signs, Nietzsche thought, of more acute discrimination. Big ears hear everything, all too much; eventually they are deafened to the subtlest sounds by the roar of all the noise in the world. The folds of cartilage around the ear hole serve both to protect the passage and capture waves of sound and spiral them around the circular bones that compose the inner ear. One of the bones looks like a snail, the cochlea, itself an emblem or an index of the ear. It was a long time before anybody thought of wearing rectangles. If you want to decorate your ears—notoriously hard to adorn—do circles. All ears benefit from wearing them.

The ringing of the ring in the ear is the circle of hearing yourself speak. Words are heard in the very instant they are spoken, they travel from inside to outside and back inside again. Speaking, you are always affecting yourself from without by what comes from within, as your words travel back to you through the ear. The ring or circle that goes from mind to mouth to ear to mind, hearing myself speak, is the circle or ring in which I feel most present to myself. That is why a lot of people feel alive only as long as they hear themselves talk.

Hearing myself speak, silently, is another name for thinking, says Kant, as if we had an ear in our mind. Wherever there are ears there are earrings. Do we wear jewelry in our mind's ear? An ornamental earring for the mind, that's what I'd like to fashion, with my jeweler's art of braiding, weaving strands of jewelry talk around the ear. But after all, maybe it's only an illusion that thinking is in the mind. The natives of Tahiti, Kant claims, call it talking in the belly. No wonder so many these days are putting rings in their navels.

The little boat earring from Tarentum in the fourth century may be the most dramatic one ever made. You've seen statues of Roman women, with their hair, like the Venus de Milo, piled on top of their head or gathered in a bun at the back. Statues of Venus are unadorned, but imagine the lady in flesh and blood smiling dreamily over at you from her couch at the banquet, imperceptibly swaying her head in order gently to roll the elephantine boats at her ears.

Half of the earring's circumference is a sturdy gold band that hooks in the holes of the ear. The bottom half crescent is an elegantly curved boat embroidered on its surface in exquisite arabesques with delicate gold thread, and dotted with tiny granulated beads. At each end of the boat stand figureheads at the prow—tiny figures that could be mistaken for Cupid. They are emblems not only of love but victory over a sailor's risk of death. This boat in the ear is a siren song that invites the wearer to dream of setting sail.

Each little Victory or Cupid is supported by a pedestal which in turn rests on the shoulders of an even tinier Atlas-like figure—love's slave. The inside of the boat is decorated at each end with exquisite rosettes of gold, scores of petals gathered around a central bead. Between them arches a golden palmetto leaf—it could be drowsy hemp—spreading its fronds to the wind. Beneath the boat, like many anchors, hang large pendant trophy beads, crowned with rosettes, attached by multiple tiny golden chains (each link minutely forged) to the curlicues and spirals that swirl around the keel of the boat like waves.

The drama comes from the extraordinary effects of volume achieved by the play of light and dark across the uniformly golden surface of the earring. No precious gems or splashes of polychrome serve to complicate the golden unity of the piece. Only the exquisite applications of gold leaf embroidered with corded wire, chains, and tiny heads of granulation modify the surface in an infinite chiaroscuro. The earring is a single thing, you can hold it in your hand, but examined closely it is composed of many discrete and innumerable small things that lend it, in its very smallness, the grandeur of the mathematical sublime—evoking feelings of awe and pleasure in the presence of seemingly infinite differences, contained within a miniature domain.

There is a rhythm to the piece, the way the eye is constantly invited to move in symmetrical and haphazard ways from one point to another. The earring commands a kind of wandering attention, one that allows itself, simultaneously, to be closely directed and aimlessly distracted by the extraordinary intricacy of the tiniest details.

Watching the way the earring boat captures the light and plays with shadow across its surfaces stimulates the imagination to evoke musical metaphors—late symphonies of Beethoven or Mozart piano concertos—ennobling joy. Each rosette and palmette is a trophy bursting like a little golden sun across the face of the earring, or like trumpet blasts in a symphonic crescendo. Against entropy the crescent boat sweeps upward, with heroic energy, like the bull's horns, tipped at their points by the little angels of victory, poised at the prow to lead upward and onward at all cost. The beads, hanging down, obsessively worked with granulation and embossing, seem to represent the weight of gravity, the gravity of graves, mortality and all its entropic falling, to which the spirit is complexly chained. Is there any jewelry made today as beautiful or as technically complex?

Granulation reached its apogee in the sixth or seventh century B.C. Certain alloys could form a eutectic bond (at the lowest possible temperature of solidification) when heated in a reducing atmosphere. This permits the precision fusion of incredibly tiny spheres of gold, sometimes microscopic, onto a surface. Ordinarily, when solder is used to attach small gold beads, it tends to fill in corners and blend their shapes. In the cold fusion process, the granules are attached only at very small contact points, giving them the effect of floating above the surface, like balloons on a quiet lake. It was only very recently that artisans recovered the technique for doing what the Etruscans were doing millennia ago with enormous precision and blinding attention to detail.

Some early earrings are gold disks with a space cut out

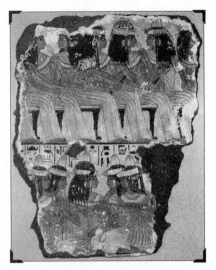

Wall painting from Egyptian tomb

into which you squeeze your lobe. They pinch the ear. They remind you at every moment that there is always someone pulling on your ear—probably whoever it is who gave you those golden hoops. Among the oldest earrings are those that date from 3500 B.C. and come from Egyptian royal tombs. They are given the generic name of leech earrings, because the crescent earring, at the bottom where it grossly thickens, is perceived to resemble a leech. Can a leech be beautiful? Thrown into the shallows of an Amazon river, submerged in the muck of Jurassic slime, I emerged unscathed with only a large gray leech, almost flat, slightly hunched, against my neck, attached by its love of my flesh. Could that be decorative? Suppose that all jewelry is a kind of lovely parasite sticking to some part of you; it's not exactly part of you, but it's up against you in a way that's different from the way clothes envelop you. Like a ring that pierces the ear, jewelry aspires to enter the body, penetrate beneath the skin, incorporate itself into you even as it remains exterior, ornamental, merely decorative and not at all essentially you. But the aspiration of jewelry to become a part of you is also resisted by whatever it is in jewelry that wants to remain totally apart. To wear a diamond on your skin is to put your flesh in intimate contact with the least flesh-like thing in the world. The sharp angles of diamonds on the flesh can be painful, as it often is to queens, who nevertheless rarely complain of the pain they endure, obliged to wear on their necks many strands of heavy stones that pinch, and press, and scratch the skin. Yet the whole chic, say Simmel and Chanel, of the diamond is in its indifference to the flesh it adheres to, its hard exteriority, that raises it up and out of the messy morass of subjectivity, the particularity of idiosyncratic selves with all their specific warts and individual farts, to the universal realm of what is generally regarded as chic. The diamond is impersonal and, thus, universal, bestowing on its wearer some power that raises her to a higher plane, that allows me to participate in a more purely beautiful form of the beautiful. I am not my jewelry, in the way that I am my dress.

In antiquity, the ear was pierced with a needle, while a piece of wood, later cork, held behind the lobe braces it for the prick. The system of piercing the ear started in the Orient, and remained the principal mechanism for suspending decoration on the ear, until clips became common in the eighteenth century. Benvenuto Cellini, the artist goldsmith, may have invented them in order to dress up a friend who was impersonating a woman for a party given by Michelangelo. He writes in his autobiography: "In his ear I placed two little rings, set with two large and fair pearls: the rings were broken; they only clipped his ears as if they had been pierced." Oh, what I'd give to have seen the drag that Cellini devised for him! What woman was ever better dressed? And imagine her earrings, little golden circles set with luminescent pearls.

In Africa, ear decoration is sometimes wound around the ear. In ancient Egypt, tomb paintings show women whose earlobes have been hollowed out to leave room for large solid circles of wood or metal, devised with ridges around the edge allowing them to be held in place by the flesh into which they are stretched. Instead of poking out of the ear at 90 degrees, like an earring, an ear disk is set in the plane of the ear, as if the jewelry desired to be seen as part of the flesh, or vice versa. Tutankhamen was found to have very large holes in his ears.

There are women with adorable earlobes, perfectly crescent shaped and slightly plump, with a pinkness that reminds her lover of other pink appendages one can nibble. They cry out to be adorned. The Romans had a professional class whose principal cosmetic function consisted in administering balms and remedies to the martyred earlobes of Roman aristocratic women, obliged for decades to wear heavy earrings; they were called "auricolae ornatrices"—decorators of ears.

At certain moments in fashion, the earring becomes impossibly large, usually in conjunction with moments that sweep hair upward off the face and neck. That upswept hair creates a vacuum between the brow and the shoulder, setting the stage for the appearance of dramatic jewelry.

Pliny tells us that Roman women fashioned wearing two or three pearl drops hung from the ear, which rattled gently as they moved their head, and hence were called *crotalia,* the Latin word for rattle-snake.[14] To hear a lulling rattle in the ear is a way of dancing to your own beat.

An earring is even less significant than a bracelet or a necklace. An earring is the purest, vainest, most ephemeral jewel, the one that most closely resembles the airy breath of talk. Earrings talk in the ear. A woman chooses her earrings as a function of what she most wants whispered in her ear, which, of course, changes—perpetually: La donna è mobile.

I briefly went with a woman who ordinarily wears earrings that are excessively small and discreet—not only during the day

---

14. Cited in Danela Mascetti and Amanda Triossi, *Earrings from Antiquity to the Present.* New York: Rizzoli, 1990, p. 19.

but at night. One night she appeared at the door in pair of hugely long cubist ones. They must have been lighter than they looked because they only stretched her earlobe slightly. A large triangle plugged in the ear set above two tight spirals, one hung beneath the other. Three elements hanging down: triangle, circle, circle. I mean, please! Archetypically, for Jung, a circle above a triangle makes a keyhole and for him that's always a hole into which someone wants to insert his key. Triangle/circle is a sign of coitus; it was the extra circle she added to her earring that reinforced the message she was sending herself, that told me she wanted to be flattered into bed.

Earrings vanished in the Middle Ages, as women covered their heads, and as hair covered their ears. The disappearance of a woman's ears, beneath hair or veils, is a reliable measure of her degree of freedom. It was not until the end of the sixteenth century that women began wearing earrings again.

Men, of course, never stopped. In portraits, you can always recognize the French king Henry III by the ring he wears in his right ear. He's frequently painted surrounded by his *mignons,* elegant, mincing young men, with their velvet caps, lacy ruffs, full-length stockings, and very high doubloons, who lovingly imitate their king. The fashion comes and goes with great regularity: in the seventeenth century English sailors mocked the French whose officers still wore a single golden earring. Today, a sole ring in a man's ears has passed, like long hair in the sixties, from being a sign of effeminacy to being a token of the contrary—high-test male, with the air of pirate ready for anything. Two rings in the ear are another story: this boy is cruising.

The most extraordinary thing happened to women's earrings when they revived. Rather than being circular, as they mostly had been since the dawn of time, they hung down off the ear, became pendants or chandeliers. The first and simplest was the

Gold & jeweled earrings

pendant earring, an element suspended from a support in the ear, imitating forms already familiar in Renaissance pendant brooches. It is this shape that lends itself most lustrously to the iridescent display of long pear-shaped pearls or elliptical diamonds, both of which became more widely available in Europe in the seventeenth century.

But for nearly two centuries, the favorite earring was one based probably on Roman chandelier earrings: the girandole. It's often a precious stone set in gold from which hang three other stones—a prominent central element from which are suspended three smaller ones—in the interest of accumulating more light. In the seventeenth century when the girandole began to reappear, it enlarged and enlightened the space in which one could admire large gems at the ears of beautiful women.

The girandole is often seen as being a sort of bow in the ear. Earrings in the seventeenth century often featured bows of satin or velvet on which metal and gems were hung. After the fashion faded, the form of the bow was frequently incorporated into earrings of all kinds and became a recurrent motif in jewelry, even today. The thing attached falls away, but the attachment remains. Wearing bows in your ears you attach an attachment, a sign to any whispering lover that you love the knot he ties.

In the seventeenth century, women like Anne Carr, Countess of Bedford, wore matching sets of double pearl earrings—two hanging in each ear, called a "union d'excellence"—earrings of four perfectly matched pearls. During the French Revolution, the earring "à la guillotine," favored in monarchist Nantes, rather than in Paris, consisted of a small guillotine surmounted by a red Phrygian cap, with a pendant below in the form of a decapitated head. A way of telling yourself to watch out for your neck.

By the end of the eighteenth century, women's taste shifts away from the enormous size of girandoles that tired the ear. The ring in the ear returns at the end of the nineteenth century and remains the most commonly worn earring. The girandole, with its aesthetics of brilliant light, and its superb size, was fashionable for two centuries, as women became significantly independent of men—a sign of the more ambitiously articulated speech they wanted to hear in their ear. The return of rings in the ear at the end of the eighteenth coincides with the renewed subordination of women after the French Revolution—as if wearing rings in your ear were the condition, once more, of becoming enslaved.

Following the Revolution, during and after the Directory, under the influence of Napoleon's promotion of French fashion, earrings became flat and angular, designed to complement the neoclassical style of dress "à la Grecque," flimsy white dresses modeled after the chemise dresses worn by Attic goddesses. Sometimes to enhance the effect of drapery clinging to their body, women of the Empire wore their clothes wet.

It is true that twentieth century rings in the ear speak more complexly and often at greater length. The circle of rings is a mysterious thing; since antiquity it's been seen to be magical. Witches and fairies dance in one. Where does its magical mystery lie? Imagine you're racing round a track. You are going down the straightaway behind the competition, and steadily losing ground. So instead of continuing neck and neck, straight ahead, you cheat, veer sharply off, take a detour across the infield, and rejoin the track at a point much farther along. Now, however, you are going backwards, opposite the direction you were going, but way in front of those who are still going straight ahead, because now you're farther along the circumference of the circle. Turn back to leap ahead—that's the circle's secret. Every step you take forward leads you inexorably backwards, on a circle. That's what makes it a symbol of eternal union, the place where there is no beginning and no end, where here is no longer entirely distinct from there. The downside is that the circle allows you to cheat and be cheated. It is the principle behind many sorts of traps that lure you into thinking you are going in one direction when you're really going in another.

The easiest circle earring to make is a penannular one, which is to say, a ring that is almost perfect—as a peninsula is an almost perfect island. Take a thin rod and curl it around until the ends almost touch and you've made an ornament—something to attach to finger, wrist, neck, or ankle. But if from one perspective a penannular ring is an almost perfect circle, from another perspective the two ends of the rod, which once were pointing away from one another, suddenly confront one another—head to head. So what does a jeweler do? He turns the ends into two heads facing one another. Whenever two identical things are seen to front one another, humans see a face to face, a confrontation of foreheads. And so you have, from the earliest times, animal head bracelets and neck rings, or torcs. From ancient Greece to the present, bracelets (not bangles, which are solid) have been decorated with heads at the terminals, abutting one another, often rams' heads with delicately carved fleece and florid horns.

Big bangly hoops mean you're very interested in the other person's noticing that you're exclusively interested in yourself. A simple gold stud in the ear is the tiniest sign of that elemental wish to be seductive. It's not very ornamental, almost hygienic, as if you only wanted to hit the acupuncture point with the gold, in order to improve your eyesight. Earrings tell you what she wants you to think about the ways she loves herself. The bigger the earrings the more she is interested in attracting attention; the bigger the lie the seducer can tell, the louder she's asking to be told the most extravagant things. But most of the time it's not clear. Hepburn's occasional earrings, for example, are always small and bright.

Like no one else, Katharine Hepburn exercised the art of attracting attention to herself, the greatest star, through the power of her fiercely narcissistic disinterest in others; seeming not to want to seduce, she seduces. What we love are the films where she seems so unconscious of her charm, so determined in the pursuit of her own interest, that she becomes a tyrant, and other people's interests get trampled in the process. It's only a miracle in the end that her refusal to acknowledge others—even reality—doesn't bring the comedy crashing down to terrible tragedy. She persists in being who she is.

A woman like her doesn't want to be a woman the way men expect her to be. She's only slightly transgendered, but significantly. She's not quite a woman, rather her own man, and the most desirable woman in the world, like Wallis, in a more modern style. For millennia, men endowed woman with a certain beauty at the price of her being diminished, as in China. Men agree to give away what is most precious to them, their wealth, if women will agree to be the sort of woman they want—one who wears the ornaments they give her so kindly and cruelly, crippled feet or heavy jewelry. She is all the more desirable by virtue of the adornments he lays on her—his girl. Traditional female beauty is the creation of man's love of himself: he makes the women beautiful by giving her what he wants to see her wear. This addition, this supplement he adds to her beauty, is what Luce Irigaray, the French philosopher, following Freud calls the Phallus a sign of castration.

Oh God! Zeem, I'm sorry I used that word. How am I ever going to explain it to you in a way that doesn't seem ridiculous, that doesn't make you laugh or cringe? But you can't avoid the thing, or its absence, in any theory of jewelry, or gender for that matter. But in the future I'll avoid the C word—at least I'll try. I'll try and say "be-jeweled" for when you have it "de-jeweled" for when you don't. Even if you don't buy this, find it absurd, you've got to try to understand. The truth, Zeem, often lies in what seems most absurd.

Irigaray says that traditional women are the creation of men's homosexuality. The man gives her a phallus, which she accepts, in order to become a be-jeweled woman who protects him against the threat of being de-jeweled—a possibility he discovers when he learns she doesn't have a penis. I'm not making this up, Zeem. Men make women into women designed for men, the way they want them to be, so they don't have to face the way they are—differing from men. The man gives the woman a phallus so he doesn't have to acknowledge, in the unconscious, that she doesn't have a penis.

What's the difference between a penis and a phallus? I knew you'd ask, Zeem. Asked by his daughter Anna what a phallus is, Freud took down his pants. She looked at her father's endowment and said: "Oh! I see, Daddy, a phallus is like a penis, only smaller." It's a joke, but not so dumb. A penis is real, a phallus is fiction—what's authentically real is always somehow bigger than any mere imitation, even when it's big.

For Irigaray, jewelry is traditionally a sort of a fetish, a holy veil that a man attaches to a woman. Her jewelry veils her bijou, hides it and shows it at the same time. For Irigaray, men have made all sexual relations into a sort of male compromise with the feminine, desiring it only on the condition that it have a phallus.

Accepting his gift of jewelry is the gift girls give to their daddies, to all "men." Their jewelry is the award they get, a medal for being women like Chanel, like Wallis Simpson, or Elizabeth Taylor, that men move mountains to love.

The style of Katharine Hepburn says that she refuses to accept to be a phallic woman—the one men want a woman to be. When you go out in the world, wearing no jewelry talks; it says that this beauty needs no adornment. It says: this lady won't play the role of the phallic woman or wear signs of accepting its props. Irigaray puts it like that and I can't find anything better to understand the motive behind the style of Katharine Hepburn. Of course, there are periods of fashion when it's fashionable not to wear jewelry; at those times it becomes all the more interesting and necessary to try—but differently, oddly, more subtly or blatantly. Katharine Hepburn grew up in a world where jewelry was *de rigueur.*

Katharine Hepburn would never let herself be a phallic woman. Instead, she rather grew up to be Jimmy. She gets her fierce intensity from the way she refuses to be taken as (just) a woman. It reminds me of drag queens, who won't dress down; she won't dress up—slouches along in her mannish leisure suits. Neither the drag queen nor the slouch king dresses "appropriately," with respect for the conventions of decorum; they don't play the role or don the costume assigned to their gender.

I learned how to be a man by watching Amad trying to become one, by modeling himself on Katharine Hepburn. It was she who taught me how to become a masculine woman with a maleness that isn't effeminate, or butch. I learned it from watching Amad model himself on her. She taught him how to be a woman who could live and play as a man, could be as determined and tough as a man needs to be, while still being beautiful and irresistibly feminine. We ended up living happily as a successful "heterosexual" couple, in which the usual hierarchies pretty much maintained but where I was the woman and s/he was the man.

In her twenties, Amad used to go to Leatherdyke, S&M parties with sons and daddies whose bodies are recognizably female. She saw it as part of her training on the way to becoming what she thought she planned to be: a surgically and hormonally altered transsexual FtM. The parties allow women in transition to practice being adolescent boys. A thirty-five-year-old woman insurance company executive bottom is on her knees, wearing boy scout shorts, playing at being a submissive fourteen-year-old boy, asking to be disciplined and punished with a riding-crop by his big-breasted, mustachioed, daddy scout master sadist top. She is learning how to be the adolescent boy she never was, since the hateful moment she entered puberty and her tomboy pre-pubic body blossomed with feminine attributes and softened with girlish curves. She could never grow up to be a tomcat like the rest of the boys. She had to live the tortured life of an adolescent girl who discovers her maturing body with an extra powerful dose of shame and loathing. But down on the forest floor, with the scouts—her ass in the air, waiting for the sharp slice of the leather against her bared skin—she becomes the boy she never was but will need to have been once she's had her operation. After she becomes transsexed, anatomically transformed, she will need to have been what she never was, except too late, and only in play. Not only her sex, her feminine body, her whole sexed past is erased or written over. Amelie became Amad—became a woman becoming a man. "Becoming" is the word that's confusing, mixing up sex and gender.

Amad used to tell me that growing up she seethed. She knew in her heart she was not a feminine female but a masculine one, and butch—a stone butch. From her earliest childhood, people looked at her and asked, Is this a boy or a girl? She insisted on dressing like a boy and acting like one, playing with trucks not with dolls, wanting to be more and more what she was most often taken to be, more often boy than girl. Eventually, she came to hate the body she received. For a while, she was a lesbian, but unlike other lesbians she took no pleasure in her femininity. Growing up, she was doubly different, not exactly female, not exactly lesbian, all the more grotesque.

Growing up a gender freak in a society that violently enforces the distinction between masculine and feminine makes you a particular focus of anxious aggression from those who revere the difference you seem so naturally to violate. You have the effrontery to act as if you had no control over trying to be what you are manifestly not, as if it weren't your decision at all— as if you assumed no responsibility for dressing and acting like a boy. That's what enrages people, that you won't control your perversity, that you seem to be male so spontaneously. You're a willful pervert, the worst kind, who uses the wrong bathroom. And yet you've known since you can remember that you are male at the core. But the worst price you pay for being stone is not the persecution, which is terrible at the hands of some men and all kinds of police, but the contempt of many women. The greatest danger arises from your success at becoming stone butch: you turn to stone, or "granite," as Amad used to say. You become numb, indifferent and obdurate, irrevocably cut off from your own emotional and sexual feelings by the inescapable knowledge that in your deepest being you are seething with humiliation at finding yourself in a female body. Whenever you take the risk of giving or asking for love, you are deathly afraid that the beloved will confirm your own hatred of your self. Instead, you become a diamond, perfectly self-enclosed, brilliantly cold.

In the logic of the stone butch, it makes perfect sense to want a technological answer. It makes all the difference in the world in terms of your feelings of social security. A pre-op stone butch can't go into a man's bathroom, without arousing aggression. But neither can she stand in line at a woman's toilet without evoking fear and loathing. Urinary segregation is the cruelest, most visible, persistent affront to the self-respect and civil rights of TGs. Once she's been trans-sexed, hormonally and surgically transformed, a stone butch can pass as a man. For the first time in his life, he can feel the ease that comes from being the sex he is. That's why she gives her body over to the risks and opportunities the new technologies provide. She starts by getting shot with testosterone; she grows a stubby beard, her voice deepens, her fat shifts and becomes muscle. Eventually she has a mastectomy—a double one (Amazons only sacrificed one of their breasts to their warrior ideal). Her chest is reduced and siliconed to resemble exactly a male's—except for the two scars that run across it like railroad tracks.

Amad went so far as to start the hormone treatments, and almost immediately started feeling like she was two different people: Amelie on the inside, still locked in there with all her wounds and fears, but Amad on the outside. Before hormones, Amelie was trapped inside a hated female body, but one that was nevertheless hers. Then, even though the hormones made his life a lot easier, it was no longer her body—the one she grew up with. She loved that familiar body, even if growing up she hated its curves and cushions, but she always loved its surprises, its unexpected delights and pains, and its indomitable good health.

Even though life gets easier once you've had the operation and received a prosthetic penis, from a certain political point of view it stinks. Getting a penis in order to pass is seen by many lesbians, and by certain feminists, to be a betrayal. For them, a surgically altered FtM has gone over to the enemy, identified with the most primitive, anatomical forms of macho phallocracy, with cock-centered masculine rule. For these lesbians, the very masculinity they admire in their butch girlfriends turns them off when the woman gets a penis. That is why a lot of stone butches stop their transition at a point before getting one. They have chest reductions, take hormones, but they remain lesbian genital women. Like many dykes, they tend to dislike most men, and identify only with women in their respective roles of butch and femme. They not only resent operated transsexuals for having gone over, they prefer dildoes to the (so-called) real thing.

Amad could only learn about strapping on a dildo from a stone butch. A dildo is a tool, of course; it also adorns, and like a jewel it is never exactly bought but always given—always received as a gift. A dildo is the gift one butch gives to another, passed down as if from father to son. In the life of every stone I know, there's always the moment when she-he receives her first strap-on dildo from another older butch who knows the straps. Like most jewels, a dildo must be worn with a certain discretion and decorum. "Don't be like those bulldaggers who put this on and strut their stuff. Use a little decorum, you know what I mean?" is the last bit of fatherly advice that the tough Buffalo butch named Al gives Leslie when she gets her first one.[15] A bulldagger is a stone butch who's too cocky.

Radical lesbians want to keep both their sex and their strap-

---

15. Leslie Feinberg, *Stone Butch Blues.* Ithaca, NY: Firebrand Books, 1993, p. 30.

on. It's the role-playing in relationships—parodying conventional arrangements—that seems to them to be the most radical form of intimacy, a private political gesture. For them, gender distinctions are a social habit that requires repetition to persist. They love the stone butch who stops short.

On the other hand, those transsexual FtMs who have had the operation often see themselves as having had the courage the lesbians lack, a determination to go all the way to the end of their deepest conviction. Many FtMs never for a moment thought of themselves as lesbians before they got a penis; sometimes they even despise dykes and disdain the perversion that consists in two women playing at being butch and femme—man and woman. Unlike them, the FtM, choosing surgery, proves he has the balls to take the decisive step, make the most radical gesture, with psychic risks and consequences far greater than those of mere playacting. It's a Promethean ambition, this brave determination to use the current technology actually to alter gender and choose one's own. Constructed TGs look with suspicion on queer theorists who vaunt notions of gender fluidity, leaving them, FtMs, nowhere to go. For them, living unambiguously as a fully endowed man is a dream to which they have always aspired, ever since the moment they knew of their gender dysphoria—the anguish of thinking you're trapped in the wrong body.

Anatomy biases our choices, reinforces distinctions, lends its imperatives to social distinctions: the doctor says, "It's a boy" because of the jewel hanging there attached, the indifferent detail that makes a significant difference. We may be approaching the moment in human history when it will become evident that the division of the sexes is a half-truth invented to serve the interest of some. Many women still desire to play the role their anatomy assigns them. But they aren't obliged to anymore. What once was a mad idea, or a novelistic fiction—that a woman could become a man—has become a technically practical possibility. Not only can you choose your gender, it doesn't have to be male or female. There are all the possibilities in between and, who knows?, beyond.

What's fluid and what's rigid? The only certain thing in these political wars is that the first is better than the second. But which is which? Is it better to be a bulldagger and leave your body intact, in order to dissolve the gender rules, or like a stone butch to change the shape and disposition of your body, at the price of becoming a fully fixed male. Besides, there are plenty of transsexuals who pass fully clothed whose bodies, naked, are totally ambiguous.

The old distinctions between masculine and feminine, which have seemed immutable, may be dissolving into a plurality of genders. If I'm taking estrogen and live like a woman, with breasts and no beard, but I love only women who beat me while I'm lying on my back, what is my gender or sex? I asked myself that question for a long time, before I decided I couldn't decide. At times I've felt like an alien, like the cult followers in California, who erased their gender into unisex uniforms and cyborg lives that aspired to the unthinking indifference, the sexless repetition of robots. Do robots have sex, and genders, I wondered. Most of them do. They are mostly male, like Hal and R2D2; some are women, most are as children, like C-3PO, whose gender is often vague. Maybe it's time we started learning to live like robots, to love the new chance we have to manufacture genders—to celebrate the possibilities technology gives us to widen the horizon of our imagination and enhance our options for pleasure.

Amad and I both took hormones for a while; she took testosterone; I took estrogen. After a while we stopped because neither one of us could stand swallowing daily large doses of power-ful drugs—that weren't recreational. Even though we liked the way they made us look, we couldn't bear the way they made us feel, the persistent low-level symptoms they produced, the fuzzy mouth, the odd pains, the nervous buzz. Years after having stopped, our bodies retained shadows of the effects hormones wrought on our flesh.

Conclusion:

Adieu

Ouf! I've been running on again, postponing the end too long. Now I'm in a hurry to conclude. You may have guessed, Zeem, by this point, that I don't give a damn about jewelry anymore. I only deeply care about you. Katharine Hepburn possesses the quality to which I aspire, what the *I Ching* calls simple grace. It's the perfection of feminine form that comes at the farthest limit of grace, when exterior ornamentation surpasses itself and vanishes. The woman's beauty no longer needs any external ornament or jewelry. In its place is the perfect fit of form and content, the admirable fitness of a woman who is athletically graceful. She puts off the adornment that conceals her beauty, and allows the full value of her intrinsic beauty to emerge. It's only after spending a life devoted to jewelry that I feel happy renouncing it now. I want to be my own ornament, adorned by nothing other than the beauty of myself. As that diminishes, as energy flags and flesh sags, I find myself increasingly eager to leave this jewelry to you. You probably caught the hints along the way and realized already what I'm about to tell you, and why I've taken the trouble to instruct you, with these memoirs, and to endow you with my gems.

Naturally, I assumed the position of the woman in my relation to Amad, and preferred to receive him, to feel the doughty thrusts of his baroquely shaped dildoes, worn proudly and expertly manipulated by a man who knew how to give pleasure to a woman on her back. That did not however preclude my entering him from time to time; my small but incessantly hard little penis became another toy in our games of fucking and sucking. Amad became pregnant; abortion was out of the question. He was a Muslim, and would have this baby at whatever cost. I knew in my heart I would love it like a mother, but that we couldn't possibly raise the child given what we were, given the times and the lives we were leading in Paris. Amad and I agreed to abandon the child, if we could find it a good home. My sister, God bless her! agreed to adopt it and keep the child in the family. That's you, Zeem. I'm your father, biologically speaking. Your actual father, the sonofabitch you grew up with, is not your real father, but he's more your father than I, whom you will never have seen. But that's the thing with fathers, you can never be entirely sure who they are, or what they are supposed to be.

Amad took giving you up very hard. Three months later he stepped off the curb on the rue des Écoles and was hit by a galloping milk truck. We buried him in the cemetery in Montparnasse, not far from Baudelaire's tomb (where every week someone lays a small bouquet of evil-looking flowers) and Gainsborough's (where a cigarette is kept eternally burning); I had a small dildo in gold leaf engraved on Amad's stone. Someday you'll visit, Zeem. I'll be lying right next to him. So don't worry too much about this. You haven't lost much and you've gained new parents you'll blessedly never know but now will wear like secret charms around your wrist. I've left you a golden bracelet with charms of A's and Z's. Remember the Duke gave Wallis a golden charm for her bracelet on every important occasion of their lives. I've told you all you need to know. I can put down my pen, as they say. And I think I'll pour myself a drink.

List of Illustrations

Page 160. Elizabeth Taylor applying makeup for a scene: © Bettmann/CORBIS

Page 166. Queen Mary: © The Society of Antiquaries of London

Page 185. Katharine Hepburn playing golf: Archive Photos

Page 186. Katharine Hepburn playing tennis: © Bettmann/CORBIS

Page 189. The Canning Jewel: © Victoria & Albert Picture Library

Page 189. Hans Holbein brooch: © The British Museum

Page 198. Wall painting from Egyptian tomb : © The British Museum

Page 202. Gold & jeweled earrings: Courtesy of the Trustees of the Victoria & Albert Picture Library

Acknowledgments

I am the shrink Abby briefly mentions in this
memoir. She made me the executor of her will,
charged with conveying her jewelry to Zema
along with these pages. Having been paid all too
infrequently over the years for listening to her
rant, I've decided to profit from Abby's demise by
publishing her thesis, for whatever it's worth. With
little competence in these matters, I would never
have succeeded in editing and composing this
text without the infinitely precious help of Debra
Helfand and Harvey Young. I am blessed to
have had the ear of Erroll McDonald and Kim
Witherspoon—and Altie Karper's brilliant attention. I needed Emoretta's generosity, Marie-
Anne's support, and Carolyn's admiration. Most
of all, I am adorned by Jonah's love.

Bibliography

Bapst, Germain. *Histoire des joyaux de la couronne de France.*

Bloch, Michael. *The Duchess of Windsor.* New York: St. Martin's Press, 1996.

Bocca, Geoffrey. *The Woman Who Would Be Queen: A Biography of the Duchess of Windsor.* New York: Rinehart & Co., 1954.

Bonhême, Marie-Ange. *L'art égyptien.* Paris: PUF, 1992.

Choisy, Abbé de. *Mémoires de l'abbé de Choisy habillé en femme.* Toulouse: Ed. Ombres, 1995.

Darys, Katherine, and Michèle Cohen. *Le guide de vos bijoux.* Paris: M.A. Editions, 1989.

Diderot, Denis. *Les bijoux indiscrets.* Paris: Garnier-Flammarion, 1968.

Feinberg, Leslie. *Stone Butch Blues.* Ithaca, New York: Firebrand Books, 1993.

Furbank, P. N. *Diderot: A Critical Biography.* New York: Alfred A. Knopf, 1992.

Halberstam, Judith, and C. Jacob Hale. "Butch/FTM Border Wars: A Note on Collaboration." *GLQ: A Journal of Lesbian and Gay Studies* 42 (1998): 98.

Harlow, George E. "Following the History of Diamonds." In *The Nature of Diamonds,* edited by George E. Harlow. Cambridge: Cambridge University Press, 1998.

Hegel, G. W. F. *Introduction à l'aesthétique.* Translated by S. Jankélévitch. Paris: Flammarion, 1979.

Hepburn, Katharine. *Me.* New York: Alfred A. Knopf, 1991.

Heymann, C. David. *Liz: An Intimate Biography of Elizabeth Taylor.* New York: Birch Lane Press, 1995.

Jung, Carl. *On Synchronicity.* Princeton, New Jersey: Princeton University Press, 1973.

Kanin, Garson. *Tracy and Hepburn: An Intimate Memoir.* New York: Viking Press, 1970.

Kant, Emmanuel. *Anthropology from a Pragmatic Point of View.* Translated by Victor Lyle Dowdell. Carbondale: Southern Illinois University Press, 1996.

Lanllier, Jean, and Maie-Anne Pini. *Five Centuries of Jewelry.* New York: Leon Amiel Publisher, 1983.

La Rochefoucauld, Duc François de. *Oeuvres complètes.* Paris: Editions Gallimard, 1964.

La Rochefoucauld, Duc François de. *Maximes.* Paris: Impr. nationale editions, c. 1998.

Lewin, Susan Grant. *One of a Kind: American Art Jewelry Today.* New York: Harry N. Abrams, 1994.

Louis XIV. *Mémoires de Louis XIV pour l'instruction du Dauphin.* Paris: Didier, 1860.

Mascetti, Danela, and Amanda Triossi. *Earrings from Antiquity to the Present.* New York: Rizzoli, 1990.

Mauriès, Patrick. *Les bijoux de Chanel.* London: Thames and Hudson, Ltd., 1993.

Morel, Bernard. *Les joyaux de la couronne de France.* Anvers: Fonds Mercator, 1988.

Morton, Andrew. *Diana: Her True Story.* New York: Simon and Schuster, 1992.

Palatine, Princess. *Une princesse allemande à la cour de Louis XIV: Lettres de la Princesse Palatine.* Paris: 10/18, 1962.

Parker, John. *King of Fools.* New York: St. Martin's Press, 1988.

Philips, Clare. *Jewelry: From Antiquity to the Present.* London: Thames and Hudson, 1996.

Rudoe, Judy. *Cartier 1900–1939.* New York: Harry N. Abrams, 1997.

Ryan, Joel. *Katharine Hepburn: A Stylish Life.* New York: St. Martin's Press, 1999.

Saint-Simon, *Les Mémoires du Duc de Saint-Simon.* Paris: Bordas, 1965.

Sancton, Thomas, and Scott MacLeod. *Death of a Princess: The Investigation.* New York: St. Martin's Press, 1998.

Simmel, Georg. *The Sociology of Georg Simmel.* Translated, edited, and with an introduction by Kurt H. Wolff. Glencoe, Ill., Free Press, 1950.

Simpson, Wallis. *The Heart Has Its Reasons.* New York: David McKay, 1956.

Soto, Donald. *A Passion for Life: The Biography of Elizabeth Taylor.* New York: HarperCollins, 1995.

Tavernier, Jean-Baptiste. *Six voyages en Turquie, en Perse, et aux Indes.* Rouen: J.-B. Machuel le Jeune, 1724.

Vickers, Hugo. *The Private World of the Duke and Duchess of Windsor.* New York: Abbeville, 1995.

Windsor, Duke of. *A King's Story: The Memoirs of the Duke of Windsor.* New York: Putnam, 1951.

Zbinden, Véronique. *Piercing: rites ethniques, pratique moderne.* Lausanne: Editions Favre, 1997.

About the Author

Richard Klein is the author of _Eat Fat_ and _Cigarettes Are Sublime._ A professor of French at Cornell University, he lives in Ithaca, New York.